ROMANCING THE HOLIDAYS

A First Coast Romance Writers Anthology

ALYSSA DAY   C.L. THOMAS   DEBBY GRAHL

P.K. BRENT   MELODY JOHNSON   LEAH MILES

KAREN RENEE   LIA DAVIS

GLORIA FERGUSON   MAGGIE FITZROY

SARA WALKER   VICKEY WOLLAN

Romancing the Holidays
A First Coast Romance Writers Holiday Anthology

Published by First Coast Romance Writers
Jacksonville, Fl.

Cover Art by Abigail Owen at Authors On A Dime
Editing by Nancy Quatrano at OnTargetWords.com

VALENTINE'S DAY IN ATLANTIS

A Poseidon's Warriors paranormal romance
short story

ALYSSA DAY

Valentine's Day in Atlantis

When Atlantis's fierce warrior and captain of the king's guard Marcus finally decides to go after the woman he's loved for more than a decade, the only thing stopping him is the very odd human ideas about how to celebrate Valentine's Day... and the lady herself. Can a love that's deeper than the ocean find its way in a second-chance romance? Find out in *Valentine's Day in Atlantis*!

VALENTINE'S DAY IN ATLANTIS

ATLANTIS

Marcus, who had been the captain of the Atlantean King's Guard for longer than this woman had been alive, stared at the human in disbelief.

"This is a holiday where people proclaim their love to each other? And yet it's named after a martyred saint?"

Jaime bit her lip in a way that told him she was trying not to laugh, which didn't help his mood. At all. The purple-tipped strands of her dark hair floated around her shoulders when she shook her head. "No. But, yes. It's complicated. He's the patron saint of love, you see. And, actually, beekeepers. And epilepsy."

She wrinkled her nose in a way that he might have thought was appealing if every word out of her mouth hadn't been so completely ridiculous.

"*Epilepsy?*"

"And happy marriages," she rushed to add. "But, um, also plague."

He folded his arms over the deep blue of his uniform shirt—no silly gold braid for him, what *had* they been thinking with these new uniforms? Just because Atlantis had risen from the depths of the ocean after eleven thousand years and now had *tourists* didn't mean the guards needed to dress like fools at a drunken feast—and gave her a stern look.

"You're pulling my foot now, aren't you? Your idiot husband, Liam, told you that you could make up some ridiculous story—"

"Leg." She narrowed her eyes. "It's pulling your leg, not foot, and no, I am not pulling any of your body parts, and Liam is not an idiot. You said you wanted to know about Valentine's Day, so here I am. I can't help it if the tradition is confusing. It's mostly about writing things on hearts and giving gifts of jewelry and candy, anyway."

Marcus scanned the area around them—warrior's habit, impossible to break even in the safety of the palace gardens—and then returned his gaze to her.

"Thank you, then. I have what I need."

She blinked. "But... aren't you going to tell me who, I mean, what—"

"Thank you," he repeated, bowing and then turning to stride off through the fantastical riot of color and scent of the flowering bushes and trees in the queen's garden. When he glanced back over his shoulder, he grinned to see her still standing there staring after him, no doubt frustrated that she didn't get any gossip out of him to take back to her husband

and the rest of Poseidon's newest crop of warriors and their families.

Now, all he needed was a trip to the artisans who worked with jewels, those who worked with sweets, and then a stop at the game park. The whole thing sounded ridiculous to him, but the queen herself had suggested that perhaps his lady would appreciate the romance of a Valentine's Day surprise, and that Jaime, the new fete planner, might have some ideas. After all, everyone knew that Queen Riley had a special knack for matchmaking. After nearly two decades of waiting to make Neela his, Marcus was going to follow the queen's advice to the letter.

Even if it didn't make a damn lick of sense.

NEELA, THE HEAD HOUSEKEEPER OF THE ENTIRE palace and, she felt sometimes, mother to the royal family, the warriors, and their families, had decades of practice handling every single situation that Atlantis and its residents could offer, both below and above the surface of the sea.

Until now.

Of course, she'd never had a fifteen-year-old son before.

"*Mom*," the boy in question groaned, his teeth a startling white in his mud-covered face.

His entire body was covered in mud, actually, from head to overly large feet. Trying to keep the boy in shoes was a constant trial, not helped by the regular disasters that seemed to befall his clothing.

Case in point: today.

"What in the... " she broke off, not willing to break her vow to keep from swearing in front of her son. Nine hells *was* a mild enough expression, but a vow was a vow, especially one given to her late husband before he... died.

Abandoned them.

Left her alone.

She shook off her uncharacteristically melancholy mood—it had been nearly ten years since they'd lost Niall—and focused her attention on her wayward child. The child who was now nearly a head taller than she. She blew out a breath and glanced around the sunroom at the front of their house—the floor of which was currently covered with mud, too.

"Nicholas. I specifically asked you to stay away from the warrior training grounds. You're not old enough—"

"I'll be sixteen in a month!" He glared at her. "All my friends' mothers allow them to train. Why can't—"

Her turn to interrupt. "If all your friends jumped off the palace turrets, would you follow?"

Unexpectedly, he grinned at her, his blue eyes sparkling. For a moment, he was not just her beloved son, but he was also a cherished memory come to life, looking *exactly* like his father had when Neela had first met him, and her heart ached in her chest.

"Probably," he admitted. "I'm more loyal than smart."

She laughed, unable to remain stern in the face of his good nature. She knew she was luckier than most— Nicholas had never gone through a rebellious, angry phase in his teen years, like so many. It had been just the two of them for most of his life, and they were more than mother and son—they were friends.

"All right," she said, relenting. "Go get cleaned up, and we'll have dinner out. Those musicians you like are playing at the outdoor amphitheater tonight."

He started to hug her, but she sidestepped him neatly, not wanting to be covered in mud.

"I knew you'd come around," he said, still grinning as he kicked off his shoes. "Marcus said—"

"Marcus?" The sound of the warrior's name seared flames through her good mood until it lay in dust around her. "You have been discussing me and my parenting rules with *Marcus?*"

Her son blinked and swiftly tried to backpedal. "No, not exactly. It's not like that. It's just that he... I..."

"Never mind." She flung out one hand and pointed in the direction of the bathing chamber. "Go. I'll take care of Marcus *myself.*"

"But—"

"*Go. Now.*"

He went.

She slammed open the front door and marched down her front walk, not taking time to enjoy the flowers she'd so carefully planted to border the small but welcoming porch of the little house she loved so much. Not thinking about all the reasons why confronting Marcus right now—or ever—was such a bad idea.

Not even surprised when, as if her anger had conjured him like an evil spirit—a ridiculously handsome, masculine, hard-bodied, evil spirit—he suddenly appeared from around a turn in the path, coming from the direction of the park.

She stopped, fists clenched at her sides, and waited for him to come to her, telling her traitorous heart to *stop it, now*, when it leapt at the sight of the light in his dark green eyes when he saw her. The touch of silver in the rich, black hair at his temples only served to emphasize the hard lines and sharp angles of his striking face, and his lips—she *would not* think about his lips.

Nothing about his lips. *Ever.*

The light in his eyes turned to caution as he slowed and then stopped directly in front of her, no doubt instantly picking up on her body language—he *was* a trained warrior—and realizing this was going to be no happy encounter of old friends.

"What in the nine hells are you doing telling my son he can train with the warriors, when I have specifically and repeatedly told him he cannot?"

A slow, wickedly sexy smile spread across his unfairly gorgeous face. "Nice to see you, too, Neela. Happy Valentine's Day."

❦

"DON'T YOU... WHAT?" A LOOK OF CONFUSION BRIEFLY replaced the anger on her beautiful face. "What are you talking about?"

He drank in the sight of her. It had been far too long since he'd been this close to the woman he could finally admit he loved. The years had been good to her. She wore a simple blue dress that hugged her curves and concealed more than it revealed, making him want to touch. Her golden hair, loose around her shoulders instead of pulled up and away like she always wore it to work in the palace, was touched with just a hint of silver now—long years alone since Niall's death and raising a son on her own had left a mark there and in the fine lines at the corners of her vividly blue eyes.

She was even more lovely than she'd been when he'd first met her.

When she'd already been in love with his best friend.

He'd never let either of them know, by word or gesture, even a hint of his feelings. But Niall had been gone for a decade, and Neela deserved a chance to move on.

Dammit, *he* deserved a chance to finally—*finally*—claim her for his own. To tell her exactly how he felt.

"It's a human holiday," he said, instead, like a damn fool. "I'm surprised you didn't hear about it at the palace, when Jaime—"

"Forget Valentine's Day!" Her eyes narrowed. "What in the nine hells are you doing telling my son he can train with your motley crew of thugs, after I specifically told him that he could not?"

He blinked. Forgetting Valentine's Day was *not* on the evening's program. And who was she calling thugs? "I just thought—"

"You thought? *You* thought?" She took a step closer to him and poked him in the chest, startling him to stillness.

The only time anyone dared touch Marcus, the much-feared captain of the guard, was to spar with him.

He realized in that instant that it had been years since he'd been touched with any caring or gentleness.

She poked him again, harder, nothing of caring or gentleness about it, and he wanted to laugh. He wanted to lean forward and inhale deeply until her scent of wildflowers and cinnamon filled his lungs.

He wanted to pull her into his arms and kiss her until she couldn't breathe.

Instead, he tried to remember what she'd asked him.

"Neela. Lovely one. He's nearly sixteen, not a youngling anymore. He wanted to train. I didn't think it would harm anything to allow him to learn to defend himself. If he decides to become a warrior—"

A look of sheer panic crossed her face, and she stumbled back and away from him, crossing her arms over her chest. "No! No fighting! His father died fighting. I won't have Nicholas become a warrior. I can't lose him, too."

He started to reach for her arm but stopped when she flinched. "Neela. You'll lose him if you don't let him find his own path. You of all people know that. You defied your parents to marry Niall."

"You don't get to throw that in my face," she said, her face flushed and her breath coming too fast. "I can't —this is my son. My responsibility. All mine, for so many years now."

"I know. I'm just offering help as a friend." He glanced around and saw a bench set back from the path. "Let's talk over there."

"I don't want to—"

This time he did take her arm, nodding to the couple walking toward them on the path. "Just for a few minutes. I think we don't want to have this discussion in front of all of Atlantis."

She bit her lip but then nodded and walked over to the bench and sat, pulling her arm away from him. "You never, ever get to tell me about how to be a parent. Or speak to me as a friend—you have been no friend to me for years."

Her words sliced through him like the edge of a freshly sharpened blade. It was true. He'd spent so much time with her just after her husband—his friend —had died, but the guilt had become too much and, slowly but steadily, he'd pulled away. Although he'd only seen her from a distance for the past year or so, she'd been in his mind and heart every single day.

How could he admit that? Now, after all this time?

He was making a terrible mistake.

He rose and bowed. "I'm sorry, my lady. I will not disturb you further."

But when he turned to go, she stood and grabbed his arm. "Stop. You don't get to do that—you don't get to retreat into formality and court manners, when you're finally talking to me again."

She stared up at him, her lush pink lips parted, breathing hard, and his body tightened. Of all the ridiculously wrong and inconvenient times to fall prey to the wanting that nearly drowned him every time he saw her—the *needing*—this was one of the worst.

"Why did you stop coming to see us?" She took a deep breath, and he realized that it must have taken its own kind of courage to ask him that, in spite of how proud and independent she was. "Was it me? Why did you—Why did you abandon us, too?"

The tears she refused to shed shimmered in her eyes, each one a crystal-edged dagger to his heart. The words he'd buried deep inside himself for a decade rasped their way out of his throat. "I couldn't face you. Not after I failed your husband. Failed Nicholas's father. I should have protected Niall."

He wanted to double over against the pain that was like a sucker punch to his gut, but he stood frozen. A condemned prisoner awaiting her judgment.

Her contempt.

Instead of anger and disgust, though, her widening eyes told a different story—one that he could scarcely allow himself to believe. A story of... forgiveness?

She shook her head and then took his hands in hers. "Marcus. Oh, my dear friend. No, you can't think that— please tell me that this hasn't been weighing on your heart for all these years! How can you feel guilt for how he died? You almost died yourself!"

He swallowed hard, past the boulder that was suddenly lodged in his throat. "No. I was his captain. I should have—"

"You should have known about the secret nest of vampires that *nobody* knew about? You should have left those lost children to die?" Her hands tightened on his. "Marcus, you can never feel guilt for that. You fought through those vampires and nearly died just to bring his body home to us. How can you think we blame you for that?"

Relief and disbelief combined to weaken his knees— he, a warrior who'd faced countless dangers over his long life, brought low by the grace of forgiveness.

Of understanding.

"I thought—I thought seeing me, when Niall was gone... I thought my presence caused you pain."

She pulled her hands from his, and then raised one to touch his cheek. "Your *absence* caused me pain. Both of us. Nicholas needed you, too."

"Neela. Please give me a chance to try again. To be what—who—you need." He leaned his face into her touch, but in an instant she pulled away.

Her eyes darkened from forgiveness into withdrawal. "No, Marcus. I can't. It's better to just leave things as they are, now."

No.

"Please. Give me a chance. Tonight, I wanted to ask if you'd—"

But she was shaking her head and backing away. "No. It's too late. For ... so many things. There are too many years between us. Between then and now."

"It's never too late. This is Atlantis—the city of dreams. Give me one more chance, please. Just one. If you say no—if you tell me to stay away—after this evening, I'll never broach the subject again." Every fiber of his being rejected this idea, his soul shouting refusal, but he would do what she wanted, even if he didn't believe it was what she needed.

What *he* needed.

"Yes, this may be Atlantis, but some dreams are unrealizable," she whispered. And then she reached out, as if to touch his face again, but instead she turned and walked away from him, at first slowly and then almost running.

He stood and watched her until she turned a corner on the path and was lost to his view. And then he stood a while longer, waiting for the pain to subside so he could think logically about the situation.

A warrior might rush in, but a captain was strategic.

A leader thought, and planned, and analyzed.

As he did all of those things, still standing there by the bench, realization struck, and he felt a fierce smile spread across his face. *'Some dreams,'* she'd said.

And she'd cried.

If she didn't care about him, she would have shed no tears.

She didn't blame him for Niall... and she'd cried... and she'd said 'some dreams.'

And then she'd run.

But Marcus had not become the fiercest captain of the Atlantean guard ever to hold the role by giving up.

Five minutes later, he strode up to a group of boys hanging around the perimeter of the training grounds and pointed at one of them.

"You. You're a friend to Nicholas, aren't you? Neela's son?"

The boy's overly large ears reddened, and he gulped. "Yes sir. I'm Hanson, sir. You said I could come train with the warriors in three months, when I turn sixteen, sir, and—"

Marcus nodded. "Why wait? You can start training now, if you'll do me a small favor..."

NEELA SWEPT THE SKIRT OF HER FAVORITE WHITE dress out of the way as they left the outdoor café. She'd been surprised when Nicholas and his friend, Hanson, who'd dropped by unexpectedly just when they were leaving the house, had wanted so badly to meet up at the park after dinner instead of go to the concert, but she'd been in too much emotional turmoil from her encounter with Marcus to do anything but shrug and agree.

She wasn't much in the mood for music, anyway. A long walk around the park would be just what she needed to calm nerves that were frazzled—*No.*

She had to be honest, even only with herself. It wasn't mere frazzled nerves that had disturbed her so much. It was the whisper of a promise of something more—something new—on Marcus's face that had sent her fleeing for the safety of her home.

Her lonely, lonely home.

Apparently it was the day for difficult truths.

Yes, she'd been lonely. Yes, she'd missed Marcus, about whom she'd built up so many guilty fantasies for so long, after she'd come out of deep mourning for her husband.

But it was too late for that.

Wasn't it?

And was that even what he'd offered? Perhaps her foolish heart had read far too much into a simple offer of renewed friendship.

But the look in his eyes when she'd first encountered him... that hadn't been friendly. It had been almost feral. A predator encountering his prey.

Or a man finding the woman he'd wanted for a very long time?

She stumbled over a stone in the path and realized twilight had fallen. The boys' chattering as they walked along in front of her was now paired with the calls of birds and insects settling in for the evening.

She wondered what Marcus was doing.

Enough.

She needed to put all this romantic nonsense out of her mind. She was a woman grown with a child who was almost a man. She held a very responsible position as head of the palace staff. The last thing she needed was to derail any part of her life with fanciful notions of a second chance at love.

Odd, though, how that realization sank like a stone in her stomach.

She shook her head, ridding herself of the melancholy musings, and walked faster to catch up with her son and his friend.

"Why are we so excited to go to the park, anyway?"

They both looked at her like she was daft.

"The unicorns? Mom, remember I told you the Siberian unicorns were going to have a baby? It happened! The gamekeeper is allowing them out for a public showing this evening, but only for a little while." Nicholas grinned at her, eyes shining, and for a moment the little boy he'd been stared down at her.

But then she realized what he'd said. "Mom? Since when am I *Mom*?"

He laughed. "It's what the humans call their lady mothers. It's a pet name, indicating affection, I believe."

"Maybe not," Hanson said darkly, tripping over his own feet again. The boy was like an overgrown puppy, and he kept looking all around them like he was searching for something. "I heard some of the really bratty ones say 'Mom' when they were having temper tantrums. I think the king should stop letting them visit."

She turned to give him an admonishing look. "I think perhaps diplomacy is best left to the king and queen, don't you?"

The boy gulped, probably suddenly remembering she was high up in the royal household. "Um, sure. Sorry, Lady Neela. I, ah, oh. Look! There are the guys! See you later, Nicholas."

He ran off and Neela shook her head and then smiled at her son, who'd remained by her side. "Baby unicorns, of course. How could I have forgotten that?"

As they approached the game preserve, where no hunting had ever been allowed, the din of conversation rose, and Neela realized that far more people must have come out to see the unicorns than she particularly felt like dealing with right then. Her emotions were still pulsing just beneath her skin, sketching possibilities in her imagination that she had no right to think of at this time in her life.

She was a mother. She'd been a wife.

It was enough.

It would have to be.

When they walked through the open gateway to the park, she saw that the crowd wasn't in fact very large, just boisterous.

"The park's not open to everyone tonight, just to the king and queen and Poseidon's warriors and their families, since Dare saved the unicorn pair from drowning."

"It's remarkable how you can't remember your

history lessons, but you know every exploit of every single one of the warriors," she said dryly.

He grinned. "I know, I know. If history lessons were more exciting, I'd probably remember them, too."

"Neela!"

Neela looked over at the sound of the queen's voice and smiled. The human who'd stolen King Conlan's heart had become a friend to her in the time since Queen Riley had come to live in Atlantis.

The queen, arms full of a squirming toddler who desperately wanted to get down and race around, smiled and beckoned.

Neela and Nicholas crossed the lawn to where the king and queen stood talking to the king's brother Ven, the Lord Vengeance.

"Good evening, Your Majesty. King Conlan." Neela curtsied and elbowed Nicholas, who bowed.

The king smiled, but the queen rolled her eyes. "Neela, I keep telling you to stop 'your majestying' me. How are you, Nicholas? My goodness, you've grown half a foot since I saw you last!"

Nicholas glanced down at his feet, his brows drawing together in puzzlement, and Prince Ven roared out a laugh. "Not an actual foot, kid. It's human speak for a measurement. She means you're taller."

Ven held his hands apart a small distance to demonstrate, and Nicholas, his cheeks reddening, grinned. "Maybe not that much since I saw you last month, Queen Riley, but definitely a little."

Little Prince Aidan, who'd clearly had enough of grownup talk, held his arms out to Nicholas. "Down! See cornies now," he demanded.

Nicholas bowed again, laughing. "Yes, my prince." He turned to the queen. "May I?"

"With my gratitude," she said. She kissed the top of her son's head and then handed him to Nicholas, who kissed Neela's cheek—making her mouth fall open in surprise—and then walked off holding Aidan's hand, the little boy babbling away next to him and shouting about the 'cornies.'

Her son was so good with children. If things had been different, and she'd been able to give him a brother or sister... She pushed the thought away to join the other inappropriate thoughts she'd been having since seeing Marcus and realized the king was speaking to her.

Conlan, smiling, was watching their sons wander toward the peacock enclosure. "That boy is a credit to you, Neela. Please give us any tips you have on raising a son so he grows up so well."

Neela flushed as a wave of pure pleasure swept through her. "The only tip I have about raising children is to love them, Your Majesty. Just love them."

The thunder of many galloping hooves interrupted anything else they'd been about to say, and they all turned to see a small herd of Atlantean spotted deer break through the edge of the woods and run straight toward them.

"Stampede," the queen called out, sputtering with laughter. She glanced sideways at Neela and then away so quickly Neela wondered if she'd even seen it.

A sharp whistle sounded, and a pair of herding dogs raced out to corral the deer in a bit of sharp maneuvering. The herd slowed and then stopped, milling around in a small group just in front of where Neela stood with the king and queen and Ven.

Someone gasped. "Are they bleeding?"

Neela turned from chatting with Queen Riley and focused her gaze on the deer, who seemed to be perfectly healthy, but who indeed had red blotches on their sides. But it didn't look like blood, it looked like...

"Why are there letters on the deer?" Lord Ven put his hands on his hips and stared. "And what is happening now?"

A series of whistles sounded, and the dogs quickly herded the deer into a row, so that the letters on their sides formed a word.

ENALE.

Somebody pointed. "What does Enale mean?"

At this point, Riley was laughing so hard she was doubled over, clutching her stomach, and Neela started to get a sinking feeling in her own stomach when she saw Marcus, his mouth flattened into a grim line, come marching out of the woods holding a box of some kind.

The king shook his head. "No, I think it's Leane. And why are you laughing so hard, my love?"

The queen, completely unable to speak, pointed at Jaime, the human who was now the palace party planner.

Jaime's mouth hung open. "That's not—I don't know what's happening."

By this time, Marcus had reached them. He stopped directly in front of Neela.

Ven shook his head. "Maybe it's Elane? Do we know anybody named Elane?"

"It's meant to spell *Neela,*" Marcus roared, his cheeks dark red.

Neela, who wanted to sink into the ground, raised her chin and cleared her throat, instead. "Why in the *world* is my name spelled out on the deer?"

Marcus pointed at Jaime. "She told me to do it," he growled.

Jaime blinked at him and clutched her husband's arm. "What? No I didn't! What are you talking about?"

Marcus narrowed his eyes. "You said humans write things on harts to celebrate this love or plague-inspired holiday!"

"What? Yes! *Hearts*! Not deer," Jaime spluttered.

"These are harts," Marcus exploded. "They're all adult males!"

The queen made a weird choking sound and grabbed King Conlan's arm, all but hyperventilating with laughter. "No. Oh, God, I'm dying. No, wait, let me breathe."

They all stood staring at the queen with varying degrees of impatience until she could speak. "Marcus, the *hearts* are little heart-shaped candies with things like *Be Mine* written on them. Jaime, *hart* is an archaic word for an adult male deer. You can see how—you can see how he could get that confused."

Queen Riley had to stop to draw in a few deep, shaky breaths to keep from laughing, but Neela could see the mirth in her eyes.

Marcus, who looked as though he'd rather be dropped into a pit of ravenous sharks than continue this conversation, thrust the large box he'd been holding at Neela. "The queen said I should make a big gesture. And Jaime said write things on harts—*hearts*," he broke off to glare at the poor woman. "And chocolates and jewelry."

"But why would you do this?" Neela didn't know whether to laugh or cry or run away, standing there holding a box that smelled like the richest chocolates on Atlantis were inside.

"Because the queen told me to!"

"What? What?" Neela helplessly looked back and forth between the queen and Marcus. "Why?"

Marcus's gaze suddenly gentled, and he reached out to touch her cheek. "Because I love you."

Everyone around them suddenly found somewhere else to be. Moments later, Neela found herself alone with Marcus.

"You love me?" Her voice broke on the words she'd never even dared to think.

"I've loved you for almost fifteen years, since the first day we met," he told her, his green gaze glowing with heat and emotion. "But you were already pledged to my best friend. I kept my peace and kept my distance and then... then guilt kept me away. But today you said you don't blame me, and you gave me reason to hope."

Neela swallowed, the yearnings and desires of years rushing up to swamp her with emotions she'd believed locked away. "But I... But you never..."

"Until now. The queen suspected my feelings for you, and when she asked me, I confessed. Jaime told me about this holiday, and I stupidly got it all wrong. I know about battle and war and service, Neela. I have no knowledge of love and soft words. I—I bought you this candy and jewelry and wrote on the harts—" he starts laughing. "I'll never live this down, will I? I'm going to find painted *hearts* in the warrior training grounds for the next hundred years."

She smiled, surprised to find that she had to blink away tears. That such a fierce man could laugh at himself... that he could stage such an event—for *her*—she found herself dizzy with the power of her feelings for him.

Maybe it was time she admitted the truth.

"I always cared for you, too, Marcus. And then, after Niall died, and you were so good to us for those first few years, that caring grew into something more... but I have Nicholas. He needs me. I can't—and I can't betray Niall's memory by being with someone else."

"Lady Mother," Nicholas spoke up from behind her, startling her. He carried the little prince on his shoulders. "*Mom*. I have few memories of my father, but in those I do, his love for you is shining through. He'd never want you to be alone for the rest of your life."

She stared at him, overwhelmed at the love in his eyes. "But, Nicholas—"

Her son grinned and elbowed Marcus, who grinned right back at him. "And hey, I know I'd be glad to have somebody else to blame when the floor is muddy."

Aidan picked that moment to yank hard on Nicholas's hair.

"Ouch! Okay, buddy." He swung the toddler down off his shoulder and onto one hip and then leaned over and gave Neela a one-armed hug. "I love you."

"I love you, too," she told him, kissing his forehead, as she had when he was little.

He tilted his head at Aidan. "Wouldn't mind one of

these, either. Or a baby sister. Hey, kid, let's go see the unicorn baby."

Shock stole Neela's voice at the idea that her son wanted a sibling and had just *told* her so.

"He gave me his permission," Marcus said quietly.

"Permission?"

"To ask you to be my lady wife."

The world swirled around her in a kaleidoscope of sound and color. "To—I—Marcus, I don't know what to think—"

"Don't think."

"What?"

"Don't think," he repeated, his brave, handsome, beloved—yes, she could finally admit it, *beloved*—face so near to her own. "Just kiss me, and then give me your answer. Just one kiss."

One kiss.

One kiss, which would have to be enough to hold her forever. Because this was crazy, this was insane, this was—this was everything she'd wanted for so very long.

"Yes."

And then she kissed him, right there in the middle of the park, in front of the king and queen of Atlantis, in front of her son, in front of the warriors and their families, even in front of the ridiculous deer who'd been painted with the letters of her name.

She kissed him, and she finally, *finally*, came home again.

Home to love.

Home to a place to share her heart.

She stood kissing him for a very long time before,

laughing, they pulled away from each other for long enough to breathe in great, shuddering gulps of air.

"If we weren't surrounded by people, I'd have you right here on the grass in front of the gods and unicorns and even the damn deer," he growled.

"If we weren't surrounded by people, I might be the one to take you down to the grass first," she whispered, flashing what she hoped, though she was out of practice, was a seductive smile.

From the way he groaned before resting his forehead against hers, she guessed she'd been successful.

"Marry me, Neela. Rescue me from the barrenness of my life without you."

She looked up at him, at green eyes blazing with sincerity and passion and hope and love.

"Yes," she told him. "I love you, Marcus. I have loved you for so very long. Yes!"

Much later, after the congratulations and the laughter had all been given and shared, Neela's son looked up from the giant box of chocolate he and his friends were devouring.

"Hey, I think this might be for you."

When she held out her hand, he dropped a ring into it. Silver and gold strands were delicately intertwined to form a band, and an enormous sapphire graced the center.

Marcus took it from her. "This stone is the exact color of your eyes. But if you want something different..."

"It's beautiful," she whispered. "So beautiful."

She held out her hand, and he slipped the ring on her finger. The finger that had been bare for more than five years, since she finally, regretfully, had put Niall's ring in a box for Nicholas to one day give to his own wife.

Marcus pulled her back into his arms. "Will you spend all of your Valentine's days, forevermore, with me, Lady Neela?"

She put her hands on his face and pulled him down for a kiss. "Yes! Yes, forever and for always. I only have one request."

Her fierce, wonderful, beautiful warrior smiled down at her. "Anything. You know that. You have only to ask."

Neela bit her lip against the smile and tried to look stern. "Never, ever, paint my name on any animals, ever again."

THE KING OF ATLANTIS WATCHED THE CAPTAIN OF HIS guard embrace the woman he'd always loved, and then he put his arm around his beloved queen and kissed the top of her head. "You did this, didn't you? Playing matchmaker again?"

Riley smiled and shrugged. "I don't know what you're talking about. He was in love with her long before I ever came to Atlantis."

"Thank Poseidon that you are here with me now," he said fervently. "And always."

"Happy Valentine's Day, my love," she told him, before pressing a kiss on his lips.

"I need to go write your name on some hearts," he mused, and she started to laugh.

"Is that *harts* or *hearts*?"

"Which would help me get lucky tonight, after Aidan goes to sleep?"

She burbled out a laugh and plucked their tired son up into her arms for a kiss and then handed him to Conlan. "We're lucky every night, my love, because we found each other. And now Neela and Marcus are lucky, too."

He pulled his son close, put his other arm around his wife, and they headed for the palace. "Truer words have never been spoken in the history of Atlantis."

"Happy Valentine's Day," Riley called out to everyone and then looked up at Conlan. "I wonder what we could do next Valentine's Day to top this?"

The king of Atlantis glanced down at his wife and decided that some questions were *not* meant to be answered. Instead, he just smiled. "Happy Valentine's Day, indeed."

She whistled. "Just wait till you hear what I have in mind for the next holiday!"

Conlan started laughing.

It was going to be an interesting year.

ABOUT ALYSSA DAY

Alyssa Day is a *New York Times* and *USA Today* best-selling author with more than a million books sold, including the **Warriors of Poseidon** and **Cardinal Witches** and the upcoming **Vampire Motorcycle Club** paranormal romance series and the **Tiger's Eye Mysteries** paranormal mystery series. Throughout her seventeen-year writing career, she has won many awards for her fiction, which include Romance Writers of America's prestigious RITA™ award for outstanding romance fiction and the RT Book Reviews Reviewer's Choice Award for Best Paranormal Romance Novel of 2012. A former trial lawyer and frequent speaker, Alyssa is also a past president of Romance Writers of America.

LABOR DAY MOONLIGHT

A Sweet Paranormal Labor Day Story

C.L. THOMAS

Labor Day Moonlight

Drunk, and possibly drugged, Jessica Cane has no choice but to trust Mckale, a gentleman with kind eyes, to get her home.

It's a morning of revelations when she wakes in a strange cabin and her savior rescues her from a creature that poses as human.

Attraction grows between the pair, but when the moon rises, she discovers that the monster he saved her from isn't the only beast she should fear.

LABOR DAY MOONLIGHT

"Aye didn't order thisss," Jessica Cane said to the bartender as she delivered another Vesper Martini. Strange, her tongue wouldn't cooperate.

"Labor Day Special. Buy two get two," the bartender said as she removed four empty glasses.

Jessica pushed away the drink. The bartender's inability to count wasn't the only thing that didn't add up. Damian, the gorgeous man that she'd met that afternoon, had slipped away to take a phone call, and hadn't returned. Searching for the blue-checkered shirt and thick shaggy hair, she noted the bar's unfamiliar interior. Under normal circumstances, she'd never choose an establishment with this hillbilly décor. When had they left The Comedy Club and where were her friends?

"Are you all right, Miss?" asked a man with a well-groomed beard and piercing baby blues. His white shirt bore a dark red blotch. He tightened his lapel and secured two buttons, hiding the stain.

Her gaze wandered toward the back wall. Who had she been looking for?

"You look unwell. You need fresh air. Follow me."

The perfect day with the sexy Damian was now shadowed by his disappearance.

"I'm Mckale," he said as he offered his hand.

She placed her hand in his. The moment they touched she felt a sense of connection. He briefly squeezed her fingers and she wished she'd met him earlier in the evening instead of her disappearing date.

"I'll make sure you get home."

Home.

A good idea because she'd nearly taken that fifth drink and the events of the last few hours were blurry. Her toes snagged on the wooden floor, and she nearly toppled.

His arms wrapped around her waist and held her upright as he led her toward the back door. "I got you," he said.

Mckale, a total stranger, was there for her and not her date. All Damian did was buy her drink after drink, which seemed like a good idea earlier in the evening, but not so much now.

"Thank you," she said as she lost all strength and leaned into him. He had an earthy musk scent, better than Damian who had drenched himself in cologne.

A commotion started in the corner of the bar. Damian lay on the floor, a knife in his abdomen and blood pooled below his body.

Pain ran up her arm, and she stumbled as he pulled her out the back door and down three steps. "Stop," she said.

"We must leave," Mckale said as he dragged her through the nearly dark parking lot with the only illumination being the three-quarter moon.

She attempted to pull away from him, but he yanked her along.

"Get them," someone yelled from behind.

Suddenly, she was upside down, slung over his shoulder. A citrus taste exploded in her throat and she covered her mouth to keep the martinis from reappearing. Her entire body jostled violently.

Pain radiated along her entire back as she was thrown down. Metallic bumps were spaced evenly under her body. How dare he dump her in the back of a pickup!

The truck vibrated as the engine roared, then something slammed into the back of the vehicle. Looming over her was a pitch-black outline of a man.

Grrrrr

The truck shot forward. She crashed into the tailgate and the growling man was gone.

She pulled herself up to peer behind them, then tossed her cookies over the side. When she was finished, she was able to think a tiny bit clearer.

She'd been abducted. To save herself, she would have to jump.

Hair whipped around her face and the truck increased speed. If she bailed, it would be a death sentence.

Jessica woke to jackhammering inside her head

and severe cottonmouth. Each time she attempted to peek at her surroundings, it felt like glass shards pierced her eyeballs.

"Never again," she said. The sound of her voice increased the pain in her brain.

"Thank God, you're finally awake," a man said a few feet away.

Her eyes snapped open. A man with short brown hair and a well-groomed beard stood by a window six feet away. Mckale. He'd hustled her out of the bar the previous night. "What? Where?"

He moved toward her, and she scooted toward the opposite side of the sofa. Between them were her phone and purse sitting on a coffee table. She leaned forward to grab her phone, but he leaned toward her, and she backed away.

"My name is Mckale Brue. I'm a private investigator. Here is my ID." He produced a wallet from his back pocket and angled it towards her.

Just because he showed her identification didn't mean she would trust him. She snatched her phone, but the battery was dead. To top it off, a jagged crack marred the screen. When had that happened?

He reached for something.

Fear of him ran through her, and she moved away, trying to put distance between them, but the room spun, so she leaned on the back of the sofa.

"You're safe here," he said as he unlocked his phone, then placed it near her.

Why was she so jumpy? Because she'd never woken in a strange environment, and she would have never agreed to come home with someone she'd just met. "You should have taken me home."

Mckale walked to the other side of the one room dwelling to the kitchen. The walls, cabinets and furnishings were all made of natural wood planks, and she imagined they were in a rustic cabin in the middle of the woods. That better not be the case.

"Where am I?" she demanded.

He paused next to the mini fridge. "You were a bit under the weather. I didn't feel comfortable taking you home to be alone."

Her insides quivered and memories of the night before came in bits and pieces. As much as she wanted to argue with him, she had drunk way more alcohol than she should have.

He pulled out a soda.

Sugar. Her body needed a boost to shake this hangover.

"Drink," he said as he set the can in front of her and popped the top. She tossed aside a throw blanket and snatched up the icy can. The need for the bubbly delight was equivalent to her need of oxygen. In several continuous swigs, she consumed half the can.

"What do you remember from last night?" Mckale asked.

"He growled." What a silly comment. Men don't growl, but she couldn't dismiss the clear memory of a dark man hovering over her.

A deafening belch erupted from her mouth. Any other time she would have been appalled but she wouldn't let a burp stop her from answers. "After you threw me in the bed of the pick-up truck."

He glanced at the ground, then eyed her. "Sorry about that. At the time I was more concerned with our safety."

She studied the water droplets forming on the soda can, as visions of the previous night came back to her. People chased them. Why?

"How do you feel? You were drugged."

Her gaze snapped up to meet his, and she was shocked to see genuine concern. Never had she felt this horrible after a night of drinking, and her abnormal obsession with Damian, a man she'd just met, must have been a side effect of drugs. "You saw him drug me?"

He shook his head. "I suspected. You wouldn't have agreed to leave with me, someone you'd never met, if you were of sound mind."

It pained her to hear that she had agreed to leave with him, but hadn't he agreed to take her home? Why was she in his cabin?

"Damian has drugged women before."

She sucked in her breath and covered her mouth with her hand. Images of Damian, stabbed and bloody, haunted her. Had Mckale stabbed him? Or had that been a drug-induced hallucination?

"You need to eat," he said moving toward the mini fridge.

She stood, then swayed. Damn it! She couldn't stand up to him if she could not support herself. She leaned against the side of the sofa, then straightened her spine.

"Level with me. I have memories that can't be real, and I need to know why you snatched me out of the bar and hauled ass."

He took a frozen meal out of the freezer, ripped

open the box, placed it in the microwave, and activated the appliance in a series of quick punches.

Was he delaying? Did he think she was so hungover that she wouldn't push for answers? While he was distracted, she grabbed his phone.

"We're too far from town for a phone signal but sometimes a text will go through," he said as he picked up a computer tablet.

The display on his phone showed it was 7:00 Monday, Sept 7.

Monday?

"This is wrong. It's Sunday."

"No, it's Monday evening."

The Labor Day community pool party and cookout had been that afternoon. She'd bought a dozen packages of hot dog buns for the gathering. She texted her closest friend, but a moment later, the phone dinged, indicating that it failed to deliver the message.

"The truth won't be easy to hear. I can give you a watered-down version," Mckale said as he approached her, his gaze firm.

Somehow, she knew he would be truthful, unlike Damian that had pushed her to drink more than she wanted and had probably slipped something into one of those drinks. "I need the full truth."

He set the tablet on the coffee table in front of her and settled beside her. "When did you meet Damian?" he asked.

She swallowed the last drop of soda. "I need to receive answers, not give them."

"Fair enough," he said as he pushed a button, then opened a file. The display showed a picture of her and

Damian in the park, minutes after they met. They were both smiling. Her heart skipped. Late yesterday, or two days ago? At that moment, she would have said it was one of the happiest days of her life. She would have viewed that picture as a keepsake. Was that vision about to be shattered?

He swiped the screen to show another picture. She was walking down Main Street in her pet store work uniform. A digital imprint on the bottom displayed eight AM, before she met Damian.

She glanced at Mckale. He watched her closely, as if gauging her response.

"What do you see?" he asked.

She ground her teeth. She wasn't about to be baited into a game.

"Look closely," he said, moving his finger over the upper left corner.

Damian was in the picture, about ten feet behind her.

Mckale swiped the screen to show her wearing a red minidress. She'd worn that outfit several days ago when she went out to lunch with friends. He moved his hand in the corner of the screen. Damian was in that picture also, his head clearly angled toward her. A dozen pictures from a span of ten days, and all times of the day, went across the screen, and each one showed her and Damian.

She stood. "What the hell?"

After seeing his creepy stare in so many photos, how could she have thought he was good looking?

The microwave dinged. "You need to eat before we continue," he said as he grabbed the food out of the microwave and placed it beside her with a fork.

Did he think she could eat after she learned Damian had stalked her for more than a week?

Mckale walked to the window and peered between the curtains, he then moved to three other windows.

Was Damian outside now? No, he'd left her. Why would he return now? Or had she seen him dead on the floor when Mckale had rushed her out of the bar?

"I need to go home," she said, as she picked up her purse and broken phone.

"Eat," he said.

"How did my phone break?"

"Damian threw your belongings in the dumpster. I dug them out and stained my favorite shirt with pizza sauce. You're welcome."

What would have happened to her if Mckale hadn't interfered? Did she want to know what Damian had planned?

"I have food at home," she said, as her stomach growled at the scent of meatloaf and mashed potatoes. She needed nourishment and waiting until she got home to eat would make her weaker.

"Do you want answers?" he asked.

Her knees buckled and she plopped on the sofa. She needed every detail, no matter how hard to hear. "Yes."

"It's still not too late to get the simplified version."

Her heart raced. Did he have pictures of Damian peering in her window at night? She wasn't sure she could handle more truth, but not knowing would drive her insane. "Don't leave anything out."

He walked toward the door, checked that it was locked, then strode to the back of the room and picked up a thick file. When he settled next to her, he gently placed a hand on her shoulder. "I won't let anything happen to you. I want you to believe that."

He'd given her soda when her body had felt like she would die, he'd given her his phone so she could contact friends, then encouraged her to eat. On top of that, he'd saved her from a stalker she didn't know had targeted her, and she had treated him horribly for not taking her home after she'd been drugged.

She leaned into him, feeling his warm body next to hers. "Thank you for helping me."

He opened the file to expose a headshot of her. No, she looked again. The photo appeared to be a drivers' license picture of a woman that looked eerily like Jessica. They both had light brown shoulder-length hair that parted on the right.

Mckale moved the picture aside to reveal another woman, with a similar appearance, then continued to line up seven pictures of various women. All could pass for her sister, or even twin.

He paused before he revealed the next picture. "Are you sure you can handle the truth?"

Technically, she couldn't know that she could cope with the facts while she was still in the dark. "Yes," she said, hearing the quiver in her voice.

He patted her knee. "I know you can. I must confess that I took the earlier pictures. I followed him, and then I watched you because of his interest in you. You are strong."

Mckale's confession made her feel weak. Physically and mentally. It should creep her out to learn he observed her from afar, but after seeing the sinister look on Damian's face in numerous photos, his presence was a relief.

"These next pictures piece together the story of what happened, after the fact."

"Who are they?"

"Damian's prior interests."

Bang! Bang! Bang!

Jessica jumped. Someone beat on the door so loudly they could wake the dead.

Mckale tossed the pictures into the file folder, then shoved it underneath the sofa. Within a second, he jumped over the armrest and approached the window, then peeked outside.

She held her chest, trying to get her beating heart to calm.

He moved to another window, then glanced at her. "Did I receive a text?"

"I haven't heard a notification."

"This isn't good," he said as he moved to the window on the opposite wall and looked outside.

"Who is it?" she asked, but she didn't want to know the answer. Seeing the pictures of her being stalked were more frightening than any horror movie.

"Damian."

"He's alive?" The memory had been so real, she would have sworn in a court of law that he'd been stabbed.

Mckale turned toward her. "You thought he'd died?"

She felt like an idiot. Of course, people didn't go around stabbing each other. All her memories of that night could be false. "I clearly remember a knife sticking out of him, and a blood stain on your shirt." *No, that was pizza sauce.*

"I don't understand," Mckale said quietly, more to himself than to her.

"Give me what belongs to me," a man screamed from outside.

Jessica recognized Damian's voice. What disturbed her more than her stalker being outside was that something had shocked Mckale. "What don't you understand?"

Mckale ran to his phone and handed it to her. "Get upstairs."

She glanced around for a staircase but didn't see one.

He rushed into the kitchen, then jumped, pushing open a hinged door in the ceiling. The wooden planks had camouflaged the hardware.

He pulled himself up with brute strength and disappeared. A few seconds later, a ladder appeared, and he jumped down. "Climb up to the loft. Pull up the ladder and shut the door."

"Mckale," Damian screamed while he beat on the door. The commotion was so loud she believed he was using a baseball bat or something equally deadly.

She dragged herself up the first rung, straining with the physical effort, then hesitated. "You should come up, too." She didn't know him, but her stomach twisted at him being anywhere near her stalker.

He smiled, and his eyes twinkled as if he were shocked at her suggestion. "For a human, you have a big heart. Maybe, that's why he chose you."

She giggled at his word choice, and for a split second, she forgot Damian was outside. She moved her leg to the second rung but failed to lift herself up higher. Anger flared. She wasn't a weakling. At least she wasn't normally. The unknown drug had left her feeble. "I don't think...."

The front window shattered. From the outside, a hand appeared and yanked the red curtains, knocking out the remaining windowpane. A face appeared.

She froze.

The face, framed by thick shaggy hair, was misshapen and hairy.

"I got you," Mckale said as he wrapped her right arm around his neck. In a blink of an eye, they were upstairs, as if her one hundred and seventy pounds weren't a burden.

The upper floor wasn't an attic, but a bedroom. An open door on the opposite wall revealed a full bathroom. Mckale placed her on a queen size bed that was made up with a hand-sewn blanket.

"Mckale," Damian screamed. *Was he inside?*

Mckale turned away from her.

"No. Don't go," she said as she wrapped her hands around his neck, to keep him safe.

"Jessica," he said, as he peered into her gaze. "I won't let him get to you."

He removed her hands from around his neck.

Desperate to keep him near, she held onto his upper arm. Large muscles rippled below her hand. "Don't risk yourself for me."

He lowered his head, his gaze inches away. "Jessica."

Her name on his lips caused her body to spasm with delight.

"You're worth the risk."

A second later, he'd jumped through the opening to the floor below.

No. She couldn't let anything happen to him.

Before she could react, he reappeared, again jumping, and not using the ladder. He placed the file, the meatloaf, and another soda on the nightstand.

She sat on the bed, as she concluded she was delusional. No one could jump from one story to the next. Damian wasn't a hairy dog-man creature.

"Jessica," he said, putting his phone in her hands. "Keep calling and texting this number. It's my brother. Without his help, we're on our own."

She glanced at the phone, and she could see he'd sent a text to his brother earlier that morning. The fine print under the text indicated it had been delivered.

I hid Jessica at my cabin. Need assistance before Damian tracks our location.

Bang!

Jessica dropped the phone. The hatch had slammed closed. Mckale had gone downstairs to face Damian alone.

She retrieved the phone and texted his brother. *Need help ASAP.*

Silence enveloped her. Were the heavy wood walls and floor preventing her from hearing downstairs?

She ran to the only window. An oak tree blocked her view of the front porch. Without a view of Damian, she could only imagine he'd made it into the house. Desperate to hear what transpired below, she attempted to open the window, but it refused to budge.

She paced the tiny area, and finally decided she should eat. She grabbed the tray of meatloaf off the folder and shoved a bite into her mouth. Her stomach knotted. Refusing to spit it out, she continued to chew as she glared at the file.

Answers were in that folder and knowing what she faced could calm her stomach, or not. Answers would have to wait until she regained her strength.

Not knowing if Mckale were safe from Damian would drive her crazy. She pulled on the wrought iron handle to open the hatch but couldn't keep it open long with her lack of strength.

She knelt with her ear at the crack. Grunts and growls came from below. Something fell directly below her, but the tiny crack didn't give her enough visual clues to know for sure what she suspected.

Mckale Brue and Damian fought.

JESSICA COULD ONLY IMAGINE WHAT HAPPENED downstairs. After what seemed like forever, she continued to lay on the floor with her ear at the crack, but all sound from downstairs had ceased.

Mckale had protected her and kept her safe when she'd stupidly followed Damian under the guise of a date. If not for his interference, she had no idea what evil could have transpired.

Mckale could be injured. If he were, she had to help.

She pulled on the wrought iron handle, and opened the door a few feet, but it slammed shut. Gathering her strength, she knew she had to jerk it hard to flip open the hatch.

The door blasted open. She fell backward.

A hairy beast landed on all fours several feet away. Fur covered his body from head to toe. His nose and mouth were elongated, and his ears were pointed, like a canine, but this was no ordinary dog.

Jessica crab-walked backward until she hit the wall.

"Ggeessika," the creature said with a growl.

He'd said her name! It was a growly distorted version of her name, but it had been clear enough she had no doubt this creature had spoken to her.

He leaned on his back legs, then stood upright. That was when she noticed his clothes, tattered, torn and bloody. The same blue trousers and white button up shirt that Mckale had worn. The fur was the exact same color as his hair and beard.

Her instincts screamed for her to run, but where could she flee? "Mckale?"

He reached for her, and she forced herself not to cringe from him.

Then, he paused while he studied his own hand, as if just now noticing that he was covered in fur. His gaze jumped to her. "You are safe with me," he said, his words clearer than they were a few seconds ago, but still growly.

"What the hell are you?"

Every second that passed, his form altered, and he appeared more human.

Human

He had called her a human when he helped her climb the ladder. Which meant he wasn't human. So, that explained how he was able to jump to the second story.

"We are shifters. Wolf shifters."

If his actions weren't a delusion, then what she had seen could be real, and not a side-effect of the drugs. "Do you mean, you shift between human and wolf?"

"Exactly."

We as in him and Damian. Her gaze landed on the folder of photos of Damian's prior interests. She pointed to the file. "Them too?"

He nodded.

"Damian?" she asked, hating the fear she heard in her voice, but now that she knew he possibly had super-human strength, like Mckale, she had to know he was no longer a threat.

"Restrained. He cannot get free," he said.

A wolf howled outside.

Mckale leaped to the window.

Several more howls erupted.

"This isn't good," he said as he lowered his head, then faced her.

"Is that your brother?" she asked. Hadn't he wanted his brother to back him up?

"Yes. With reinforcements."

"That's a good thing, right?"

He twisted his lip moving his mustache awkwardly. "It is forbidden for our kind to interact with humans."

Was he in trouble for interacting with her? He'd prevented Damian from harming her. Surely, that was more of a sin than anything he'd done.

"Jessica, I need you to trust me."

"I do," she said automatically, but then she thought about her declaration. Did she really trust him? They'd just met. He'd been honest with her when he could have dismissed her queries and he'd pushed her to eat and get well after she'd been drugged.

"They know you are here. Come with me outside," he said as he offered his hand.

She placed her fingers in his, then turned his arm to study it. Dried blood blotted parts of his shirt, but his skin was unmarred.

"I will not let anything happen to you."

The firmness in his tone caused a wave of concern to ripple through Jessica. What would they do to her for interacting with him?

"Hold on to me," he said as he stepped toward her and wrapped his arm around her waist. Before she could object, he jumped down to the lower level. The sofa was upside-down and on the opposite side of the room. There would have been less destruction if a category five tornado had ripped through the cabin.

Mckale held her against his body as he waded through broken glass and debris. "How could you fight and not get cut?"

His lip twisted, as if he didn't want to tell her the answer. "Let me do all the talking, and I'll explain more later, if it is allowed."

"Okay," she agreed, only because he'd saved her life. Any other time, she would argue that no one had the right to choose what was 'allowed' in her life, except her.

He kicked open the front door, then walked outside in the moonlight. Gently, he set her on the ground, and then stepped in front of her. "Stay behind me."

She peeked around his shoulder. Twelve men stood in a semi-circle.

"Damian is inside restrained with silver. The evidence of his actions is upstairs."

One man stepped forward, his glowing eyes on her. "She's not from the same pack as the others."

Mckale reached behind him and held onto her arm. "No, she is not."

Another stepped forward and walked around Mckale. He was taller than Mckale and had pitch black hair and a jagged scar along his jawline.

"Her name is Jessica Cane," Mckale said.

Several of the men howled.

Fur erupted on Mckale's hand. After seeing the cabin's destruction, no way would she want to be in the middle of a group of wolf shifters during a disagreement over her. Instinctively, she stepped closer to him, leaning against his back.

"She works at the pet store in town," Mckale said.

"Jessica," the man with the jagged scar said. "How many Cane's are in town?"

She'd grown up in foster care and had no family except distant relatives she hadn't seen in years.

"Damian drugged her as if she were one of us. I brought her here and nursed her back to health. This interrogation is unwarranted," Mckale said through a series of growls.

"You should have let her die," a voice from the group said.

Her heart raced. She'd imagined a slap on the wrist, not wolf shifters that wanted her dead.

"I'm the pack regulator, and this is how you treat me? Do you believe I would put our pack, our loved ones, in danger?" Mckale's voice bellowed in anger.

He'd watched over her from the first moment Damian had set his sights on her. She still felt weak, but she wasn't going to continue to cower while he fought for her. She stepped forward and placed herself next to Mckale. No matter what happened, she refused to hide.

The man with the scar took a step toward Jessica. Her insides quivered just like when she first woke earlier in the evening, but she wouldn't show weakness.

"Mckale, I place Jessica Cane under your protection. She's your responsibility. Make sure she doesn't betray the pack," he said.

Mckale tightened his grip on her hand. "Yes, Alpha," he said loudly.

The man then leaned close to her and drew in a deep breath. "Interesting."

If any man had done that, she would have pushed him away, but she fought the urge, trusting Mckale would react if necessary.

He turned on his heel and ran off. Ten other men followed him, leaving one man behind.

Mckale wrapped his arms around her. "Claws and fangs. That was close," he said in her ear.

She leaned into his warmth, wanting to stay there indefinitely, or at least until she regained her full strength.

The remaining man stepped toward them. Mckale seemed unconcerned with his presence.

"Mckale, what the hell have you done? You're shackled to a Cane, now."

Mckale turned, keeping her within his embrace. "Jessica, this is my brother, Mckenny."

Jessica smiled with a nod, even though his brother continued to scowl.

"I'll deal with Damian," Mckenny said as he stomped off.

Jessica leaned her head against his chest, grateful they were alone so she could get the answers she needed. "Why did they make a big deal about my last name?"

He released a strained laugh. "Cane is a shifter name, and most shifters like to work around our four-legged counterparts, like how you work at the pet store. That is why I wrongly assumed you were a shifter. All but our leader think you are one of us."

"So that weird sniff?"

"He verified you were human."

Earlier in the evening, she'd believed she'd been delusional, and now she accepted that Mckale wasn't human. She laughed at the idea that the shifters thought she was one of them.

"Jessica," Mckale leaned into her, placing his fore-head against hers. "What am I going to do with you now?"

"You're not really shackled to me, are you, and I don't need your protection, right?"

"Can I give you the watered-down version?" Mckale asked.

Jessica thought she heard a slight squeak to his voice, as if he were highly uncomfortable. After the previous night, and the frightening day of learning about wolf shifters, she wasn't sure she could accept any more earth-shattering revelations. "For now, I'll take the simplified version"

"Before this night ends, all of my people will know that you and I are...best friends."

Her gut screamed that there was more to the story than what he was telling her, but she trusted he would tell her the rest when she could handle the truth. She stood on her tiptoes and touched her lips to his.

He deepened the kiss, allowing their tongues to caress.

"I would like to be your best friend," she said as she wondered what it would be like to be more than friends with a wolf shifter.

OTHER BOOKS BY C.L. THOMAS

Beware The Wolf

After becoming a wolf shifter's girlfriend, Jessica's nightmares
wake memories of the night her mother was killed by a
werewolf.

Scheduled for publication March 2021

ABOUT THE AUTHOR

C.L. Thomas enjoys writing Paranormal and Fantasy stories. Her first novel, Beware The Wolf, is scheduled for publication March 2021. She's been a finalist in The Sheila and Stiletto contests.

A sucker for a story with a happily ever after, C.L. enjoys creating characters that struggle and occasionally fail before reaching an unexpected and satisfying end.

An avid wildlife enthusiast, C.L. loves taking photos of wildlife near her home in North Central Florida. Pictures of fox, deer and raccoons are found sprinkled throughout her social media accounts.

When she's not writing, she spends time with her family on the porch and walks in nature.

Hearing from fans and fellow authors makes her day. Reach out anytime at: clthomasauthor@gmail.com!

Website: http://clthomas.net/
Tumblr: https://clthomasauthor.tumblr.com/
Twitter: https://twitter.com/CLThomas22
Facebook: https://www.facebook.com/CLThomasauthor

A MAGICAL FALL

A Sweet Paranormal Fall Story

DEBBY GRAHL

A Magical Fall

When nosy neighbors discover Sabrina Duncan performing magic, her coven sends her to Laurel, Colorado, to assist in her aunt's school for young witches. While preparing for the fall festival, Sabrina meets U.S. Marshal Jake Mallory. Neither can deny their instant desire, but Sabrina fears he'll discover the truth.

Jake, on the trail of a killer, isn't expecting help from a beautiful stranger. As their passion ignites, can their attraction burn brighter than Sabrina's secret?

CHAPTER 1

Sabrina Duncan, her hands covered with flour, peered into the wood-burning stove. An aroma of hot cinnamon and apples filled the room.

"Perfect." She flicked her wrist and the pie floated from the oven and landed on the counter to cool.

She wiggled her fingers, and the rolling pin glided back and forth over the dough while she reached for the fresh pumpkin filling. *Fall, what a wonderful time of year. The crisp mountain air, trees blazing with color, and the smell of wood smoke.* But her favorite of all was Samhain, a night of magic, ghosts, and mysterious happenings.

Sabrina peered through the window at the young girls practicing levitation. She laughed at Winnie Pickens whose assignment was to lift an old boot. Instead, Merlin, the school's black cat, was floating a few inches above the ground. While the girls squealed with laughter, Aunt Anoria, the founder of the school, raised her hands in defeat.

Sabrina's mind drifted back to her own childhood

and the mishaps which had landed her in one predicament after another. And here I am, twenty years old and banished from my home to Laurel, Colorado. She loved Aunt Anoria and enjoyed helping teach young witches, but, blast it all, how was she to have known those nosy ladies of the Salem Women's Auxiliary would come snooping around and catch her performing magic? Honestly, they stopped burning witches a couple of centuries ago. There was no reason in 1889 for the Witches' Council to think it prudent for her to leave, but here she was.

Sabrina smiled, recalling the scandal that had sent Aunt Anoria west, years earlier. Selling her erotic herbal elixir to the ladies of Salem wasn't bad enough, but Judge Parker's wife chasing him around his courtroom had been too much.

Sabrina slid the pumpkin pie into the stove as Anoria came through the kitchen door.

"I'm getting too old for this," she said easing down into a ladder-backed chair. "Mother God save me from twelve-year-old witches."

Sabrina grinned and wiped her hands on a towel. "The last pie is in the oven. I can teach the afternoon class."

"If you don't mind taking your life in your hands, that would be wonderful."

"The kettle is hot. How about a cup of chamomile tea?" Sabrina asked reaching for the cups.

Anoria nodded. "Thank you, my dear."

"Where are our little darlings now?"

"They're supposed to be having a picnic lunch. What they're actually doing is anyone's guess."

Sabrina kissed her aunt's wrinkled cheek. "If the stories are true, as a girl you found your share of mischief."

Anoria's green eyes twinkled. "Don't believe everything you hear."

Sabrina sliced them each a piece of apple pie and poured their tea. "The girls are excited about the fall festival."

"I know. They've been pestering me over what games and prizes there will be. I keep warning them that under no circumstance are they to use magic, but I'm fearful of what might happen."

"Yes, well, that is a troubling thought." Sabrina gnawed at her lower lip. "Perhaps we should split them up. You take four, and I'll take the others. Priscilla is perfectly capable of selling our baked goods and preserves at the booth."

"Good idea. All we need is for someone to witness one of the girls performing magic. Fear of the unknown can make perfectly normal people lose all rational thought. When I first came to Laurel, it was a small town, then it practically boomed overnight."

Sabrina removed the cups and plates and placed them in the sink. "It might be for the best. Who's going to pay attention to a school for orphaned witches?"

Anoria nodded. "True."

"Let's hope the girls behave like the sweet little fairies they'll be dressed as."

At that moment, the scarecrow, normally perched in the garden, danced past the window.

Anoria sighed. "And you were saying?"

Laughing, Sabrina cocked her head. "There's the buggy. Priscilla's back."

Within seconds, sixteen-year-old Priscilla Mead hurried through the door. "Sorry it took me so long." She removed her bonnet and coat. "I was helping organize the pickles and preserves for the booth, and Pastor Hallowell told us a deputy marshal arrived this morning from Denver. He said a man robbed a bank and killed the bank president. The marshal trailed him here."

"How dreadful," Anoria said. "With any luck, he's hiding in the mountains, and not near town."

"Pastor Hallowell said the Sheriff is placing guards at the bank."

"I hope he's caught before the festival." Anoria peered behind Priscilla. "Are the packages still in the buggy?"

"Oh, no, in all the excitement, I forgot. I'll go back."

"That's okay. I'll do it." Sabrina stood. "You start measuring the girls for their costumes."

"And tell them they are not to attempt to conjure fairy wings," Anoria stated. "We don't want any more episodes like Juliet producing bat wings attached to her head."

Priscilla tried to hold back her smile. "Yes, Miss Anoria. I'm awful at brewing potions, but I can teach them to sew by magic."

Sabrina donned her hat and gloves and went to ask Mr. Beck, the school's handyman and warlock, to hitch the horses to the buggy.

CHAPTER 2

J ake Malory adjusted the brim of his Stetson and
paused to allow a woman driving a buggy to pass.
His gaze lingered on her longer than it should
have, but damn she sure was pretty. Her copper hair
shone like fire beneath her hat, and her profile revealed
a delicate nose and creamy skin. He also had time to
admire a very nice bosom.

He made his way across the street and entered the
hotel. "Howdy, I'm Deputy Marshal Jake Malory. I need
a room."

"Yes, sir, Marshal. I heard you were in town, and we
have a very nice room I think you'll like."

Jake nodded, signed the guestbook, and took the key
to room seven. He unlocked his door and sighed. "How
did you know this would be my room?" he asked the
man seated on the bed.

"I was there when the desk clerk handed you the
key."

Jake closed and locked the door and tossed his bag on a chair. "Clarence, what if someone saw you?"

"No one seems to be able to see me but you."

"Lucky me," Jake murmured.

Jake ran his hands through his hair. Unusual abilities ran in his mother's side of the family. Originally from New Orleans, Jasmine LaDoux headed west at the outbreak of the Civil War and married a Yankee soldier from Denver. Jake encountered his first ghost when he turned ten. He decided to leave home after being punished for eating the berries meant for pies. Before long, he was cold, hungry, and scared. An old prospector happened upon him and returned him home. When he had turned to thank the old man, he had disappeared. Jake never learned who the old prospector had been in life.

"You and I trailed Slade Potter here," Clarence said. "Now you need to catch the bastard who murdered me. Damn it to hell, Jake, I was bank president, and I had a family. I need to see justice done."

"I understand and I plan on bringing Slade in. But I'm not going to rush headlong into a situation before having the information I need. I'm sorry you're dead, but I don't plan on joining you if I can help it." Jake reached for his hat.

"Where are you going?" Clarence asked.

"I have posters with Potter's description to take to the local sheriff. Then, I thought I'd get some supper."

"I'll come along."

Jake shook his head. "Great."

SABRINA ENTERED THE POST OFFICE AND GAPED AT the crowd of people milling about. Judging from snatches of conversation, the murdering robber was the only topic. She made her way to the counter and smiled at Mr. Janson. "The town is certainly riled up."

He shook his head. "It's been like this all day. I've got your packages come all the way from Salem, Massachusetts. Do you need help getting them outside?"

"No, thank you, I'm fine." Sabrina lifted the bundles and was surprised at their weight. She glanced around, then wiggled her fingers. The packages now floated just above her arms, but to anyone else she seemed to be carrying them. She stopped in front of the closed door. Did she dare use magic to open it? As she was about to do so, it opened.

Sabrina stepped through the door and stared at the most handsome man she'd ever seen. Smoky gray eyes gazed into hers, and she couldn't look away. "Thank you," she stammered as he held the door for her to pass.

"My pleasure, miss. Can I help you with those packages?"

Sabrina opened her mouth to speak, but her tongue wouldn't work. *Say something, you ninny.* "I'm, I'm fine. My buggy is right there." She pointed.

He smiled and Sabrina's knees went weak. His teeth were straight and white and there was a cleft in his chin. *Oh, Goddess help me,"* she prayed. *Get me to the buggy before I embarrass myself any further.*

He tipped his hat. "Afternoon, miss."

Sabrina nodded, hurried to the buggy, and, without a backward glance, headed toward home. Sweet Goddess, what a fool she'd made of herself. He wasn't the first handsome man to cross her path, but the first to cause her mental faculties to scatter to the four winds. She'd been drawn to him with a force that both thrilled and frightened her.

Sabrina frowned as she recalled what she'd seen but her muddled brain hadn't taken in. Obviously, that man was the U.S. marshal Priscilla had told them about. It was the translucent figure standing behind him that interested Sabrina. Throughout her life, she'd encountered ghosts, but this one pulsated with desperation.

When Sabrina arrived home, Anoria and Priscilla were seated in the kitchen. "You're not going to believe what happened to me." she said, depositing her parcels on the table.

She explained about meeting the marshal and seeing the ghost. When she finished, Anoria's and Priscilla's faces held the same expression of surprise and intrigue.

"Do you think the ghost knew you could see him?" Anoria asked.

Sabrina considered this. "Yes. It was just for an instant, but our eyes met."

Anoria tapped her lip with her finger. "Interesting. I wonder if the marshal knew he was there."

Sabrina paused in thought. "I'm not sure."

"Mortals usually can't see ghosts," Anoria stated. "So, what does that tell us about the marshal?"

Was that why I was so drawn to him? Sabrina wondered. *Is he from our world?* While she contemplated this, Priscilla squirmed in her seat.

"I'm anxious to see what the coven sent," she said.

Anoria smiled. "Hand me the scissors."

"Oh, my," Priscilla gasped when the contents were

revealed. Handmade lace, colorful ribbon, and soft fabric of forest green, midnight blue, rich red, and bright gold lay in front of them.

"The witches' council certainly outdid themselves," Sabrina said. "It's not as if we'd be able to find enchanted fabric at the general store."

Anoria grinned. "Not hardly."

Sabrina fingered the soft wool. "You two do realize there are eight costumes to make and the festival is the day after tomorrow," she pointed out. "My talent is kitchen magic, not sewing."

Priscilla beamed. "Leave it to me. The costumes will be ready on time."

CHAPTER 3

Jake sat in the hotel dining room waiting for his steak to arrive. Since his eyes had locked with hers, he hadn't been able to brush the woman from his mind. Beautiful, with mossy green eyes, milky skin, full lips, and fiery red hair, a nicely rounded bosom and thin waist. Her pull was magnetic, and his desire for her an instantaneous flash of heat. No woman had ever made his body react like that. *Hold off cowboy, she might be married. Besides, after capturing Potter, you'll be heading back to Denver.* He frowned. Why did the thought of never seeing her again fill him with sorrow? Perhaps before he left, he'd meet her again.

SABRINA AWOKE FROM A RESTLESS SLEEP. VISIONS OF the marshal's smoky eyes had her body on fire. She flung off her blanket and, still hot, opened the window. Cool air surrounded her, and she sighed. Her attraction to the man was extremely disconcerting. Something told her she'd be wise to avoid him, but she feared she'd ignore the warning. In Salem, she'd had a few men interested in her, but none made her think thoughts no proper lady should be thinking. She inhaled the crisp air, closed the window, turned, and opened her mouth to scream.

The translucent man before her violently shook his head. "Please, miss, I won't hurt you. We need your help."

Sabrina, her heart racing, held onto the dresser for support. "You're the man who was with the marshal."

He tipped his hat. "Yes. I'm the late Clarence Pratt."

Sabrina took a calming breath. "Mr. Pratt, I'm not used to ghostly visits in the middle of the night. What can I do for you?"

"My apologies, miss, but when I realized earlier that you could see me, I hoped you'd assist us to apprehend the bastard, excuse me, blackguard, who murdered me."

"I don't understand what you think I can do."

The ghost gave her a detailed accounting of the bank robbery and his demise. "I believe I wounded him as he fled. For some reason I can sense his presence, but not clearly enough to pinpoint his location. The connection I sensed between you and Marshal Malory, and the fact you can see me, convinces me the three of us could track him down and capture him."

Sabrina hesitated. Did he know she was a witch? If so, he really wasn't a threat. But it would be wise to proceed with caution. "Mr. Pratt, I'm not a clairvoyant."

He waved his hands in dismissal. "I haven't been dead for very long, but I've learned that only people with unusual gifts can see me. Please, come with me and speak to the marshal."

"It's one A.M. Can't this wait until morning?"

"You must meet in private. We can't take a chance of being overheard."

"Where is the marshal?"

"At the hotel."

Sabrina gaped with incredulity. "Mr. Pratt, you expect me to go alone to a strange man's hotel room?"

"I wouldn't ask if it wasn't important. I can't rest until the man who destroyed my life is caught. The marshal is trustworthy, and besides, I'll be there as well."

Great, chaperoned by a ghost. "All right, Mr. Pratt, please wait for me out front." *Sabrina, this is not wise.*

She ignored her conscience, quickly dressed, and slipped out the front door.

"It's quite a way to the hotel," Mr. Pratt said. "You'll need a horse."

"I can transport myself short distances. I'll meet you there." Sabrina pulled the hood of her black cape over her head, closed her eyes, and concentrated.

She landed on the deserted sidewalk next to Mr. Pratt.

"The desk clerk is asleep," he said.

They silently crossed the lobby and climbed two flights of stairs. Sabrina was following Mr. Pratt so closely, she neglected to stop when he disappeared through the door of Room Seven.

"Ouch," she exclaimed, touching her nose.

The door opened, and the man who'd haunted her dreams stood there staring in disbelief. "What the hell?"

Sabrina didn't know what to say. His thick dark hair was mussed, his shirt open at the neck and untucked. She lowered her eyes and noticed his feet were bare. She inwardly groaned, as visions of him lying in his bed filled her mind.

Without another word, he grabbed her arm and guided her into the room. He closed and locked the door and glowered at Mr. Pratt.

"Clarence, what have you done?"

"She can see me. I think she's a witch."

At his words, Sabrina felt the color drain from her face. Even though the marshal was able to see ghosts, this didn't mean he accepted witches. She glanced at the marshal from beneath her lashes and sighed with relief. His expression wasn't one of shock, more of annoyance.

"Miss..." He hesitated.

"Duncan," Sabrina said.

"Miss Duncan. I apologize for Clarence involving you in this matter. I'll be happy to escort you home."

"No." Clarence exclaimed. "Listen to me. She can help us."

The marshal sighed and indicated a chair. "Miss Duncan, would you like a seat?"

Sabrina nodded and sat down. "Marshal..."

"Malory. But call me Jake."

"Jake, I don't know if I'll be of assistance, but I can read auras. If someone is harboring evil intent, they produce a distinct glow around them."

Jake paced the small room. "There's a number of people in this town who for one reason or another might put off such a glow. How can we be sure it's Potter?"

"Mr. Pratt gave you a description, didn't he?" Sabrina asked.

"I certainly did. Around six foot, thin, with dark shaggy hair," Mr. Pratt replied.

Jake paused in thought. "It might work. We know he's wounded and probably becoming weak and in need of help. And most likely hungry as well. That combination might bring him to town."

"If it were me, I'd try and blend in with a crowd," Sabrina added. "Especially if there was a lot of food and confusion."

"Do you have something in mind?" Jake asked.

She explained about the fall festival. "Not only does the entire town turn out, there's also a costume contest."

A smile spread across Jake's face. "Miss Duncan, I believe you are a wish come true."

Clarence beamed. "See, I told you she could help."

CHAPTER 4

When Jake smiled at her, Sabrina's senses whirled in all directions. Her pulse quickened, her hands grew damp, and her body reacted in a way that screamed trouble.

"Now we need to make our plans," Clarence was saying.

But Jake's attention was on Sabrina. The giddy sensation she'd experienced when she'd first met him, washed over her. The intensity in his gaze let her know he felt it as well. The energy around them sizzled like lightning

Her internal alarm told her she needed to leave. She stood. "It's late. I should go." Instead of heading for the door, she paused.

Jake took a step toward her. "This situation is extremely unconventional, but I wanted to tell you I've been thinking about you since we met earlier."

Sabrina's mouth went dry. "I have you as well." For a

second neither moved, then as if there was an invisible force, Sabrina stepped into his arms.

Mr. Pratt sighed. "I believe I'll go look for Potter."

The desire in Jakes eyes stole Sabrina's breath. Heat surrounded them as he placed his arm around her waist and his hand cupped the back of her head. He bent his head toward her.

He's going to kiss me, and I have no will to stop him. When their lips met, every nerve in her body reacted with a delicious tingling sensation. She wrapped her arms around his neck and allowed him to devour her mouth with his.

Her body ached in a way she didn't understand. She pressed closer, and he let out a low moan. A throbbing began in a part of her body that demanded some kind of release.

His hand moved from her waist to slide up her side and cup her breast. Her breath was coming in tiny gasps and she dug her fingers into his shoulders. When his erection pressed against her, she knew she should pull away. But the feelings were too glorious, and she clung even tighter.

She let out little whimpering sounds. Jake, his breath ragged, broke their kiss.

"Come to bed with me, so I can please you properly," he said, his voice low and husky.

She met his eyes and read the passion that blazed in their depths. Not quite sure what her body was craving, Sabrina understood enough to know what he wanted.

"Yes" was on the tip of her tongue, but thankfully common sense ruled out. She swallowed hard before saying, "Jake, we're practically strangers. We can't do this. Please let me go."

Jake closed his eyes, moved his lips as if counting, then released her. "Sabrina, I apologize. I don't know what came over me."

Her emotions rattled, she shook her head. "Don't. I didn't want you to stop. I... Oh, I have to leave." She flung the door open, ran down the hall, and disappeared.

JAKE STARTED AFTER HER BUT HALTED MID STEP WHEN she vanished. "I'll be damned." He returned to his room, sat on his bed, and ran his hand through his hair. What the hell had just happened? He'd never treated a woman as he had Sabrina. Christ, he almost took her standing against a wall.

If he hadn't seen the desire in her eyes, he'd think she had him under a spell. He'd had his share of women, but none stirred his blood as Sabrina did. He had to see more of her, but first he must capture Potter. Then, they'd discover if this spark between them was love or lust.

SABRINA STUMBLED WHEN SHE LANDED IN HER ROOM. Still shaken from her experience with Jake, she fell across the bed. She'd been kissed before, but her body had never reacted like that. Was it normal to experience those wonderful sensations? She'd heard that a witch knew when she'd met her mate. Even now, she craved his touch. Mortification burned her cheeks. What must he think of her? She'd actually rubbed against him.

Oh, sweet Goddess. She buried her face in her pillow. She'd promised to help find Potter, so she'd have to see him again. As humiliated as she was, deep inside she knew she and the marshal's relationship wasn't over.

CHAPTER 5

The morning of the festival, the girls were bubbling with excitement.

Sabrina smiled. They did look enchanting. Their forest green dresses shimmered with tiny gold stars, and a circlet of flowers crowned their heads. Filmy wings fluttered in the breeze, and a sprinkling of fairy dust covered their cheeks.

"There's a taffy pull," one of the girls exclaimed.

"We want to enter the sack race, and the egg and spoon race, and we want to bob for apples," they said as one.

"Yes," Anoria said. "Patience please. You'll get to do it all."

Sabrina took in the array of booths selling everything from baked goods, embroidered towels and handkerchiefs, to jars of pickles and preserves.

The girls had just gone to watch a man carving pumpkins when Jake came up beside Sabrina.

"Good morning," he said.

His smile alone caused butterflies to take flight in her stomach. She hadn't seen him since their encounter in his room, and she had trouble meeting his eyes. She cleared her throat. "Good morning."

He lowered his voice. "About the other night."

"Not here."

He nodded and ran his gaze over her. Her dress, the color of fall leaves, emphasized her thin, but curvy, body. "You look very pretty."

Pleased that he noticed, Sabrina's cheeks turned slightly pink. "Thank you." She wanted to tell him he looked mouthwateringly handsome in his black hat, vest, and denim pants, but couldn't get up the nerve.

Jake scanned the crowd. "Any indication Potter is here?"

"Not that I've seen. I've only just arrived."

"The costumes will make it easier for Potter to blend in. Although he might be favoring his wounded arm. Also, keep your eye on the food stalls."

"I'm concerned the townsfolk are in danger. Do you think he knows you're here?" Sabrina asked.

"He doesn't know me by sight, and I'm not wearing my badge. I explained our theory to the Sheriff, and he has men here as well. I thought if we walked together, he'd think we were a married couple and not be suspicious."

Married. The images that conjured brought back that wonderful sensation in her nether regions. She fought desperately to clear her mind of memories of his kisses. She took his arm, and the feel of him sent a thrill up her spine. The knowing gleam in his eyes said he felt it too.

"There's a group of men near the booth selling stew. Shall we head there?" Jake asked.

Before they took a step, Mr. Pratt appeared shimmering with agitation. "Hurry, I believe I've spotted Potter."

"Where?" Jake asked.

"At the booth selling pies."

Fear clenched Sabrina's chest. "Priscilla." She let go of Jake and maneuvered through the crowd. She concentrated on people's auras. Most were happy, some annoyed, others angry, but one radiated malice. She lifted her dress and quickened her pace.

She arrived at the booth to hear Pricilla exclaim, "Sir, you haven't paid for that pie."

Pricilla's shout attracted the attention of others. Potter, with the look of a cornered animal, grabbed Pricilla, placing a gun to her head.

"Stay back," he snarled. "I'll kill her."

Sabrina didn't want to take her eyes from Potter. *Where are you, Jake?*

The gunman, one arm around Priscilla's neck, the other holding the gun, moved slowly away from the booth.

Sabrina stared into Priscilla's stricken face. *Use your magic to stop him, Priscilla, s*he tried to mentally communicate. But the glazed expression in her eyes told Sabrina she was overcome with fear.

As she was about to use her own magic, Sabrina spotted Jake to her right and the Sherriff to her left. But her heart nearly stopped. Directly behind Potter, eight angelic fairies lifted their arms as they had been taught.

Sabrina concentrated all her power on Potter's gun.

As it flew from his hand, he began to rise. All around her, people gasped as Potter rose higher and higher. Priscilla, no longer in danger, floated to the ground.

Potter, his mouth hanging open, and his eyes bugged out, dangled in the air as if by invisible strings.

"Tell them to lower him," Jake said, coming up next to Sabrina.

She cleared her throat. "I can do it." She waved her hand, and Potter landed in the arms of the Sherriff and his deputies.

Anoria gathered up the girls and hurried them toward the school's wagon.

"That was quite remarkable," Jake said, with a slight grin. "What will happen now?"

Sabrina gave him a wry smile. "I suppose the cat is definitely out of the bag."

"The girls saved Priscilla and captured a murderer. The town might think they're heroes."

"More likely daughters of Satan." Tears filled her eyes. "We probably won't be burned at the stake, but I'm sure we'll be asked to leave."

Jake brushed a tear from her cheek. "Don't cry. You can all come to Denver. No one will bother you there."

A lump formed in Sabrina's throat. "That's kind of you."

"I'm not being kind for the reason you think. I can't imagine never seeing you again."

Sabrina's thought process stopped. What was he saying?

"Sabrina, I don't know what this is between us, but I do know you make me feel as no other woman ever has. I can't get you out of my mind." He lowered his voice.

"I want to kiss you and make love to you, morning, noon and all through the night."

Joy bubbled up in Sabrina until she feared she'd burst. A smile spread across her face. Not caring who saw, she wrapped her arms around Jake's neck. "I'd be happy to let you do just that."

A man cleared his throat. "Excuse me," Clarence Pratt said. "I wanted to thank you and say good-bye."

Jake and Sabrina broke apart. "I'm glad you now have peace," Sabrina said.

Clarence nodded, tipped his hat, and disappeared.

Sabrina steeled herself and took in the crowd around her. Some were speaking excitedly, some walking away, and some staring, confusion and horror on their faces.

"Let's go," Jake said, taking Sabrina's arm.

Sabrina, determined not to show how upset she was, held her head high as they made their way to the street. The buggy she and Anoria had arrived on, was parked nearby. "You shouldn't be seen with me," She said to Jake. "You might be accused of being evil like me."

Jake's mouth formed a thin line. "You're not evil." He helped her into the buggy. "There will be a few who react badly, but I believe the majority will go about their lives and let you and Anoria go about yours."

Sabrina gathered up the reins. "I hope you're right."

"I need to speak with the Sherriff. Can I see you later?"

Sabrina was about to agree when Sherriff Brown approached.

"Ma'am." He tipped his hat. "I'm not sure what happened, and I'm not sure I want to know. But I'd like to thank you for your assistance in apprehending Potter."

Sabrina, temporarily speechless, nodded. "I'm glad we could help."

He turned to Jake. "Marshal, we'll keep Potter until you're ready to take him to Denver."

"I need to make arrangements for additional men," Jake replied. "I'm hoping in a day or two."

"Fine." He tipped his hat to Sabrina and left.

"May I accompany you home?" Jake asked.

Sabrina smiled. "Yes."

EPILOGUE

S ix weeks later

SABRINA HELD ON TIGHT AS JAKE CARRIED HER ACROSS the threshold. All of Laurel turned out to cheer the new Sherriff and his bride. Anoria, forgiven by the council for past indiscretions, was on her way to Salem. Sabrina, now head of the school, wasn't expecting her next class until after the Yule holiday.

Gloriously happy, Sabrina didn't realize Jake was heading upstairs. "Where are we going?"

"I'm taking you to bed. And, I'm not letting you up until hunger forces us."

Sabrina smiled and wiggled her fingers. The baskets of food left by the townsfolk, floated behind them.

OTHER BOOKS BY DEBBY GRAHL

Mountain Blaze [release November 2]

Diana falls in love with cowboy Dillon McCoy. Can they unmask a killer and save the Lazy M ranch?

His Magic Touch

Can Jared defeat the dark magic descending over the Big Easy while winning back the woman he loves?

Decorated to Death

Newcomsville is ready for their Christmas tour, but betrayal, blackmail and murder lie beneath the gentle mantle of new-fallen snow.

Rue Toulouse

Two strangers must learn to trust one another to survive in a world of family greed and ruthless revenge.

The Silver Crescent

Betrayal, murder. and a stolen fortune bring Elise Baxter to Cedar Bend to solve a family mystery.

ABOUT THE AUTHOR

Award winning author Debby Grahl lives on Hilton Head Island, South Carolina, with her husband, David. Besides writing, she enjoys biking, walking on the beach and a glass of wine at sunset. She is a history buff who also enjoys reading murder mysteries, time travel, and, of course, romance. Visually impaired since childhood by Retinitis Pigmentosa (RP), she uses screen-reading software to research and write her books.

You can find Debby at the following:
   Website -- www.debbygrahl.com
   Facebook -- https://www.facebook.com/debby-grahlauthor?ref=br_rs
   Twitter -- https://twitter.com/DebbyGrahl
   Bookbub -- https://www.bookbub.com/search/authors?search=debby%20grahl

THE HONEYBEE

A Sensual Samhain Tale

P. K. BRENT

The Honeybee: A Samhain Tale

When Connor tries to interest women at the Samhain festival he meets with disappointment. Nevertheless, he is kind to an old woman, one of the fey. She turns up at Connor's door insisting she will find him a bride. Soon Connor is performing amazing feats to prove his worth and looking forward to his wedding. Everyone in the village is ready to laugh at Connor until the bride appears – a golden beauty.

THE HONEYBEE

Connor stared at the bonfire then aimed his long knife at the platter being passed around and skewered a large slice of roast pig. He dropped the juicy meat on his wooden plate.

"You seem to be enjoying the harvest feast, Connor!" Jimmy-John pounded his friend on the back.

"Indeed, I am! The food is excellent, as is the mead. I couldn't ask for a better Samhain festival."

"We have enough of the old ways to enjoy a good party, but not so many as to yoke us with superstitions. No ghosts, no fey, no gods – just an outdoor dance, food, good cheer, and a bonfire to ward off the chill and remind us of the winter to come."

"Yes. Winter is ahead. The harvest is behind us. Cattle and sheep are moved down the mountain to summer pastures. Kitchen gardens are ready, and smokehouses are full. Now we wait for the cold to arrive full-force."

"As a married man, I look forward to winters now." Jimmy-John gave a knowing smirk. "Now I'll be plowing the field I want to plow best."

Connor choked on his mead and hastily changed the subject. "I must say hello to my sister, who just arrived."

Jimmy-John nodded good-bye to his friend. Connor hastily went to refill his mug. He did not care to be reminded that for him, winter would be long and lonesome.

Unfortunately, Connor had been striking out with the lasses, ever since his sister wed and moved into her husband's home. Now he, Connor, was left to do all the housekeeping by himself. His cheeks reddened at the thought of Kirstie Grier laughing in his face a few minutes earlier, while he looked down her loosely-laced bodice at the lovely mounds of her creamy breasts.

Her disdain had been humiliating. "Go home with you to that rat's nest you live in? So you can ride me all night and then ask me to scrub your pots and cook breakfast the next morning? I'll save myself the trouble! I have better offers."

Fortunately, Connor was not easily discouraged. The heaving hindquarters of Kendra Grant, as she frolicked and bowed in jest at the other maids gave him plenty of inspiration. Connor grabbed an extra cup of mead, refilled his cup, and just like a good sheepdog, cut Kendra out of the pack.

"Kendra love, I brought ye refreshment as ye look a might bit peaked with all the jouncing and dancing. I thought ye might like to stroll with me in the moonlight."

Kendra gave Connor an appraising look. "Aye,

Connor, I would at that, but I can do better. I have other suitors with more to offer. Thank ye for the cuppa though!" Kendra gulped down the mead quickly then just as quickly disappeared.

Truth be told, Connor longed for far more than food, ale, and gaiety. A long cold winter lay ahead, and he would be alone in his cottage, with no one for company or to share the long nights. Connor glanced at the women as they danced with lively partners, passed around the food, or gathered up the crockery. None suited him and he suited none of them. Most were either too young, too old, married, engaged, or otherwise attached. The ones he admired most were also the ones most out of reach. News travels fast and everyone knew that Connor paid an outrageously large dowry to the man his sister married, which made him damaged goods for more reasons than one.

"Your fortune for a penny?" A creaky voice startled Connor who looked down at the crone sitting on a bale of straw near the fire. She was so small and bent that she barely reached the tabletop. He recognized her as the old woman who set up a cart in the village, peddling herbs, and tinctures, while offering to tell fortunes. Connor felt sorry for her.

"What are you called, old Mother?" Connor handed the crone a penny.

"You may call me, Mother Fae. Now, hand me your palm and I will read your fortune."

Connor knew that the crone had not eaten. Perhaps she did not have the coppers required to purchase a plate.

"One moment, Mother Fae. I'll be right back."

Connor returned a minute later with a plate full of roast pork and roast chicken, bread, and mashed turnips. The crone gave him an appreciative look and cleaned the plate faster than Connor imagined was possible. Then she grabbed his hand.

While examining his hand, Mother Fae nodded and sang a lilting song to herself in a language Connor thought he knew but somehow could not entirely recall. He was nearly asleep when the crone stood up to leave.

"Well, Mother Fae, what do you make of my fortune?"

"Better than most," replied the crone. "Tomorrow evening I will come by your house shortly after sun sets. I have something for you."

The crone brushed off Connor's protests. The last thing he wanted was to host the crone in his own cottage. The things said about her were appalling.

True, her herbal remedies and elixirs were in high demand. But it was one thing to buy her a plate or purchase medicine from her. Having her visit his cottage and then have to play host, that was too much! The crone was odd and inscrutable. People whispered scandalous things about her including that she was half fey and the daughter of no man—but an elf or fairy.

Mother Fae stood and hollered for attention. She had an announcement to make. No one noticed until the crone reached into her pocket and tossed a handful of shimmery objects in the fire. A loud popping noise ensued with multi-colored sparks flying about. Everyone stopped talking and gaped. The old crone cleared her voice.

"I have an announcement to make! This same day

next week you all are invited to the home of Connor MacGraw here, for I have found a husband for my daughter and Connor has found a lovely wife. They will wed under the Rose Moon."

Connor gasped in horror. A few people murmured congratulations, while most held their hands to their face to hide snickers. They all turned to observe the hysterical mirth of Jimmy-John as he rolled on the ground chortling with glee. Connor took advantage of the distraction and fled.

❧

The next evening, at sundown, Mother Fae appeared at Connor's door pulling her little cart. A large wooden box sat on top.

"I have come to bring you a gift, but first I need a hot cup of tea."

Connor scuttled about the kitchen, boiling water, preparing tea, and setting out a plate of biscuits. Nothing good would come of this, only more humiliation. Nightmares about Mother Fae and her announcement of his wedding had robbed Connor of sleep.

"This place is a dump! Don't you have a woman come in to clean for you while you work the fields?"

"No, not yet. I've been too busy to find someone. My sister used to handle all the womanly chores. She wed two months ago. Until then, she kept house for me. She cooked and cleaned, milked the cow, gathered the eggs. I used to come home to a clean house and a hot dinner. Not so anymore."

"You need to do something about that. You need a wife."

"Hah! Since my sister left, I have paid compliments to a few lasses I know but no luck. They are not interested in the likes of me."

"Why not? You are an only son. You inherited the farm. You have arms, legs, fingers, and toes enough for a man. Your looks are average but pleasing enough. What is the problem?"

"My sister; Maisie wed two months ago, you might know."

"Yes. But what of it?"

"It was difficult to procure for her the man she desired. His family requested a high dowry. His family asked for a great deal. If I had not paid the amount, a rich great aunt of his would have paid it to marry off her sickly daughter and keep the dowry in the family, more or less."

"You gave what they asked?"

"Yes, of course I did! I love my sister and she had given her heart to this man."

"Was that reason enough to ruin your own prospects?"

"Yes. I wish for Maisie to be happy. The man she chose is honorable and they were in love. I did not want them to be separated. As head of the family it was my right to choose for her. I could have done it cheaper with a man she did not desire, a widower with children perhaps. But her happiness was worth the price."

The crone looked Connor up and down, nodding with approval. "You've made a most favorable impression on me. You clearly have the generous and kind nature I saw at the Samhain festival when you not only purchased my dinner, but you conversed kindly with a homely old woman. You were the only person there who paid me the slightest attention."

Connor blushed and looked down at his shoes. "It was my pleasure, Mother Fae."

"You were kind to your sister, at great expense to yourself. In fact, you ruined your own chances at a match this season, by being so generous to her."

"No matter," replied Connor. "Someday the right woman will come along, one who cares for me and not my lack of riches."

"Not someday, Connor. I meant it when I announced your nuptials and invited the village here for your wedding to my daughter next week."

Connor's mouth gaped open. Now what sort of fix was he into? "I thank you for your concern, but I am fine by myself. Eventually the right lass will come along."

"You are well thought of, Connor. But giving away such a large dowry has set your finances back and left people wondering if you are of sound mind. So, no one wants you marrying their daughter. My daughter is fairer than any of them, and I have matched her to you."

"How do you know so much about my reputation?"

"No one pays any attention to me, so I listen. That is what people say behind your back,."

"I shouldn't be surprised."

"Now first, help me with my cart." Connor and Mother Fae went outside. It was already becoming cold.

Mother Fae pointed to the large, wooden box that Connor had noticed earlier.

"Carry that inside, young man!"

Connor obediently lifted the box. It was made from fine wood with ornate carving all around. In the dusky light he could not quite make out the designs. It was heavy. *Was that a humming noise? How could a box be humming?*

Cautiously, Connor brought the wooden box inside and set it on a little table near the door. The box *was* humming.

"What do you have in there, Mother Fae?"

"Only my bees."

"Bees! It's a hive! That box cannot stay here!"

"My bees are my family. They will stay in the house with me, until your wedding or perhaps even longer."

Only then did Connor notice that Mother Fae had also carried in a satchel and she was making up a bed for herself on the sitting room sofa. He began to protest, but Mother Fae interrupted. "Don't you wish to know how your bride's laugh will sound, or the color of her eyes, or how she is called?"

"Yes, those things would be nice to know." In his head, Connor scrambled to think of a way to be rid of the crone and her bees.

"Her name is Orla, which means golden princess. When you meet her, you will understand why she carries that name. Orla's laugh is sweet as honey and musical, like wind blowing through a valley. She has beautiful sparkly eyes that twinkle with good nature and mischief. They are dark as the fertile ground of your fallow fields."

"Your daughter sounds lovely, Madam Fae." Dare he believe what the crone was telling him?

"You will be pleased. Tomorrow we begin preparations for your bride."

The next day, Connor woke early, before the rooster crowed. It still was dark. Perhaps he'd misunderstood the strange crone who fell asleep in his sitting room the night before. She couldn't possibly plan to marry him off to her hitherto unseen daughter a few days hence, and she couldn't hope to live with him until he married. He would have to be stern with her and send her on her way. But what was that lovely scent in the air?

Connor followed his nose and entered the kitchen to find his table set with clean dishes. There was Mother Fae with a pot of steaming tea, serving him a huge platter of bacon, eggs, and freshly baked bread with honey. Surprised but with his stomach rumbling assent, Connor sat and tucked into the breakfast, spooning extra honey and cream into his tea. Mother Fae spread butter and honey on his bread.

As he ate, Connor looked around. His kitchen was clean. Dishes that had piled up for weeks were washed and put away. The floor was mopped. The dining room and sitting room were set to rights.

"Your bride must find your home clean and lovely. No woman wants to move into a dirty house," Mother Fae advised. "All it needs now is a good dusting and I called in a friend to help. You head off to the fields. I packed your mid-day meal. By the time you return, your house will be right as rain!"

"No one can work that fast!" Connor replied.

"I can. One thing... Bring me back a handful of fertile earth."

"What for?" Connor asked.

"Never you mind. Just bring me back a handful of earth."

Connor nodded and left. He would speak to the crone tonight. The thought of a clean house and a hot dinner was appealing. Perhaps it wouldn't hurt for her to stay another night and leave the next morning.

Connor took one last look at his house. The front door stood open and, on the stoop, perched the largest eagle he had even seen. As Connor watched, the windows popped open, one by one. Connor remembered the gossip about the crone, that her father was from the shining ones. Perhaps it was true.

He crept to a side window and looked in. The eagle flapped its wings for all it was worth, blowing wind in the front door, through the house and out the back door, freshening the cottage. The crone spun in a circle with a wooden spoon held high in the hair, humming to her bees as they hovered from one place to the next, dusting in all the nooks and crannies.

In a few minutes, the house and everything in it was completely dusted, mopped, and dried, upstairs and downstairs. The crone picked up an eagle feather off the kitchen floor and placed it in a bowl under the window Then the crone put on the kettle and prepared tea.

Stunned, Connor hurried to his northern fields. It

would be a long day of hard labor for him, breaking ground in a field that had lain fallow for years. Then from behind a hillock stepped an enormous stag.

The stag looked at Connor and pawed the ground then began to speak. "Well, let's get on with it."

"Get on with what?" Connor replied. *I'm conversing with a beast! Perhaps I am still asleep and dreaming?*

"I am to plow your fields. Hop on!" The stag turned and offered its back.

Connor quaked with fear but jumped on the stag's back and grabbed onto the beast's thick coat. The stag lowered his antlers, slid them into the ground and ran forward at high speed, plowing the large northern field in record time.

Then he plowed the one remaining fallow field even further north. It was far more than Connor had planned. The extra crops would bring a good price. From the stag's back, Connor flung seeds of winter wheat into the earth and the stag's back hooves pressed the seeds into the freshly turned earth. When the work was done, Connor had barely broken a sweat. Two fields plowed and a new crop sown would go a long way toward rebuilding his finances. And all done in less than a day. Perhaps he *was* still dreaming.

"Thank you, stag," he said humbly.

"Thank Mother Fae." The stag nodded his head then turned and disappeared into the wood.

Still reeling with wonder, Connor returned to his cottage. It was just starting to grow dusky. Miracle of miracles, he remembered to grab up the handful of dirt as the crone requested.

As soon as he entered the cottage, Mother Fae took

the handful of dirt and placed it in the bowl under the feather. That evening, Connor enjoyed another delicious meal. He was proud of his home, with all the clean and polished surfaces. Even his dishes and cutlery looked new and fresh. He slept well that night, enjoying the clean, sweet smell of hay and lavender, and not a single nightmare troubled him. It wouldn't hurt for the crone to stay another night.

The next morning Connor came down to another delicious, hot breakfast. He knew not to ask about the eagle, stag, and dusting bees that he spied the day before. Questioning the fey was never a good idea, but it wouldn't hurt to find out what the crone planned next.

"Have you a busy day ahead, Mother Fae?"

"Yes! Today I plan to wash all your clothes and linens, not forgetting your curtains, cushions, and tablecloths. There is a lot to do and I need your help."

"My help?"

"Yes, you cannot expect me to do all that is required to please your bride. You must help too. Aren't you ahead in your workload now?"

"Yes, indeed!" he said with a smile. "I have plenty of time to help."

"Did I tell you the color of your bride's hair? It is gold as honey." The crone raised the lid of the honey pot, dipped in a spoon and lifted a long stream of golden honey. She twirled it around in the sunlight from the window.

"You see here, Connor, just like your bride's hair, the color goes from the darkest gold to the lightest, brightest! Both colors and every color in between. Her hair is long and shimmers from dark gold to light. Just like the bright, sweetness of her ways."

"A bride like that would indeed be lovely," Connor agreed, hardly believing that it could be even remotely possible.

"Yes! But you cannot expect me to do everything for you. This is your bride, so you must earn her. Now, load all the clothes, linens, and such onto my cart. Help me take it down the path to the river at the bottom of the hill."

"Usually the laundry is done here in the kitchen, Mother Fae. I can pump some pails of water for you."

"No! This washing is different, and you must help. Everything must be pure and clean for your bride. It must be done as I say."

Connor obliged, though he did not entirely understand. Yet, after seeing the eagle and stag he knew it was true that the crone was part fey, and it would not be smart to cross her. Who knows? Maybe she would find him a bride. If not, he soon would be the laughingstock of the village. Yet perhaps he already was being laughed at, if the things Mother Fae told him were true.

After a short walk to the edge of the river, the crone tossed all the clothes and linens into the water, at a place where a small inlet made a pool safe from the current. Next, she called in an ancient tongue and a salmon appeared. Salmon are wise. They swim the depths of the water and the mind. The salmon swam among the clothes, flipping and slapping them with his tail until they were like new. The crone and Connor wrung them and packed them back on the cart.

"Go now with the salmon. You need a gift for your bride." With that, the crone pushed Connor over the riverbank, and he fell into the water.

The first thing Connor grabbed was the salmon's fin. He was pulled under and expected to die, only to find that he could suddenly breathe under water. In time the salmon stopped at a large oyster. Connor grabbed it and tucked it under his coat, up against his chest. A moment later he was flipped onto the riverbank and the huge salmon slapped its pink tail three times, then disappeared.

Back at the cottage Connor found the crone again twirling with a wooden spoon in the air. A blaze burned in the fireplace as she called forth the fire salamanders. The tiny elemental spirits of fire emerged and mingled with the wet items, drying them swiftly. Mother Fae deftly snipped the tail off a fire salamander and tossed it in the bowl with the fallow earth and eagle feather. The bees swirled about, folding, putting away clothes, hanging the curtains, spreading tablecloths, and making beds. In a few minutes time all was clean and sweet smelling as new.

"Open the oyster!" Mother Fae directed.

Connor opened the oyster and out fell a pink pearl the size of his fist. "Wash it, and set it in the pretty dish, the one holding earth from your fallow field, an eagle feather, and the fire salamander tail."

Without questioning her, Connor did as he was told.

That evening, he ate the most delicious sea soup he'd ever enjoyed. Along with the oyster were chunks of fish, potato, and sweet seaweed. Soup along with honey cake and tea made for a fine meal.

"Your bride will be pleased with the gift you found. Shall I tell you about her skin?"

Connor nodded. His bride was beginning to seem real, but perhaps still too good to be true.

"Her skin is pink like this pearl you found. As you move the pearl in the light it shines lighter pink, and, in some places, darker. In some places it is barely pink at all, like the petal of the most delicate flower. In another place it is deep pink. Your bride's cheeks glow the deepest pink of all when she laughs."

"She sounds so lovely!" By now Connor yearned for his bride with all his heart. "When do I meet her?"

"Tomorrow about noon, just before guests arrive for the wedding. You will meet her then."

"Tomorrow? How will she get here? Will she be here on time? Are you sure?"

"Never you mind about arrangements. I have it all in hand."

"What if she does not like me, or I do not like her?"

"Don't be silly, Connor. An enchanting bride you worked to please? You both will fall in love. Tomorrow you will meet your bride at last. Now go to bed!"

On the third day Connor awoke again to a fabulous breakfast of pancakes, butter, honey, tea, stewed apples, and sausage. He noticed bowls filled with ingredients for baking on the counter.

"What are you making, Mother Fae?"

"Your wedding cake."

"I will leave you to it!" Connor said as he headed toward the door.

"No, you don't!" Mother Fae pointed to a large tub steaming with hot water. "Today you must prepare yourself for your bride. Hop in the tub and scrub until all the dirt is gone under your nails and every cranny is clean. Then nap and rest. Don't come downstairs until you are called."

Connor knew there was no point arguing with her, so he hopped in the tub, hidden from view by a blanket hung between two chairs. There he scrubbed every inch, washed his hair, brushed under his nails, and made himself clean.

The warm water made him sleepy, so by the time he was done bathing, Connor was more than ready for the prescribed nap. He hopped out of the tub and drew the blanket around himself. Mother Fae's large honeybee, the huge one, left her usual place on the wooden hive and roosted on the kitchen curtains. Connor could swear the large bee was gazing at him and he blushed.

Definitely time for the nap! Connor discovered that in the time it took for him to bathe, Mother Fae had baked a three tiered cake and prepared a feast of finger sandwiches, stuffed mushrooms, sausage niblits, cheeses, cookies, and many other niceties to eat.

"Won't the guests be here soon? I see no bride and it is nearly time!"

"Never mind about that. Your bride will be here on time. When Jimmy-John arrives, I will send him upstairs to help you dress."

Whether it was real or not, Connor knew better

than to argue with Mother Fae. He napped a bit but could not sleep, so he dressed, and came down the stairs.

"The bride, has she arrived yet?"

"No! Stop fretting. Make yourself useful and answer the door. The guests are starting to arrive."

Connor answered the door time and time again as relatives and guests from the village arrived. He saw now that tables inside and out in the courtyard were laden with food and drink. The wedding cake shimmered in front of the parlor window, iced in white with bowls of berries in sauce laid out on either side. Jimmy-John appeared and slapped Connor on the back.

"Congratulations old boy! No one knows the lass you will marry, and we all look forward to meeting her and celebrating your nuptials."

"As do I," Connor replied.

Once more Connor inquired of Mother Fae when his bride would arrive and again, he was put off.

Finally, the priest arrived. Connor ran a finger under his collar. Sweat ran down his back. *I'm going to look a fool! All these guests. All these preparations. No bride in sight!*

Connor walked into the kitchen, desperate. "Mother Fae! All the guests are here. My sister, my friends, my aunties, and uncles, even the priest. But there is no bride in sight! I will look like a fool."

"Oh, very well," replied Mother Fae, as she finished another tray of sandwiches, open faced with soft cheese spread and a thin slice of roast squash.

"Stand here."

Connor stood in one corner of the kitchen. Mother Fae lifted her wooden spoon to the top of the curtains, where the large bee roosted. The bee carefully climbed onto the wooden spoon. Next Mother Fae placed the enormous gold and black bee on Connor's hand.

"Now don't frighten the bee. Keep your arms steady!"

Lifting her arms, Mother Fae twirled the wooden spoon high above Connor's head. In her other hand she held the bowl containing dark fallow earth, an eagle feather, the salamander tail, and the pink pearl. A whirlwind surrounded Connor. A golden vortex spun around and around the bee on Connor's hand. He could not entirely see what was happening, but it was as though the bee disappeared and a larger form took its place. Finally, the whirlwind stopped and there in front of Connor stood the most beautiful bride he could ever have imagined. He gasped!

Orla's hair was gold as honey and hung nearly to her waist. As it shone in the sun, some locks were dark gold and other strands a brilliant yellow. Her eyes were black and sparkled. Her gown was pale gold with bees embroidered in black around the hem and a cream-colored ribbon tied around her waist. Tiny feet in black shoes peeked out from below the long gown.

On her finger sat a golden ring. The setting was shaped like a bee and held a single large, pink pearl. The beautiful young woman began to laugh, and the sound was sweet as honey and melodic as the wind. Connor was speechless.

"This is Orla, your bride. Her name means gold. You wanted a bride Connor, and my daughter Orla chose you. Of all the possible men, you were chosen because of your kind and generous nature."

"Orla! My sweet Orla!" he whispered.

Orla beamed at Connor and took his arm. He smiled at his lovely bride in her golden dress.

"The Rose Moon is high, and the priest is waiting!" Mother Fae said with glee. "Go and get married!"

OTHER BOOKS BY P. K. BRENT

Witch of the Western Gate: Dragon's Gift

Tagline: Twisted tales and pointy teeth

ABOUT P.K. BRENT

Pegeen grew up across the street from an old, rural cemetery in central New York. That explains a lot! How many kids play among gravestones?

Later she graduated from college and then graduate school. Pegeen worked for many years in the information technology field while raising a family. Reading and writing fiction were beloved hobbies.

Eventually Pegeen traded snowdrifts for hurricanes and moved to Northeast Florida with her rescue cats and dogs.

Now Pegeen has plenty of time to write tales of the paranormal, dark fantasy, and romance. Her heroes are strong and vibrant. Her heroines are smart, lovely, and ready to throw a surprise punch or two. Some characters have wings or fangs; some are wild and hard to tame.

Social Media Links

Website: http://pkbrent.com
Newsletter: http://pkbrent.com/newsletter/
Blog: http://pkbrent.com/pastiche/

GRAVE PROMISES

A Sweet Paranormal Halloween Story

MELODY JOHNSON

Copyright © 2020 Melody Johnson

Grave Promises

Terra Grum is three impossible things: a witch, Ash Henderson's former high school crush, and still under his skin. But she's the only person who might actually believe that a ghost is haunting his house. Despite the tension and longing that lingers between them—feelings better laid to rest—Terra agrees to help exorcise Ash's ghost. Only by working together can they hope to survive this Halloween night, but their own unfinished business is by far the more dangerous apparition.

GRAVE PROMISES

"You sure you don't want to keep it? Some people would be thrilled to have a legit ghost in their home for Halloween."

Charles Ashley Henderson III scowled through his gray-rimmed glasses and across his rather long nose at Terra Grum darkening his doorstep. From her high-collared, sleeveless lace top and tight jeans to her spike-studded combat boots, she was dressed in unrelenting black. Even the roller baggage she'd brought was black. He'd blame the holiday, except he knew from their six years of elementary school, three years of middle school, and four years of high school together that this was her normal everyday attire. And apparently in the five years since graduation, her monochromatic style hadn't changed.

"I'm sure," he said dryly. "I can't leave the house until this ghost is..."*Removed? Exterminated?* He shook his head. "Exorcised."

"Only evil spirits, like ghouls and demons, can be

'exorcised,' but we can try to lay your ghost to rest," Terra offered.

"Whatever. As long as it's gone afterward."

Terra raised her left, platinum blond, nearly translucent eyebrow, just the one, until it disappeared behind the fringe of her black bangs.

If her eyebrow hadn't been visible to begin with, did it count as disappearing?

And there he went. Less than one minute after opening his door and being reunited with his secret high school crush, those oddball questions she'd always inspired began to resurrect.

"I think you're making a mistake," she chided. "A few decorations, some electric candles, and BAM!"

Ash startled as Terra popped both hands out at him in dramatic emphasis. Without her steadying grip, the roller bag tipped over. Its raised handle scraped his wall, and what felt like two hundred plus pounds of luggage crashed onto its side on the hardwood of his foyer floor.

"A bonafide haunted house!"

Ash squinted at the wall and suppressed a sigh. She hadn't gouged the paint, just smeared something—tar? Blackberry jam? What was dark and viscous and could conceivably be on a roller baggage handle to smear about his formerly spotless walls?

He shook his head. Focus.

"The house *is* haunted. Why would I need decorations and candles when it's already, as you just stated, bona fide?"

"For the kids." She snapped her gum between her teeth.

She was a child. Who above the age of ten chewed bubble gum?

Terra Grim, that's who.

Grum, he corrected himself. Terra *Grum*. Jesus, had they even graduated high school?

Ash would have determinedly kept his feelings for Terra and her goth hair, cupid bow lips, that sassy tongue, and all his damned frustrating unanswered questions about her buried to rot. But there was the ghost to consider. Terra was the only person he knew who would believe him, even if he had thought her slightly insane for the past twenty-four years.

So, he'd called her. Now here she was, regret and temptation personified.

"Listen, Ash, I'm not the only witch in Thornton. Our little corner of southeast Georgia has two covens, actually."

His eyes rolled up on a surge of impatience, but the air had never had any answers, not concerning Terra. Besides, wasn't that exactly why he'd called her? She claimed to be magic, and that's what he needed, no matter how implausible—a witch to exorcise his ghost.

"Mona or Jen could be here tomorrow, I'm sure, and then we—"

"I can't wait until tomorrow," he snapped. There was no *we*. Not anymore. Not after she'd killed everything they'd almost had. "I want this ghost gone tonight. Now, if possible."

Terra blew out a hard breath from those lush lips, and her black bangs fluttered. "Sure. If that's what you want, you got it."

"It's not what I want, but it's what I'm asking for," Ash growled under his breath.

He rolled his wheelchair back and pivoted it to the side, giving her enough room to step around her baggage—and him—without touching.

TERRA GRUM CROSSED THE THRESHOLD INTO ASH'S home, invited in even if not wholly welcome. She didn't stare at the bulge and flex of his powerful arms, the lower half of which were on display from the rolled up sleeves of his white and gray plaid button down. He hated it when people stared, so she *didn't*—she soaked in as much of him as she could at a glance—but holy mother of earth and rain how she wanted to! Her eyes hadn't feasted on him at such close range in five years, and being this close now, within touching distance, made her heart trip and then stumble to catch up.

The first button at his collar was undone, baring the long cords of tanned neck muscle that dipped into his throat on either side of his Adam's apple. His light brown hair was just a bit too long, curling over his brow. The sharp cut of his square jaw could knock someone out with its jutting disapproval. His thick brows cast a perpetual shadow over the deep set of his aquamarine eyes, and that voice! Oh, his voice had always been deep, even in high school, but now with a thick, barrel chest to match, it had roughened and richened. Even cast in censure, the vibrations of his words did wicked things to the pit of her gut that some men couldn't even achieve with their tongue.

He would have seemed untouchable in high school, but his giant schnoz had saved him. He was cold and remote, polished to a glossy shine by his infallible pride, but she'd never been able to take him completely seriously, not with a nose like that. Not as seriously, anyway, as he took himself. Which, as he'd just reminded her, had always been the problem.

It's not what I want, but it's what I'm asking for, pretty much summed up their entire, well, she couldn't even honestly call it a relationship. People had to have conversations and mutual trust and regard for one another in a relationship. They could never be friends because Ash lit her soul on fire, but knowing each other since preschool went well beyond mere acquaintances. So what did that leave them?

Nothing. It left them with a stinking, aching, cesspit of nothing.

And apparently, for better or for worse, he hadn't changed a bit. Not his muscles and not his stubbornness, anyway. Although, she supposed one thing had certainly changed. After a lifetime of enduring his skeptical derision, he now believed in ghosts.

But she hadn't missed the old huffing eye roll at her mention of witches. A spirit of the dead, that was real; but witches, oh, now that was crossing the line.

Her acrylic, ballerina-tipped nails bit into her palms.

No matter. She was here for his ghost, not for him.

"You said the first time you felt its presence was in the kitchen?"

He nodded. "You remember the way?"

"Of course." She strode past, grabbing and dragging her roller bag behind her.

She'd heard from Mona, who'd heard from her boyfriend, Clyde, who attended church with his friend Rye, who was an old debate club buddy of Ash's, that the elder Hendersons had crossed the border and relocated to a retirement community in Florida last year. They'd sold the home to Ash, like a legit sale, not some dollar family deal. All four bedrooms, two baths, garage, back patio and pool were his, not that you'd know it by its looks. The foyer, dining and living rooms were exactly as she remembered. He hadn't changed anything —not the textured mint curtains, not the cream paint, not even the shell and sea glass décor—since taking ownership of his childhood home.

The only difference she could discern from how his parents had kept this house and how he kept it, was the clutter. There wasn't any. Books were stacked on their shelves. Throw blankets were neatly folded in a basket next to the couch. Dishes were in their cupboards, not in the sink and certainly not forgotten on an end table. Everything had its purpose and was kept in its place.

Terra reached the kitchen, sweeping a discerning eye over the counters and stainless steel appliances. Her attention caught and held on a dark maroon vase on the window ledge.

"That's new." She turned to face Ash and pointed at it over her shoulder with a hitchhiker thumb.

Ash stopped in front of her, gripping the wheels of his chair with the firm command of his leather, fingerless gloves. He followed the line of her thumb with his gaze.

His lips flattened into a thin line. "Yep."

Apparently he didn't plan to expand on that.

Terra bent to unzip her luggage. "Of all the things to add to your house, of everything that you could change —the furniture, perhaps—why a random vase in the kitchen?"

He blinked those big aquamarine eyes at her, nearly the matching shade as his curtains, actually, and his long black eyelashes swept the insides of his glasses. "What's wrong with my furniture?"

"Nothing. Except that it's the same couch you grew up with. Don't you want to, you know, make this place your own?"

He stared at her like she'd suddenly begun speaking fluent Mandarin.

"The vase doesn't even match the beach theme." She pulled out her infrared thermometer, digital voice recorder, EMF detector, and night vision camera from her luggage and lined them up on his kitchen table.

"What theme?" Ash's scowl deepened, and an errant curl flopped over one eye.

"The beach theme of your house." Terra straightened, spare batteries in hand, and picked up the recorder.

He frowned at her equipment. "What's all this?"

She swapped out the old batteries for new. "You want me to help your ghost find peace, don't you?"

Ash transferred his glare from the equipment to her face. "I want it exorcised from my house."

Terra popped her gum to check her gut response to that comment and met his hard look with one of her own. No compassion in that no-nonsense glare of his. Another thing to add to the long list of attributes that hadn't changed.

"In order for the ghost to leave you in peace, it must *find* peace." Terra readied the camera next with both fresh batteries and a new SIM card.

He swiped up the EMF detector and held it aloft. "And this, this—"

"Electromagnetic field detector," she said, snatching it from his hand. Her thumb accidentally grazed his wrist, and a thrilling bolt of electric heat snapped her spine straight.

"You've got to be kidding me. What else is in here?" He bent, rummaged through her luggage, and finding it empty, shot upright to re-evaluate the items on his kitchen table. "No holy water? No garlic? No wooden stakes?"

"You said a ghost was haunting your home, not a vampire." She cocked her head, managing to keep a straight face only by the thinnest thread of her self-control. "Did I bring the wrong vanquishing kit?"

He narrowed his eyes on her sarcasm. "No wand?"

Ah, so here it came. Considering that nothing had changed—not his muscles, not his house, and certainly not his selective deafness—why hadn't she expected this fight?

"Or do you just twitch your pretty little nose?"

Oh, this man! "That's not how it works, and you know it."

"What do I know about how being a witch does and doesn't work?" His lips stretched to reveal his perfectly straight white teeth. "Was it being a witch that made you stand me up that night or was that just you being you?"

Terra knew from experience how deceiving those

lips could be. They looked hard and unyielding, but they were actually soft and warm and perfect that one time he'd wanted them to be.

Now was apparently not going to be the second time.

She snapped in fresh batteries and set down the EMF detector on the table. "I've apologized. I've explained what happened that night, why I was detained—"

He sniffed just as she was recalling Jeffrey's sweet face and that terrible night she'd avenged his murder. Hot, heady rage spiked through her heart at Ash's disdain, a reaction that was probably out of proportion to the situation, but she'd had enough of him poking at old bruises.

She whirled to face him straight on. "You called me here. You wanted *my* expertise."

"As if I had such a wide selection of people to choose from." The muscles in his shoulders flexed as he edged closer to her. "They don't list ghost whisperer between carpenter and plumber in the yellow pages."

"I can't believe I gave up my Halloween for you," she hissed between gritted teeth.

"The faster you finish here, the faster you can hop back on your broomstick and enjoy your night."

"You know what, Charles Ashley? If you're such an expert on *ghost whispering* then you can do it yourself!"

Terra stormed past him, through the kitchen and across the living room, leaving her equipment, baggage and all, behind with him. She'd give him an hour before he called her back. The tools of the trade were useless in the hands of someone without the right intentions, and Ash, no matter his pure, true heart, never could see through the shroud of his own certainty.

"Terra." Ash made a rude noise in the back of his throat. The turn of his chair's wheels followed her. "Wait."

She ignored him, reaching for the front doorknob.

The EMF detector crackled.

"Terra!"

Something solid, something obviously there in front of her besides air, but something she couldn't see, gripped her under the arms, picked her up off her feet, and shoved her across the room.

Terra backpedaled fast enough that she didn't fly like a rag doll, but it was a near thing. She landed on her feet, fell from the momentum, hit the floor, and slid into the kitchen on her backside. Her elbow caught the edge of the doorway and sang with a sharp, splitting pain.

Ash pivoted in front of her, between her and the front door—between her and what was obviously his ghost—but the EMF detector stopped crackling. The air settled. The only thing that broke the silence was the gasps of her heavy breathing.

❧

"YOU *LITERALLY* CAN'T LEAVE THE HOUSE," SHE whispered.

Ash whipped around and approached Terra. She hadn't hit her head. She wasn't bleeding. No limbs appeared to be broken, but she was still on his floor, sprawled in nearly the same spot where the ghost had pushed him that first time he'd tried to leave. Granted, he'd had the cushion of his chair for protection against the hardwood. "Are you all right?"

"And you let me enter, trapping me in here with you?" She inhaled a trembling breath. "Idiot."

He offered her a hand up. "How would I know you'd get trapped, too?"

She cut him with a look, ignoring his hand. "Like I said."

He let his hand drop.

She returned her attention to the front door, and her eyes widened with something that looked suspiciously like wonder. "That's some ghost."

"I told you so," he grumbled.

Her gaze sliced back to his, the wonder stripped from her face. "You've got some nerve."

He startled, taken aback by the fury in her expression. "Excuse me?"

"I've told *you* so for years!"

She lifted her arm, her index finger extended, undoubtedly about to shake in his face, when something dripped in a long stream from her elbow to puddle on his floor.

"You're bleeding."

"I—what?"

He pointed, and she followed his gaze to her split elbow. The thin skin over her bone was gaping in a gruesome, bloody grimace. As she twisted her arm for a better look, she bent her elbow, and the wound stretched into a smile.

"I am." Her face blanched.

"Well, don't just sit there, staining my floor," he

called back, having already zoomed to the bathroom for what little first aid supplies he had stocked. She'd need stitches, but in the meantime, hopefully arguing with him would snap her out of her shock. "Get up, sit down on a chair, and hold it over the sink."

"Stand up. Sit down," she groused, but a chair scraped across the kitchen's tile.

When Ash returned with gauze pads and a roll, she was indeed sitting, her elbow hanging over the sink. But her head was lying on her arm. Her pallor was stark against her black hair and red lips.

"Squeamish much?" he asked, infusing his voice with as much chiding mockery as he could muster.

She swallowed and closed her eyes. "Yes, actually." And then promptly listed to the side.

"Oh no, you don't." Ash rushed to her, his heart leaping to clog his throat. He blocked her fall, gripping her firmly by the shoulders. "If you pass out, who will exorcise my ghost?"

That did it. Her eyes snapped open to meet his, all thoughts of passing out forgotten. "I'm not exorcising anyone. We're *laying it to rest*."

He ripped open a packet of gauze. "It tried laying *you* to rest."

"No, it prevented me from leaving your home." Terra pursed those distracting lips in thought. "Who died in this house within the last year?"

"No one." Ash pressed the gauze firmly to her split skin.

She hissed. "Someone did. You didn't have a ghost for twenty-three years and now you do. Something

144

changed from then to now, and in the case of ghosts, that usually means someone died."

He peeked under the gauze, but of course, the wound was still bleeding. Profusely. He'd need to bandage her up, then drive her to the ER, and—

He cursed under his breath, realizing he wouldn't be driving her anywhere, not while they were still trapped in this damn haunted house.

Keeping pressure on her elbow with one hand, he ripped open another packet with his teeth and layered more pads on her wound, then reached for the gauze roll. Her skin was naturally pale, making the bright smears of her blood seem nearly neon in comparison. Terra was the palest person he knew with her fringe of blond lashes, invisible eyebrows, and translucent complexion. A web of blue veins was actually visible beneath her skin in some places, the underside of her wrist and around her collarbones especially.

He wondered, not for the first time but for the first time in a long time, what other places her skin might be especially translucent.

He shook away the thought and glanced up at her face to see how she was faring. She was staring at his forearm, of all things, and blushing.

Before he'd even considered speaking, his mouth had opened. "If you didn't want to keep your date with me, I'd have preferred you just say so, not—"

She straightened. "I did want to keep our date."

"—stand me up and make up some ridiculous excuse."

Her flush deepened on a frown. "Nothing about my excuse was ridiculous. Jeffrey had *died*."

"The week before!"

"Ow!"

He loosened his grip on her wound. "Sorry," he muttered and began wrapping the gauze roll around her arm, securing the bandage to her elbow.

"My aunt had hunted down and detained Jeffrey's murderer." Her voice was steady and low and calmly rational despite the insanity of her excuse. "It was up to me to avenge him."

"To avenge your *cat's murder*."

"Jeffrey wasn't my cat. He was my familiar. An extension of myself and my magic. Losing him was like losing a limb."

Ash's face hardened, and he very determinedly didn't look at his legs. "Don't you dare compare losing your cat to—"

"My *familiar*!"

Ash knotted the gauze with a swift tug.

"Ow-a!" She yanked her arm from his hands.

"It needs to be secure. You don't want to bleed out before I can get you to the hospital, do you?"

She reared back. "The hospital?"

"You need stitches."

She stared at him for a long moment, long enough that the piercing chill in her icy eyes seeped into his nerves. It pained him to hold her gaze, but he'd endured worse from her. He didn't look away.

"Why did you even care that I stood you up?" she whispered. "I'm just a freak."

He reared back this time, the tone of her grief-soaked words like a physical slap. "You're not a freak."

"Oh, no?" She asked, her voice regaining its usual

strength and sarcasm. "But you don't believe in witches and familiars or anything else, so what am I then if not a freak? Insane? Confused? A *liar*?"

"No! I—" He shook his head. "I don't know! You—"

"*You* said you liked me. That I was special and unique and, and you looked at me with those damn eyes of yours like promises of a future, like we had *something* at least." She narrowed her gaze until only the pinprick of her pupils glared at him. "But when push came to shove, at the first sign of something you couldn't immediately comprehend, you found the easiest exit and ran. Suddenly, you didn't have anything to give but your scorn, like everyone else."

"All I know is that this ghost has been haunting me all damn day!" he burst. They didn't have time for this. Her blood was already seeping through the gauze. "Stuck here with one ghost is bad enough. If we don't get you to a hospital soon, maybe we'll have a dead body in this house after all!"

Terra held up a hand. "Back it up. How long exactly has the ghost been haunting you?"

"I, er—" he blinked. "I first noticed my inability to leave the house at 7 a.m. this morning, so—" Ash glanced at his watch. "About fourteen hours."

Terra gaped. "Your house has been haunted for less than twenty-four hours?"

"Well—" He blinked. "Yes."

She stared.

"What's that look for? How long do you think I waited before calling you? *I can't leave my house!* "He took a deep breath. "I would have called you sooner, except, well—" He glanced at her and then away.

"Fourteen hours." She lifted her uninjured arm and rubbed her temple. "Okay, so who died in this house yesterday?"

He released an exasperated cough from the back of his throat. "No one. I told you, *no one has died in this house*. Not today, not yesterday, not ever."

"Fine," she snapped. "Then what did you do yesterday?"

"I attended my grandfather's funeral," he snapped back.

"Oh," she said, the righteous wind having been suddenly sucked from her sails. "I'm sorry to hear that. Pappy Charles, your namesake?"

Ash nodded. He compressed his lips, suppressing their sudden urge to tremble. "Wiley old bugger. He outlived his wife, my Mimi Bethany, by over a decade. He should've died years ago, but he only just now got around to it. He was too busy living."

Terra grinned. "Sounds like something he'd say."

"He did, actually. I was there at his bedside when he passed."

"Oh?"

"He asked me to take Mimi's ashes—" He gestured absently to the kitchen window ledge. "—and then, just as he was about to say something else, he inhaled a rattling breath and died."

"Your Mimi Bethany's ashes?" Terra perked up and glanced at the window. "That vase? It's an *urn*?"

"Yeah." He took in her expression, and the hairs on the back of his neck rose to attention. "What?"

Terra turned on him slowly. "You bring the incinerated remains of your dead grandmother into your home directly after the passing of her husband, and a ghost begins haunting you the morning after. And you're just *now* mentioning it?"

Ash sputtered. "I hadn't made the connection, but I mean, when you say it like that…"

She snorted, stood, and strode to the urn.

"But that still doesn't make sense," he argued. "Pappy Charles had her ashes for twelve years, and he wasn't haunted. He came and went from his house just fine."

Terra rolled her eyes. "Mimi Bethany was with her husband, content at the time with the placement of her ashes. I'm sure that when Pappy Charles asked you to take her ashes, he'd intended you to take them *somewhere*, but not here with you."

"Where, then?"

She blinked, thinking. "Was Pappy Charles cremated?"

Ash shook his head. "No, he was buried in St. Christopher's cemetery on Willow Lane."

"Well, let's try there then." She picked up the urn, pivoted back to him, and plopped Mimi Bethany on his lap, heedless of his groin.

Ash yelped. Before he could find his breath, Terra gripped the wheelchair and drove them toward the door.

"Careful, your arm," he gasped out.

"I'm fine."

"You don't know this will work."

"There's only one way to find out," she muttered, and then louder, she announced, "Mimi Bethany. I'm sorry your grandson is ridiculous and brought you here

149

instead of to your husband, but thank you for making us aware of his insensitivity. As I'm sure you know, he didn't part you from your Charles on purpose."

"You're apologizing to her?" Ash whipped his head around, frowning. "She threw you into a wall and split your elbow."

"And got my attention, smart woman," Terra said, and then under her breath she hissed. "Shut up. Don't insult her now. We're nearing the threshold."

"Jesus Christ." Ash muttered.

Terra grimaced, but Ash faced front and shut up.

"We're bringing you to your husband now," Terra said in her loud, I'm-speaking-to-the-spirits voice. "If you let us pass, we'll go directly to where your Charles is buried in St. Christopher's cemetery, and scatter your ashes over his plot." She squeezed Ash's shoulder. "Tell her you're sorry."

"I'm sorry," he parroted, feeling ridiculous.

"Mean it, and tell her that we'll spread her ashes."

"You just did!" But at her blazing look, he complied. "We'll spread your ashes over Pappy Charles. Assuming we're able to leave the house," he added churlishly.

Terra reached over him and opened the front door.

Ash held his breath.

She pushed them through the doorway and onto his front porch without incident.

"Huh." Ash released a pent-up breath, relief like an aphrodisiac rushing through him.

"Trick or treat!"

Terra shrieked.

Ash spasmed in a full-body lurch, nearly losing his grip on Mimi Bethany.

The four children on his porch smiled, holding out their plastic jack-o-lantern collection buckets.

Ash slumped in his chair and patted the lid to Mimi's urn as his heart relearned how to beat. He glanced up at Terra and chuckled, sounding only slightly hysterical. "Exorcising my ghost wasn't a matter of magic after all."

Terra dropped her hand from her chest. "It rarely ever is."

ST. CHRISTOPHER'S CEMETERY ON WILLOW LANE WAS the second largest of four cemeteries in the county but the most beautiful, named for the weeping willow trees that lined its entrance from the main road and surrounded the cemetery itself and its west-facing pond.

During the day, the sun speckled the tombstones, plots, and walkways in dappled light through the swaying droop of tree branches. During the evening, the sun dipped into that pond, bleeding the clouds as it seemed to disappear into those still waters. The sun had already set that Halloween night, the golden hour having passed, leaving only the meager glow from decade-old lamp posts against the darkness.

Terra knelt beside Ash as he leaned forward, carefully sprinkling his Mimi Bethany's remains over his Pappy Charles' grave. He straightened, gazing over his handiwork for a long silent moment.

He grunted. "I don't feel anything different."

Terra suppressed a grin. "This wasn't done for you. It was done for them." She shifted her hand from the wheelchair's arm to Ash's hand still cradling the now-empty urn. "I'm sure *they* feel it."

Ash turned his head, glancing down at her hand on his, then lifting his eyes to her face. The heat of his gaze bloomed over her cheeks in a heady rush. Her breath caught.

She turned her face to meet his gaze.

His aquamarine eyes were black in the gloom. His expression unfathomable. "I'd like to, or rather, would you—" Ash cleared his throat. "How would you feel about starting where we left off five years ago?"

She raised her eyebrows. "You want to take me on a date?"

He swallowed, and his Adam's apple bobbed. "Yes."

"So you believe me now? About Jeffrey and why I stood you up that night?"

The sharp jut of his jaw clenched.

Terra glanced away to study their entwined fingers. "For years you thought I was crazy or hyper imaginative or—"

He raised his other hand and swiped it down his face. "I don't know what I thought."

"But now you know that ghosts are real, right?"

He huffed. "Unfortunately."

"Is believing in witches, too, so far-fetched?"

She lifted her gaze, but he was already looking at her again. Suddenly his lips were inches away. She felt the puff of his breath and its absence when his breath caught.

"I don't have a magic wand," she whispered. "I can't twitch my nose or say abracadabra or slap my arms together and blink. Well, I suppose I *could,* but nothing would happen. That's just not how it all works."

"Then how does it work?" he asked, his eyes searching the depths of hers.

"I'd need to show you. You'd need to trust me. You'd need to believe me when I say that Jeffrey was more than just a cat, that my grief for his loss was devastating on a visceral level, and that I didn't stand you up lightly." Terra took his hand from the urn and held it to her chest. "And that when I tell you I'm sorry, that I never wanted to ruin things between us, that I mean it."

He raised his other hand and cupped her cheek. The supple leather of his glove was smooth on her jaw. He swiped a calloused thumb across her lower lip. She leaned in, and he met her halfway, the pressure of his mouth against hers like crystalline water: flooding her senses, buoying her spirit, catching her fall. Delicious. Essential. Elemental.

She moved her mouth over his, matching his caresses, meeting his need with her longing. He licked her tongue. She nipped his lower lip. Five long years of imagining what might have been came to light.

Their lips parted. Terra opened her eyes, and lost what little breath she still had. She'd never seen such intense certainty in his expression, not aimed at her.

"I trust you. I know you're sorry, and I, I can remain open minded about everything else." His jaw line firmed with resolve. "I *will* remain open minded."

She grinned, the thrill of his words making her heart take flight. "Is that a promise?"

"Cross my heart and hope to die," he whispered gravely.

She startled back, glancing around the cemetery. "You shouldn't make such a promise. Not here, not at night, and not on Halloween."

"Doesn't matter." His lips moved against her ear, and Terra stilled, her fear forgotten. Her blood ignited. "This promise, I intend to keep."

Love Beyond Series

Beyond the Next Star

Delaney McCormick is not an animal, but after being abducted by aliens and witnessing the murder of her only friend, she pretends to be one. She endures the humiliation of being washed, the tediousness of being trained to "sit" and "come," and the intrigue of hearing private conversations. But in her owner's care, she finds something unexpected on this Antarctic planet, something she never had in all her years on Earth while house-hopping between foster families: a home. Must she continue the charade, acting like an animal to hide from the murderer waiting on her misstep? Or can she trust her owner with her secrets... and her heart?

Night Blood Series

The City Beneath

Sweet Last Drop

Eternal Reign

Day Reaper

As a journalist, Cassidy DiRocco thought she had seen every depraved thing New York City's underbelly had to offer. But while covering what appears to be a vicious animal attack, she finds herself drawn into a world she never knew existed. Her exposé makes her the target of the handsome yet brutal Dominic Lysander, the Master Vampire of New York City, who has no problem silencing her to keep his coven's secrets safe. But Dominic offers Cassidy another option: ally. As the battle between vampires takes over the city, Cassidy will have to decide where to place her trust... in revealing the truth or in Dominic's capable talons.

ABOUT MELODY JOHNSON

Melody Johnson is the author of the "out of this world" Love Beyond series and the Night Blood series published by Kensington Publishing/ Lyrical Press. The New York Times and USA TODAY Bestselling Author, Lynsay Sands, "laughed out loud" reading Beyond the Next Star (Love Beyond, book 1). The City Beneath (Night Blood, book 1) was a finalist in the "Cleveland Rocks" and "Fool for Love" contests.

Melody graduated magna cum laude from Lycoming College with her BA in creative writing and psychology. Throughout college, she wrote contemporary love stories, but having read and adored the action and dark mystery of vampires and aliens her entire life, she decided to add her fingerprint to the paranormal and sci-fi genres.

When she isn't working or writing, Melody can be found swimming at the beach, hiking with her husband, and exploring her new home in southeast Georgia. Keep in touch with Melody on social media or sign up for her newsletter to receive emails about new releases and book signings.

Social Media Links
Website: http://authormelodyjohnson.com

Newsletter Sign Up: http://
authormelodyjohnson.com/newsletter
Blog: https://authormelodyjohnson.wordpress.com
Facebook: https://www.
facebook.com/authormelodyjohnson
Instagram: https://www.
instagram.com/authormelodyjohnson
Goodreads: https://www.
goodreads.com/authormelodyjohnson

A PUG THANKSGIVING

A Sweet Contemporary Thanksgiving Story

LEAH MILES

Copyright © 2020 Leah Miles

A Pug Thanksgiving

Sidelined by an injury, Navy SEAL Echo Sanders is not looking for a serious relationship. His priority is returning to his team and the job he loves. Or was before he meets an interesting woman.

Carefully balancing her time between making money and self-improvement, Janny doesn't think she has a chance with the handsome SEAL. When she realizes their attraction is mutual, all bets are off.

With the help of an adorable pug, Janny and Echo might find something more precious than just a holiday.

A PUG THANKSGIVING

"Come on sweetheart, I know it's hard, but you can take it." The warm bass of his voice encouraged her to continue.

"Ahg…" She huffed, unable to catch a full breath.

"Yeah, just like that, yeah that's good." His breath floated over her face in a minty breeze.

"Ah…I need to stop…agh." Janny's entire body felt like it was vibrating. Unpleasantly.

Just when she was sure she couldn't take it anymore, the handsome bastard laughed and sat back on his heels, releasing her knees.

Glaring at him from her sprawled position on the mat, Janny sucked in oxygen and attempted to subtly unstick her bangs from her forehead. Why the heck did Echo have to look so good? Scruffy beard and close-cropped mahogany curls, she could probably dip him in chocolate, and he wouldn't look any more delicious.

"Forty sit ups are a big improvement." Tapping the side of Janny's leg as if to punctuate the statement, he continued. "We'll keep working on building your wind for faster recovery."

"Huh." She mumbled, because truthfully, she was just happy about not *'breaking wind'* while struggling thru that last set of reps.

"You're scheduled for two more sessions, right?"

Janny nodded. "I appreciate your help with training." *Mostly.*

"Sure thing. Here, take my hand." And he was on his feet, waiting to lever her up.

Reaching out, she clasped his hand with both of hers and let him pull her effortlessly to her feet. Just a passenger on a ride, a ride with the most beautiful brown eyes she'd ever seen.

Down girl. Jericho 'Echo' Sanders is way out of your league.

"You okay?"

The concerned look on his face, coupled with his question, completely destroyed her fantasy.

Yes sir, I'm a lunatic.

"I'm all good," Janny replied a little too loudly before snatching back her hands to pluck at her shirt. "Same time tomorrow then?" she added, gesturing inanely towards the digital clock inside the stylized 'O' of the 'San Diego Fitness Center' banner.

"Tomorrow yes, but Friday it'll be an hour earlier for the group training. Don't forget, the gym is closed next week on Thursday and Friday for Thanksgiving." Stooping to retrieve some loose hand weights, Echo paused to look back in her direction before adding. "I posted signups for the next round of training, you in?"

"Not yet, but I'm thinking about it." She tried to

keep her voice casual when she added, "Will you be coaching?"

"Possibly." Echo's smile reached his eyes. "Does that make a difference?"

Holy Moly, his teeth are perfect.

"Ah…" Awkwardly she reached for her abandoned sweat towel, trying to think of something else to talk about. Anything. "So, how'd you get the name Echo?"

Hands full of dumbbells, he hesitated, face completely blank. "You don't think my mom called me that?"

Janny was speechless. *Shit. Was she being rude?*

Echo grinned at the look on her face. Her pretty eyes were wide as saucers and her lips were rounded with confusion. He'd looked forward to seeing her in the mornings over the last few weeks; Janny might be the only thing he'd miss when he finally returned to his real job.

"Gotcha!" he said. Grinning, he snagged some cleaning wipes before stepping over to rack the weights he was holding. "Just pulling your chain. It's the handle my team tagged me with." He frowned and gestured at the thick brace strapped over his knee. "If not for this, I'd be with them right now."

"Navy, right?"

"Is there any other?" Finished with the equipment, Echo turned back to find her moss green eyes locked on his leg, as if noticing the brace for the first time. He watched as she leaned closer to flutter her fingers over the wide hinge, something he definitely shouldn't be able to feel.

"Do you mind telling me what happened?" Janny asked.

"Nothing too exciting. Training exercise with the team and yours truly screwed up the landing." He reached down to readjust some of the straps on the brace before grinning up at her. "Combat injury would make a better story."

Straightening, he realized Janny wanted to hear more. "So, they operated right after, but the doc wasn't able to fix everything all at once. Which put me here, working at Craig's gym for 'rest and rehabilitation', at least until the first of the year." He paused. "Then I go back for round two."

"You'll be going back then, after the surgery?"

"Back? To my team?" He tipped his chin to wipe some moisture off on his tank. "That's the plan." He checked the clock. "Hey, I've got some things to take care of before the next class, you good?"

"Sure. I mean, I have things to do, also." She began to vigorously rub her sweaty towel across pink cheeks.

This woman is funny and interesting, how often does that combination come around?

"Hey, any chance you'd be interested in going to breakfast with this broken-down Navy SEAL?"

The question caught Janny off guard. "Breakfast?" *Did Echo just ask me to breakfast? Please God don't let me be hallucinating. Or lying unconscious on the mat.*

Echo smiled and gently pushed her shoulder with one hand. "You know, eggs, coffee?"

She couldn't help the stupid grin splitting her face. "I love coffee. Do you mean today? Now?" *Not now, not now, not now...crap! I can actually smell the sweat soaking my shirt.*

"How about a late breakfast?" Echo stopped talking long enough to toss a weighted ball towards the edge of the mat. "I'll meet you over at Dooley's Kitchen, say in about an hour? I've got to do some things for Craig first."

Score!

"I can do that, I mean yes, I want to do that, breakfast." Knowing she sounded like her IQ had been purchased in a snack machine, Janny twisted her towel between clenched fingers and tried to think of something halfway intelligent to add. "Ah...when will Craig be back?"

"Not for a couple weeks, he's enjoying the sun in Puerto Rico and apparently his new wife's family have rolled out the red carpet for them. They might never come back."

"Eva loves it here, they'll come back, but I think it's great he has you to manage things," she said.

A cloud seemed to pass over Echo's face. "Not like my plate was full."

Damn. She never seemed to know when to shut up. Not wanting him to change his mind about breakfast, Janny began quickly walking backwards towards the lockers. "Okay, I'm going to go home and shower. Bye!"

"OOF!" And she plowed into the corner of the ab machine.

"Hey, easy there." He took a step towards her.

"No, I'm okay!" Tossing a casual, "See you soon." over her shoulder, she concentrated on not limping as she walked away.

"Roxy please! Do your thing so we can go inside already. If you don't hurry, I'm gonna be late! Late for an actual date, with him!" The man who filled her every waking fantasy. Janny did a fist pump with her free hand, which Roxy took as a cue to start enthusiastically barking at the neighbor's devil cat.

"Hush girl, you know the rules. Mrs. Carver will kick us out if you wake her up before nine!" She probably wouldn't really kick them out, but Janny didn't want a lecture either.

Finally, the little pug found a good spot for her business. When she was done, Janny scooped her up and hustled them both back inside, just as her cell began to vibrate.

"Hello?"

"Janice?" Mrs. Carver sounded annoyed with someone.

Janny hoped it wasn't her.

"A man is coming to look at the AC this morning and the last time your dog barked incessantly. Can you to take her away somewhere for a couple of hours?"

"Ah sure. That's no problem. I'll take care of it." Still holding Roxy, Janny plopped down on the single chair in her kitchen and checked the time. Not many options.

"Well girl, here's hoping Echo likes dogs."

Leaning against the brick façade, Echo tucked his hands deep in the pockets of his denim jacket, enjoying in the cool morning air while he waited for Janny to arrive. It surprised him how much he was looking forward to spending time with her outside of the busy gym. She'd only been a member for the last month, but he'd found himself looking forward to seeing her in the early morning sessions. Her determination was inspiring, and he found her curvy little body very appealing.

His nine years in the military had him scanning the street in both directions while he waited for her arrival and it wasn't long until he spotted the bright beacon of Janny's white blonde hair when she exited the parking garage. He could see her laughing as she shifted a bulky pack over one shoulder. *What was that?*

JANNY MOVED THE HEAVY PURPLE CARRIER TO HER other shoulder and powered thru the exit at a brisk pace. "You have to behave. Absolutely no barking, understood?"

The pup ignored her. Her shiny black eyes were swiveling joyfully in all directions as she wiggled against the constraints of the too-small bag. From half a block away, Janny could see Echo squinting in their direction and laughter bubbled up her throat.

"There he is Roxy." She waived and picked up her pace.

She'd met the handsome Echo after joining San Diego fitness and promptly signed up for his morning training sessions. It was a stretch on her budget, but she needed the exercise and the motivation of tall dark and handsome helped to get her out of bed. Her heart soared at the thought that he might return her interest.

"Hi! Sorry I'm late."

"Haven't been here long." Echo straightened away from the wall and quirked an eyebrow. "Whatcha got in the bag?"

"Oh, this is Roxy. Roxy meet Echo." *And I just introduced my dog like an actual person.*

Echo watched as the pug rolled enormous eyes, head and shoulders straining at the opening of the bag as she rocked it with what he had to assume were full body wags.

Eyes crinkling at the corners, Echo rubbed his chin with a serious expression. "I'm not sure dogs are allowed inside, unless they're service dogs. Is she by any chance a service dog?"

Janny grinned and tapped her lip with one finger as if considering the question. "She isn't an actual a service dog, but I did purchase a certificate online designating her as an anxiety companion; so technically, she could be a service dog or maybe a dog with a fake ID."

"That could work." Echo laughed. "Are you feeling anxious or is there another reason you brought her along?"

Janny swatted at his arm playfully. "No, not anxious. The AC guy is coming." She grinned and nodded sagely as if that explained everything.

Echo extended a hand to Roxy. "Is that code for something?"

Janny shrugged, looking chagrined. "No, he's really coming, and Roxy barks at strangers, so my landlady asked me to get her out of the house for a few hours. Is this okay? We could do this another time, but I've brought her here before. They don't mind as long as we sit outside."

Woof Woof Woof

Echo realized that he must have been staring at the dog through this exchange, because now she was barking at him with frantic enthusiasm.

"Roxy, no!" Janny sounded agitated.

Woof Woof Woof

This was hilarious! He considered pulling out his phone as he watched Janny trying to muffle the barking dog by shoving her back inside the carrier; but a quick glance at her face told him the woman was ready to scrub the meal. He wasn't going to let that happen.

"Wait." Completely unable to clear his expression, Echo stepped forward and gently lifted the carrier off Janny's shoulder. Then he put his own big hand on the dog's face, fairly certain she wouldn't bite him.

And she quit barking to lick his fingers.

"That's a good girl." Scratching the little dog behind the ears, Echo did a chin lift in the direction of the almost vacant patio seating. "The dog's fine. Come brave the elements with me over there."

Without giving her a chance to refuse, he headed in that direction and just as he'd hoped, Janny trailed behind him.

"I don't know what's gotten into her. Normally, well mostly, she's well behaved." Janny sighed. "At least she stopped barking."

Roxy was definitely calmer now, tongue out, sniffing the air. Echo assumed she was hoping to taste some of those breakfast smells as they wound through the tables.

The restaurant's hostess spotted their progress from her podium and trotted after them with a stack of menus. "Hi Janny. You and the beast here for breakfast?"

The beast?

"Hey Ruth. Yes, for all three of us."

Ruth turned and regarded Echo as if he'd just dropped from the sky. "Oh, you're together?" Her gaze filled with interest. "Your jackets are the same. Cute."

Echo winked at the older woman. "Am I cute or am I the beast?"

"Oh honey, I was calling the little guy beast. You'd be more like...hmmm...a young Will Smith." She cackled with delight and handed him the menus, patting his arm companionably.

Echo shook his head, still amused, and zeroed in on a table. *This is definitely an interesting date.*

FACE WARM WITH EMBARRASSMENT, JANNY HURRIED after Echo, pleased to realize he'd selected the table in the best position for blocking the wind on the patio. And, in spite of being encumbered by the dog carrier, he had a chair pulled back, waiting for her to take a seat.

"Uh, thank you." *Where has this man been all my life?* "You can put the carrier down here." She indicated the space at her feet.

Instead of just setting it down, Echo crouched

beside her chair, his fingers deftly scratching the best spots behind Roxy's ears. Janny knew they were the best spots because her dog was moaning in ecstasy.

Janny's own fingers were tingling with the desire to touch the neat line of dark curls on the back of Echo's neck. She could smell him too, some woodsy cologne or maybe that was just his scent?

"Janny?" He was watching her with questioning eyes.

He'd asked her something, but what was it? She was going to have to ask him to repeat it. "I'm sorry, what?"

He grinned. Probably realizing the effect he had on her. "Do we let her out of the bag?"

"Yes, we can." Peeling her eyes away from the handsome man, Janny glared down at the hopeful face of her pet. "Girl, you need to behave."

In response to their combined attention, Roxy wiggled enthusiastically and when Echo reached to unzip the top, Janny stalled him with a hand over his.

"Hook this on first." Grinning, she held up a leash.

Finally liberated, Roxy tried to scramble from the bag into Echo's arms, clearly deciding he should be her new best friend.

"Roxy, down!" Janny snapped in frustration.

Echo just laughed, easily catching the dog's wiggling body and holding her up so they were eye to eye. "Roxy is it?"

Black eyes studied brown ones before Roxy swiped her tongue over his nose.

"Nice." He rubbed the dog saliva on his shoulder and grinned at Janny. "Wonder if I can get a kiss from your mistress just by staring at her?"

Probably.

Flustered, Janny fiddled with the end of the leash. "I see you've completely enchanted my dog." *Which makes two of us.*

"Have you had her long?" Echo asked, before gently handing over Roxy and rising to move to his chair.

Did he hesitate? Sexy man loves dogs. Be still my heart.

"Only about a year, but she's a rescue. The vet thinks she's closer to eight or nine. I promise she usually behaves better. Unless she sees a squirrel, then all bets are off. Squirrels are apparently her vilest enemies." *Do I never shut up?*

Echo grinned, tipping back his chair, keeping his good leg on the floor for balance. "I think we're safe from squirrels, for the duration of this meal anyway."

Gah, he's so everything when he smiles.

Just then an overworked waiter arrived with two cups and a small pitcher of coffee. "Good morning, I'm Toby. Do you guys want to move inside where its warmer?"

Janny indicated Roxy. "We can't but thanks for the coffee," she said as she snatched up the full cup as soon as he set it back on the table.

The waiter pulled out his pad. "Okay. Well, are you ready to order then?"

"You first," Echo said.

"Okay. I'll have the special, with scrambled eggs and bacon."

Echo nodded and handed both menus to the waiter. "I'll have what she's having."

"Good choice. Looks like I'll need to bring more coffee too. It'll be right up."

The waiter rushed away as Echo reached for the sugar packets. "You don't take cream or sugar?"

"Nope, my dad was a cop and I always wanted to be like him. He thought coffee should be enjoyed in its natural form and I acquired the taste for it."

Echo began. "Where is he..."

"Oh, no!" Janny exclaimed. Handicapped by the steaming cup in her hand, she couldn't prevent Roxy from scrambling up and over the small table, probably in search of possible snacks.

Echo laughed and set his own cup to the side—*clever man*—before lifting Roxy up, all four legs wiggling with delight. She licked the air in his direction until he tucked her up under his chin, where she immediately began to lick the underside of his beard in earnest.

"Roxy, NO!" Janny moaned.

"It's fine." And it was. Miraculously the dog settled into the crook of his arm, no licking or barking—just absolute adoration on her furry face.

Janny had no idea what to do. Coffee cup in one hand and tightly strapped leash around the other—which in turn was pulling her forward over the table—effectively attaching both woman and dog to the handsome Echo.

Maybe I should climb over there and lick his chin to see if he snuggles me.

Clearing her throat, she carefully placed her cup on the table so she could unwind the leash. "Here, give her to me."

"No, we're good." He indicated the leash. "Just hand me that," he added before tossing her a heart-stopping grin and kissing the top of Roxy's head.

She couldn't reply, just handed it over. The man had been great before. Sweaty and all male power at the gym. But kissing her little roly poly dog?

Janny wondered if he had plans for the holidays, or even the next twenty years? Maybe she could entice him with the best Thanksgiving turkey he'd ever tasted. Then perhaps feed him her special dark chocolate cream pie...

Echo tapped the table. "Janny? Hey?"

Pop went that fantasy when she realized both he and Roxy were staring at her.

"Just woolgathering there for a second, thinking about..." What the heck was she thinking about? His lips wrapped around a fork full of chocolate? "Something."

Good grief, he'll be thinking I'm a nut case if I don't stop daydreaming already...

"Tell me about it?" He shifted the heavy dog to a more comfortable position and waited for her response.

"Oh, I just, my mind wandered." Janny fluttered her hand and shook out her napkin.

THE WAITER REAPPEARED WITH PLATES COVERED IN eggs, bacon, toast, and hash browns and the dog's heart started beating fast, thumping against his hand. *What the heck?*

Echo lifted Roxy towards Janny, concerned. "Something's wrong with your dog."

Janny leaned forward, her hand fitted to the side of her mouth and whispered. "It's the food. You can't tell it by looking at her, but she's starving. Haven't fed her in days."

He laughed. "Oh, funny girl, no way this dog has ever missed a meal." He hefted Roxy up to gauge her size. "What, about fifteen pounds?"

"I don't want to hear anything about healthy weight. I get enough of that at the gym. Here, give over. I'll put her in the bag with a treat to keep her occupied."

Echo stood to hand the dog to Janny. "Well, you haven't heard me talk about your weight. You look good to me."

Moving to kneel beside her chair, he waited until the pup was secure before catching Janny's fingers with his own. "Right now, I'm just trying to figure out why this is the first time we've shared a meal."

Her smile could power the room, he thought.

"This is nice."

Reluctantly he released her hand to return to his seat so they could dig into their breakfast. They were silent a few minutes. Even Roxy was quietly chewing a bone.

Echo wagged his fork at Janny. "Hey, should I ask if this is where you two usually bring your dates?"

"No!" Janny huffed, laying a piece of bacon on a napkin. "We've only been here a couple times, just me and Roxy. Until a few months ago, we lived way north of the city. Eva found this great apartment for me and since I work from home, it was an easy decision."

Echo put some jelly on a piece of toast. "What do you do from home?"

"Freelance graphic designer. Sounds fancy, but it

basically means I get to pick my own hours, no benefits, and the pay sometimes isn't the best."

"Do you like it?"

"I love it," Janny said with a grin.

"You mentioned your dad? Is your family here in San Diego?" Echo found he wanted to know everything about her.

She fiddled with her water glass. "My mom passed a long time ago, and dad's new wife is from Florida. They live there now." Reaching for the coffeepot she hesitated. "Now you tell me something."

Echo extended his cup for her to refill. "First, tell me about Roxy. How did you two wind up together?"

Just as she was about to launch into the tale, his cell buzzed.

Checking the screen, he stood. "Excuse me, I've got to take this." He stepped to the edge of the patio with his phone to his ear. "Yes?"

He didn't say much and wasn't on the phone long before he returned to their table.

Echo was frustrated, he didn't want to leave Janny. "I'm really sorry. I've got to go. One of my buddies was just in a car accident."

"Oh, no. Is he okay?"

"From the amount of cussing I heard, he's probably fine; but he's confined to a chair and his truck was t-boned. Guy can't just hop out and call a cab." Echo crouched to rub the dog behind her ears.

"If you'll give you me your number, I'll call you later to beg forgiveness for ditching you at breakfast. Maybe an apology dinner for you and the beast?"

"You don't have to do that."

"Well if I wanted to do that, I would have to have your number."

"Okay then." Janny smiled and began to rummage in the side of her bag for a pen and paper.

While she was doing that, Echo pulled out a couple of twenties to pay for breakfast and slid them up under his mug.

"This is me." She held out a torn piece of blue envelope and damn she was cute, with her hair snagged back in a messy bun.

"You're the sweetest thing." Echo leaned down and stroked a finger across her cheek. "Thanks for not giving me crap about having to leave."

Janny frowned. "I wouldn't do that."

Leaning close, Echo gently framed her face with both hands. "Is it alright if I kiss you?" He waited, hovering close enough to feel the sweet rush of breath over her lips when she whispered her response.

"Yes."

One kiss. A gentle brush of lips, once, again.

Regretfully, he relaxed back on his heels and smoothed a hand over her soft hair. "Now I'm having trouble leaving."

She just watched him with those moss green eyes, two fingers on her lips.

Echo dropped a kiss on her forehead as he stood. "Janny, I hope you never play poker."

"What?" She sounded confused.

"Gotta run, beautiful. I'll call you."

DAMN SHE HAD IT BAD. WAS THERE ANYTHING wrong with the man? Loves dogs. *Check.* Rescues friends. *Check.* Sexy as hell. *Check.*

Janny's cellphone rang just as she was placing some cut circles of dough into a round metal pan. "Hello?"

"Sorry it took me so long to get back to you."

He sounds exhausted.

"Is your friend okay?"

"He will be—just banged up and needed a few stiches. His truck is totaled though, and it's a pain in the ass to get a custom one like that. He's pissed as hell."

"That sucks."

"So, we missed dinner."

"Well, you said you *might* call, so I put something in the slow cooker. I mean, is that weird? Inviting you to my house and you may not feel like it anyway? It's totally okay, if you're tired, or maybe you ate already?" Her knuckles were white on the phone as she willed herself to stop talking.

"Relax Janny. I'd love to see you tonight and no, not weird at all. Quick, give me your address before you come to your senses."

"Eighty-six-A, Oleander Lane, just a couple blocks west of that big dog park. Come around the side. I live above the garage."

"That's close to me, I can be there in twenty. Don't let Roxy have my dinner."

Setting down the phone she turned in an exuberant circle. The soulful eyes of her dog watched from the bed where she was sitting at one of the TV trays.

"You waiting for your plate? Dream on doggo. Let

me put this in the oven and we can take a walk before Echo gets here."

⚜

AFTER PULLING HIS TRUCK UP BEHIND JANNY'S CAR, Echo immediately spotted the pair waiting for him on a wide manicured lawn. He had parked on the opposite side of the busy street and had to wait for several cars to pass before he could cross.

Why does it feel as though I'm coming home to someone?

Janny waved and called out, "We decided to wait for you out here."

He grinned like a schoolboy. The woman was definitely happy to see him and her pup was dancing and flipping on the end of her lead.

Until she wasn't. It happened so fast, the collar must have snapped because the next instant Roxy was flying in his direction, free of any restraint.

Unfortunately, a big yellow tabby appeared from nowhere and took that opportunity to streak down the sidewalk and Roxy went berserk. She bolted after the cat, following when it headed into the street, diagonally away from his truck.

"Oh God! Roxy!" Janny dropped the useless lead to charge after her pet.

Echo shouted. "Stay right there, I've got her!" Then he did what he hadn't done in months. He ran. At full speed, dodging one, two cars, trying to reach the pug before she got flattened.

The dog was fast, but he was determined. Also, she stopped running and crouched in terror in the middle of

181

the road when she realized just how desperate her location had become.

The stupid cat was long gone.

Echo was able to snatch her up, not even breaking stride as he tucked her into his chest like an oversized football, barely avoiding a collision with a blue sedan.

When he finally came to a stop, they were still on the wrong side. He could see Janny waiting across the street, tears streaming down her pretty face and her hands fisted at her sides.

Echo whispered to the trembling dog. "You mutt, are in deep trouble. The lady looks pissed, but don't worry, we're friends now, so I've got this."

Reassured by his voice, Roxy could barely contain her enthusiasm. She began licking his face and hands and when he finally was able to cross over, Janny launched herself at him in a hero's welcome.

"Thank you, thank you!"

Wrapping one arm around the woman, Echo made it all the way onto the edge of the grass before his knee buckled. *Not good.* With the dog tucked into his chest and Janny under one arm, he rotated to drop down onto his butt.

"Oh my God, are you ok?"

"I need a minute. Okay—yes." *My knee not so much.* "Here, take Roxy." Gently pushing the wriggling dog towards Janny, he concentrated on not grimacing while he stretched both legs out into the grass.

"You're hurt." Now her eyes were dripping again.

"None of that. I'm a damn SEAL woman, you're going to embarrass me." In an effort to prove the point, Echo rolled over onto his good knee, balancing his weight and using his hands to propel upwards, while keeping pressure off the braced leg.

A move which might have failed if Janny hadn't been right there, tucking herself up under his arm for support. Thankfully the dog had ceased struggling, or Janny would've been hard pressed to hang on to them both.

"Come on, let's get you inside. Or do we need to call an ambulance?"

Hell no on an ambulance.

"Inside."

The stairs were tricky, but they finally reached her apartment door and Janny paused. "I should warn you, my place is well, pretty cozy."

Echo opened his mouth to reply and caught a fantastic aroma. "Cozy smells good."

"That's our dinner."

He inhaled deeply and grinned. "Then I love cozy."

Her apartment was an explosion of color and books. As soon as the door was secure, Janny set down her dog and wrapped both arms around Echo's waist and propelled him towards a nearby bed.

His knee was feeling better, but since he liked the way her soft body was pressed against him, he shuffled a little slower and pulled her closer to his side.

When they reached the destination, Janny shoved a TV tray out of the way so he could sit. "My place is small, so the bed sort-of doubles as a couch."

With a wicked grin Echo pulled her down on the soft surface beside him. "Now that we're here, and our hands are dog free, I need to tell you something."

"What?"

Framing her face with gentle fingers he leaned down to nuzzle her cheek. "I need to kiss you." He murmured softly before settling his lips over hers.

Her body shuddered and that was all the invitation he needed to wrap her in his arms and lift her crosswise over his lap. She arched closer to him and with a satisfied groan he plundered her mouth, seducing her lips until her body sagged against him in surrender.

JANNY TRAILED HER HANDS THROUGH ECHO'S SHORT curls, dragging her fingernails over his scalp. He wasn't just kissing her, his lips were possessing her, and her body was plastered against him. When he finally pulled back to press his forehead against hers, she was glad his strong arms were anchoring her.

She wished the moment would last forever.

Rrrummph.

Startled, Janny tipped her head back to whisper. "What was that?"

Echo grinned unrepentantly. "Haven't eaten since breakfast and by God whatever you have over there smells good." His stomach issued another loud rumble.

A timer beeped.

Echo leaned back on one elbow and slid his other hand through the loose wave of her hair. "What's with the beeper?"

"That's the bread."

"You made bread?" Echo's face was incredulous, and she could see his eyes were now dancing with anticipation.

"Biscuits actually. Let me up and I'll get the food and an ice pack for your knee." Panic lit her eyes and she scooted off his lap. "Oh Gosh! I can't believe I was sitting on you! Did I hurt you?"

He tossed a pillow at her. "Didn't I already say your size was perfect? Besides, SEAL, remember?" Twisting sideways he propped the braced knee over another pillow. "What about that dinner? I mean, I did save your mutt, that should be worth a few biscuits."

"Dinner for a hero coming right up."

"You realize I may never leave?"

Reaching for an oven mitt, Janny smiled in anticipation of that very thought. Echo staying seemed like a fantastic idea to her.

Dumping the biscuits in a basket she glanced back at him. "If you like this dinner, how about Thanksgiving next week?"

"Wouldn't miss it. Hey!"

She turned to see her dog wiggling up Echo's chest, tongue swiping everything she could reach.

She laughed at the sight. "Unless you already have plans? I mean I understand if you do."

"Didn't I just make plans with this beast and her beautiful mistress?"

ABOUT THE AUTHOR

Leah Miles enjoys reading and writing in multiple genres. In 2021 she plans to publish the Romantic Suspense, *Win in Danger*, in addition to co-authoring a science fiction novel, *Angie's Ace*, with her favorite brother.

She loves the happily ever after in romance with sometimes humorous and always interesting characters who evolve in their relationships.

Former CNN news production supervisor and now insurance agent, Leah prefers quiet evenings with her husband and visits from her three adult children, whenever said children find the time to come visit the small town she calls home.

She loves to hear from fans and fellow authors. Writing is an uphill adventure and encouragement is appreciated! Reach out anytime at leahmilesauthor@gmail.com.

Facebook: https://www.facebook.com/Leah-Miles-Author-112468937186855

A FRIENDSGIVING RIOT

A Sensual Contemporary Thanksgiving
Story

KAREN RENEE

Copyright © 2020 Karen Renee

A Friendsgiving Riot

Suzy Combes struggles when her friend Turk invites her to a Friendsgiving party hosted by his motorcycle club. Recently, his flirting has escalated, but she knows they're just friends. As much as she wants him, she won't jeopardize their relationship.

When she declines his invitation, he's furious. His crazy reaction baffles her. When did everything change? To get answers, she must go to the party.

Will Suzy risk their friendship for a shot at love?

CHAPTER 1

"Are you sure, Suzy? I'd be there by two," my sister said.

I snuggled into my bed with the phone at my ear, shaking my head. "You forgot about the time zones, Stephie. It would be three before you got here, if you're lucky."

"Oh, right," she muttered. "Well, I'll leave by six."

My brows arched. "Don't you have to work on Black Friday? That would mean, assuming I have food ready, you'd eat and then have to be back on the road by four to get back before midnight. It's the first Thanksgiving we've spent apart from one another since Mom died, but it's been bound to happen eventually."

She sighed. "I don't have to like it."

I grinned. "As your older sister, I can tell you, you've made that clear since birth."

"Shut it," she chuckled.

"You, shut it."

"Well, you should go with Turk to Friendsgiving."

My eyes widened, and I suppressed my sigh. These bikers shared info more freely than anyone I knew.

"I don't know how you found out about that, but I'm gonna pass."

She scoffed. "You *think* you're gonna pass. He'll be by to pick you up. Mark my words."

"Why would he? It's the holidays. He's a nice guy, but I'll tell him I'm cool."

"Do you ever listen to me, Suze? He's into you."

I tilted my head back and said to the ceiling, "Not a chance, little sis. We're just friends. He was always here because of *you*."

I could hear the smile in her voice. "If that were true, he would have *left* whenever I went to bed. He stuck around chatting with you and always watched NBA games with us. There was no reason for him to do that. He told us, outside football season, he made most of his money on basketball."

I opened my mouth to speak, but she beat me to it.

"No, big sis. He likes you. And now that I'm outta the way, he'll make his move."

I rolled to my side. "You live in a fantasy world, Steph. So, it's good you went out to Biloxi as a card dealer. I mean where else can adults pretend they can bet a hundred dollars and get double or more back?"

"Vegas," she deadpanned.

"You know what I mean. He was into you, and it was *me* who needed to be out of the picture. Now, you're the one who got away."

"Wrong. He's gonna throw down and go all alpha male on you since he doesn't have to worry about me barging in or anything else. Besides, he's hot. You need to give him a chance."

"What are you talking about? You said he was too skinny."

"He's lean, Suzy. I never said he was skinny. Too flippin' tall, sure. But you're four inches taller than me, and you've always gravitated to really tall guys."

"Whatever. You're wrong, and in the morning I'll tell him not to bother dropping by for Friendsgiving."

"Friendsgiving isn't on Thanksgiving, Suze. The Riot MC does it the day after."

If *that* didn't say it all! The way he thought of me was front and center in the name of this thing, "*Friends*giving."

"Oh," I chirped, grateful she couldn't see my face.

He didn't want to be with me on a holiday, just the day *after* one.

"And I'm telling you he'll be coming for you," Stephie said, pulling me from my thoughts.

"Whatever. If I don't talk to you, have a fabulous turkey-day with your new man."

"I will. Happy Thanksgiving, Suze. I love you."

Stretching out on my bed, I couldn't stop myself from pulling up his voicemail and listening to it again.

"Hey, Suzy, it's Turk. It's last minute, but I wanted to know what you're doin' for Thanksgiving and stuff. Know Stephie's in Biloxi, so you're welcome to the 'Friendsgiving' we're havin' at the clubhouse. Call me. Later."

My eyes closed. I should have listened to my gut the past two years. Problem was that my heart kept drowning out my gut because that fickle organ held hope Turk would someday want more than friendship. Yeah, I was not doing this "Friendsgiving" thing with him. The time had come for me to open my eyes.

❦

THANKSGIVING RANKED AS MY FAVORITE HOLIDAY now that I was an adult. Not that Christmas lost its luster when I hit adulthood. Quite the contrary. More like Thanksgiving grew on me since it stopped being the longest, most boring day of the year. Plus, I understood why other women loved watching football.

Thanksgiving meant a shorter day at the small gym where I worked. Watching from the front desk, the cross-fit class inspired me to be healthier, but not enough to do burpees or anything.

Fifteen minutes before closing at noon, Turk walked into the gym and I did a double take.

"What are you doin' here?"

He grinned, and I admired the dark stubble around his face. "Thinkin' of joining up. Rumor has it, a smokin' hot chick works the front desk, but only on holidays."

I rolled my eyes since he said things like that a lot lately. "Gimme a break, mister!"

"Break from what? It's the truth, Suze. You get my message?"

I nodded.

He lifted his chin. "Good. We'll talk at your place."

"We will?"

He grinned. "We will."

Today I had to lock up for the owner of the gym

which meant I didn't leave until after four when the cleaners finished.

I lived close to the gym. By quarter to five, I poured myself half a glass of fancy-dancy Sauvignon Blanc, which I only treated myself to at the holidays since that was when it went on sale.

As I put the bottle back in the fridge, I realized I had nothing to eat. Opening the freezer, I spied a Lean Cuisine Turkey and Stuffing dinner. Before I could split the box open my cell rang showing Turk's name.

"Hey," I greeted.

"Tell me you haven't eaten yet."

"No. Not yet."

"Well, don't," he bossed.

"What? Why?"

"It's seventeen minutes door-to-door, woman. Don't eat anything. I'll be there soon."

"Turk! You don't need to do that."

"Know that. I *want* to, now are you gonna obey?"

Obey? What was that all about?

"Turk—"

"Do not make me put on a Bluetooth enabled helmet, Suzy. I hate helmets, but the tech ones are even worse. Later."

I peeked into the fridge looking for some fancy cheese, which also became semi-affordable only during the holidays, but I had none. If Stephie were here, I'd have bought some Boursin at the store without thinking; but when it was just me, I couldn't justify the expense. However, I needed to eat something because the wine had gone to my head already. With a block of cheddar cheese, some green olives, and Club crackers, I had a quick snack before the doorbell rang, long and loud, indicating Turk held his finger down on it. Anyone else, I would be annoyed, but with him, it was almost cute.

I opened the door and Turk herded me inside with his long, lanky build. He turned, closed my door, and threw the deadbolt home. I took a step back, and when he faced me, I thanked my lucky stars for the distance.

I stood at five-foot eight, and even though I never asked, I put Turk at six-foot four and a half. The half was mainly because he didn't get regular haircuts, and when those unkempt chocolate brown waves were left to their own devices, they added another inch. My sister was not wrong, I *loved* really tall men.

That affinity happened early in my teen years and was the number one reason I went to every basketball game I could get into without breaking the bank. By the time I had wheels, I became a basketball team manager, which allowed me free access to not only the games but also the practices. Little did I know, my time spent as a basketball team manager would later make me fast friends with a beautiful, tall biker who earned much of his living from being a bookie.

"What are you thinkin' about so hard, Suzy Q?" Turk asked, and I jolted from memory lane.

He had closed the distance between us, looming over me like he never had before.

"What is with you?" I asked.

"Not a damn thing, except wanting to know *you* got some Thanksgiving turkey in your belly. Without your sister here, I can only imagine what you were planning.

Probably the piss-poor excuse Lean Cuisine offers up as Turkey and Stuffing."

I bit my lower lip to keep from reacting. My gaze skittered down his arm to see he held a brown grocery bag.

"Are you eating too?"

"Maybe. You comin' to Friendsgiving?"

I looked away from him while sighing. When I looked back at him, his whisky brown eyes looked different. Assessing.

"You should forget about me."

His chin dipped, and he stared at me. "'Forget about you?"

"For the Friendsgiving thing, yeah. Don't worry about me."

He turned his head an inch and arched one brow. "Don't worry about you?"

I nodded. "Yeah."

He folded his arms on his chest, which put the bag of food nearly under his armpit and forced the aroma of warm, roasted turkey to my attention.

"You talk to Stephie about this?"

"A little bit. Why?"

"What'd she tell you?"

A weird vibe rolled off him, and I sensed my answer mattered more than I realized.

"That this event happens the day after Thanksgiving. Not on the actual holiday."

He unfolded his arms, stepped back from me, and sighed. My gut clenched and my heart twisted because I was pretty sure I did something wrong.

His chin tipped up, and he examined the ceiling. "Damn it," he muttered.

"Uh... what?" I whispered.

He looked at me, the anger in his eyes palpable. "Women analyze, then *over*-analyze every damn thing a man does, says or doesn't say. Why do you think I dropped by the gym today? Why the hell do you think I'm here right now?"

I pressed my lips together, not following him.

"Susan," he snapped, and it was the first time he'd used my full name in over eighteen months.

"What?" I whispered.

"Why would someone bring you food? On any day, let alone a day like Thanksgiving?"

I blew out a breath, then said, "Because they're nice?"

With his free hand, he thumbed the name patch on his leather cut. "This doesn't say I'm a nice guy. Doesn't say I'm *not* nice either, but most will assume it says I'm mean. You serious? You *really* don't know why I'm here?"

"Friendsgiving?" I answered with a question. Again... damn it all!

After a long blink, he turned his head and growled. Then he leaned over, and put the bag of food on a short ledge which led off the foyer and stalked to the door. Before he opened it, he turned back.

"Eat the food, Susan. It'll beat the frozen dinner you had planned. You want to ditch the Riot MC Friends-giving, go ahead. If by some miracle, you pull your head outta your ass, swing by. You could be glad you did."

From the amount of food inside the bag, Turk must

have planned to eat with me. Realizing that and knowing I somehow messed that up made me feel every level of guilt on the spectrum. I scarfed some food down, then packed it up and stored it in the fridge.

With a glance at the stove, I knew Stephanie had likely just sat down to dinner. This crazy day couldn't end soon enough, so I downed the rest of my white wine, rinsed the glass and put it in the dishwasher.

After a long, hot shower, I felt better. The mundane task freed my mind enough to see problems from a new perspective. By the time I toweled off, I realized Turk was just as much in the wrong as I was, if not more so – the jerk.

How could I know about Friendsgiving? And if he wanted more from me, then he couldn't expect me magically to know that. I mean, the past two years he'd been coming and going, hanging with Stephie and me when it suited him. His recent comments about me being a hot chick were random and not to be believed. Men lived to tell women they couldn't read minds, but that certainly went the other way, too.

Wearing my softest pajamas, I crawled into bed and turned on the TV. *Thursday Night Football* was on, and for the first time I couldn't stomach it because it made me think of Turk. I took a calming breath after I turned it off since next up was calling Stephie; I didn't want to unleash my anger on her.

She answered my call within seconds. After we wished each other a happy Thanksgiving, I told her about Turk dropping by.

"Girl! You've done it now," she said.

"What?"

"All the brothers know Turk, honey. They love him because he is the calm in the storm. To hear these guys tell it, I'm stunned his road name isn't Calm."

"Whatever, Steph. I don't even know what I did to piss him off, and now that I've thought about it, I'm angrier than he is."

Stephanie belly laughed, and I pulled the phone from my ear until she finished.

"I was serious," I muttered.

She exhaled. "Yeah, I know. I wish I were in town to see the clash of the Titans."

My eyes rolled. "Listen, drama queen, he and I are not the clash of the Titans. And that's another thing that makes me angry. We get along great, now suddenly he's towering over me, accusing me of having my head up my ass."

The humor abruptly left her voice. "Um. What?"

I paused, but Stephie launched in.

"Suze, you need to tell me what he said. You are the *last* person with their head up their ass. Hell. If it weren't for you, we'd never have been able to afford living in that house, and I don't know how you're doing it now. You pinch every penny so well; I'm surprised you haven't harvested blood from pennies. Knowing you, you'd donate that newfound blood to a blood bank, such is your awareness of the outside world."

I bit back a giggle. "Stephanie, stop!"

"Fine," she huffed. "But you *start.*"

I shared what he said about women, and when I finished my sister was uncharacteristically silent.

"Hello? Earth to Stephanie…"

"Well, shit," she finally whispered.

"What?"

I heard her loud inhale and exhale. "I want to say I was right, but really I was a little wrong, too."

"You know I never liked riddles or word problems, so how about you say it straight?"

"He was making his move on you, Suze. And you kinda did have your head up your ass because—"

"I did not!" I yelled.

"He wasn't *looming* over you, dingbat! My guess? He was moving into your space, but he's so tall, you misinterpreted it."

"Whatever. He could have, oh I don't know, told me that."

"For once, learn from your little sister. Bikers don't use words when actions speak far, far louder."

I shook my head. "So, should I go to this thing tomorrow? He said I '*could* be glad' I did. What does that mean? Why am I gonna waste my time when he's being so damn mysterious?"

She took a long time before she answered. "You're gonna do what you want to do, because you always have, but the only way you're gonna find out is by taking a chance."

"But I don't want to lose his friendship," I blurted.

"It feel like friendship when he left?"

I said nothing.

"That says it all, doesn't it, sissy?"

CHAPTER 2

"Yo, Combes," my boss yelled from the other side of the gym.

When I turned, his index and middle fingers made walking moves for me to leave. My brows furrowed. "You sure?" I called.

"Go! You closed up yesterday. See ya!"

I fired up my car, and the clock showed the time as three-thirty-three. While I drove home, my mind dwelled on whether I would go to the Riot MC compound or not. My sister mentioned Turk might pick me up, but his parting shot to me made it clear showing up was all on me.

If ever a double-edged sword existed, getting what you always wanted was it. I'd fantasized about being with Turk, in every way I could be. On the back of his bike, eating breakfast with him, and of course, going to bed with him. If we did this, there would be no going back to watching NBA games together or lengthy phone calls at night. I had enough built-up anticipation that I wanted to take the risk, but my fear of letting either of us down held me back. In my world, reality *rarely* delivered on the promise of the fantasy.

After I collected my mail and went inside the house, I made a rash decision. I texted my sister asking for the address to the Riot MC compound, then I hit the shower and gussied up for a night out on the Westside of Jacksonville.

My sister's text included the address and instructions to bring an unwrapped new toy. Apparently a Toys for Tots drive was the primary reason the Riot MC hosted Friendsgiving. Two hours later, I pulled in behind the clubhouse and parked my car next to a blue Jeep Liberty.

I popped the trunk and retrieved the *Paw Patrol*® Lookout toy. The box was large and unwieldy, which forced me to watch my feet as I trudged to the building.

"Hey, baby, you need help with that?" a jovial voice called from a few feet away.

I lowered the box from in front of my face and saw a mountain of a man with long wavy golden brown hair, playful hazel eyes, and plump lips surrounded by golden stubble. *Yowza.* Tall, lean men might have been my male flavor of choice, but something about this guy screamed he'd be a fun time.

"I've got it, thanks. It's not heavy, just awkward."

He grinned and I pressed my lips together. His brow arching made it clear he noticed my reaction.

"I'm Yak. Believe me, I can help you whether it's heavy *or* awkward." His tone hinted at a double entendre.

"Susan!" Turk hollered from ten feet away.

I turned, and so did Yak, who chuckled. That seemed curious to me, but the look on Turk's face held my attention prisoner. His eyes flared at me with what looked like hunger.

"You his?" Yak asked.

My eyes shot to Yak's. "No. I'm not anyone's."

His hazel eyes danced over my face while his chin dipped. "Don't be so sure, babe."

As he drew closer, Turk ordered, "Take that thing from her, Yak."

My every instinct was to pull away and carry it myself, but I let the toy go without a fuss. Yak ambled away and Turk stood toe-to-toe with me, his eyes glittering.

"You eat the turkey?"

"Some of it," I muttered.

"You stickin' around?"

I shrugged. "Thought I would."

His fingers delved into my hair at the side of my head and he tilted my face toward his. "You here because I invited you?"

My eyes narrowed. "Yeah."

"Good."

My eyes slid to the side and back to him. "What are you doing?"

His eyes widened, and he shook his head in tiny shakes. "Showing you why I invited you."

Our eyes locked, and my belly filled with butterflies as I watched his face come closer.

A female voice said, "Turk, what did you do with... oh, I'm sorry. I'll just find—"

He yanked his head back and turned to the woman. "Jackie, it's okay. What do you need?"

I gazed past him to see a tall, heavily pregnant brunette standing behind him. She caught my eye, and a tentative smile curved her lips.

"Nope, nope. It's good. Volt can handle it."

"Sweetheart, do not make the president do something if I can do it instead."

She gave him a pointed look. "You literally have your hands full. Believe me, he'll understand. Besides, he loves this party more than the others we have, so he'll be cool."

Turk gently let go of me and turned toward Jackie, but she scurried away. He reached back, grabbed my hand, and we followed her.

I stopped and tried to wrest my hand from his. He stopped and glowered at me.

"What are we doing?" I asked.

He put his hands on his hips. "I need to know what my president's old lady needed from me, and then—"

A sense of relief washed over me and I realized I had been worried about who she was to him.

"No, Turk. I mean before that. What is going on? I thought we were just friends."

His jaw clenched. "Yeah, except I don't have female friends."

"My sister, me and Jackie seem to be your friends."

He shook his head. "Jackie's my president's old lady. She's family. Your sister is your family. And having two sisters myself, I know better than to ignore one of them."

"But you like being around both of us. And you only came by to watch games with us."

He ran his hand through his unruly curls. "No. I only came by to watch games with you two *after* I helped you get a decent deal on a flat screen. *That* should've been your first clue, Suzy Q. A man doesn't watch the game just anywhere."

I shook my head. "But you always watched Stephanie like a hawk. I figured you had a thing for her."

"Watched her 'cause in the little time she worked for me at the Flat Iron Bar and Grill, I knew she was accident prone. Plus, she was always watchin' me like she knew what was in my head about you."

"About me?"

Turk's eyes widened with exasperation, and the next thing I knew he pulled me to him and kissed me.

His warm mouth on mine surprised me, but my mouth opened and he slid his tongue along mine. My breath hitched, and I tangled my tongue with his. Turk tasted great, faintly of beer mingled with a flavor all his own. My hand roved up his torso while my other arm wrapped around his back. His arm tightened and the hand at my face slid into my hair where he yanked gently, but enough so I would pull away from him.

His heated brown eyes narrowed at me. "That say 'just friends' to you?"

"No," I breathed.

"Your head finally outta your ass, Susan?"

My lips pursed, and my eyes widened. I tried to jerk out of his hold, but his grip tightened.

"Bryant Hughes, my head was never—"

He pressed his body against mine to kiss me silent. Even though it was shorter, the second kiss surpassed our first.

When he pulled away, a shit-eating grin spread across his face.

"I don't want to ruin what we have, but what really scares me is possibly losing you, Turk."

His hand in my hair let go so he could cup my cheek. "We could make what we have better. Suzy, I don't want to lose you either. But I can't bide my time any longer. Had we eaten turkey together last night, I'd have told you *you're* what I'm most thankful for, and we'd have damn sure taken the next step. That didn't happen, so ultimatums aren't normally my style, but either you want this with me, or you don't."

Before I could respond, he added, "And another thing, Suze, don't think using my given name gets my attention. If anything, it's less likely to do it. Now, let's go."

He pulled me around the side of the extensive building and through the front door of the clubhouse. We walked into an open room with two pool tables to the left and a grouping of couches to the right. An older couple sat on a couch, but they were oblivious to us since they were making out like teenagers.

Turk guided me to a bar. "Wine tonight, or some-thin' else?"

"I'll have a Diet Coke, thanks."

He dropped my hand, but curled his hand around my neck. His eyes bore into mine. "If you're with me, you're stayin' tonight."

"Here?"

He nodded. "Have a room, and our parties get rowdier the later it gets. You can let your hair down, Suze. Or you can stick with Diet Coke."

"I'll stick with a diet for now."

He shrugged a shoulder and told one of three men behind the bar our order. Those men were also wearing leather vests like Turk's, but theirs had no Riot MC patch on the back.

I looked back to a grinning Turk. "They're prospects, honey. They earn their patch, they get a road name and a kick-ass party where they don't have to work the bar or do grunt labor."

"Oh," I said, nodding.

A burly man with shoulder-length brown hair, chestnut colored eyes, and a full beard sidled up to Turk.

"Jackie tells no lies. Appears you do have your hands full. This your woman?"

My spine straightened at the words and the tone, but Turk's arm around my shoulders pulling me to his side forced me to look up at him.

"Workin' on it, Volt. Sorry I didn't help Jackie with whatever she needed—"

"Not a problem," he said, reaching a hand toward me, "I'm Volt. It's nice to meet you..."

"Susan," I answered, putting my hand in his.

He nodded. "Well, enjoy yourself. Way I hear it, we'll see a lot more of you."

Before I could correct him, Volt moved down the bar. A prospect put our drinks in front of us.

Turk let go of me, grabbed them and said, "C'mon."

We moved out of the bar area of the enormous

room down a wide hallway. A kitchen was to the right and we went down a long, narrow hallway to the left. Turk handed me my soda and pulled keys from his pocket. We stopped at the third door on the right. While he unlocked the door, Jackie came out of a room at the end of the hall. She smiled widely.

"We didn't get the chance to introduce ourselves. I'm so excited that you're here. I'm Jackie. You must be Suzy Q, but I'm guessing that's a code name Turk gave you because he's so damn secretive."

She held her hand out to me, and even though I didn't know what to say to her, I put my hand in hers.

When we shook hands, my brain kicked into gear. "Um, no. I'm Susan, and every so often even my sister calls me Suzy Q, so not a code name."

A door on the other side of Turk's room opened and a woman with purple streaks in her brown hair stuck her head out. "Did you say Suzy Q? Turk actually brought his 'Suzy Q mystery girl' here? Get out. This I gotta see!"

I swallowed, but Jackie leaned closer. "That's Trixie. She's pushy, but don't let it scare you. She's great."

"Ladies," Turk grumbled.

Trixie hurried over, shaking a finger at Turk. "Oh, no, mister. You don't get to tell us how great Suzy is, and not expect us to find out more. We won't bite her."

From behind me, Turk wrapped an arm around my chest. His thumb grazing the side of my breast sent intense heat curling through my torso. "Anybody's gonna bite her, it's gonna be me. Now, go. You can inter-rogate her in the morning."

"In the morn—" Jackie started, but stopped. "Fine. Have fun," she said to me with a wink.

My stomach pitched as Turk moved us both into his room. It looked like a hotel room, and the most prominent piece of furniture was a bed.

Staring at the bed, lost in thought, my sister's situation came to mind. She landed her fantasy. She found happiness beyond her wildest dreams, so if it could happen for her, why not me?

I heard the thunk of Turk's beer bottle hitting a table, then he took my soda and put it down too. His hands cupped my cheeks, tilting my face to his.

"The first time I make love to you is *not* gonna be at the clubhouse, Susan."

My eyes slid to the bed, but my facial expression must have been something because he added, "Unless you want me to."

I looked up at him. "You talk about me," I blurted.

"Why wouldn't I? I love you, and you love me, too."

My eyes narrowed. "Making assumptions aren't you?"

An admonishing look crossed his face. "Not hardly. I go to you after a long-ass day. Your sister argues with you about LeBron versus Michael Jordan, but you only argue that shit passionately with *me*. You care about what I think, and you always have."

My mouth opened, but his thumb pressed against my lower lip. "You keep me hip to new music, and I force you to appreciate the classics."

"Z.Z. Top–"

His thumb moved and his face dipped so his lips

brushed mine. "Shut it. You aren't bad-mouthing Z.Z. Top the first time you're finally standin' in my room."

I smiled, my arms went around his neck and I kissed him *hard*.

The kiss lasted quite a while, long enough for Turk to shift us onto the bed. He pulled away.

"Got somethin' you want to say to me?"

I smiled. "I'm thankful to have you in my life, too, honey. I love you."

He smiled and his eyes twinkled like I loved. "That's what I thought. And I'm damned glad to hear it."

ABOUT KAREN RENEE

Karen Renee is the award-winning author of the Riot Motorcycle Club, Beta, and O-Town series. She once crunched Nielsen ratings data but these days she brings her imagination to life by writing books. Karen spent years working in the wonderful world of advertising, banking, and local television media research.

She is a proud wife and mother, and a Jacksonville native. When she's not at a soccer field or cooking, you can find her at her local library, the grocery store, in her car jamming out to some tunes, or hibernating while she writes and/or reads books.

For more information about Karen Renee, sign up for her newsletter. Or visit one or all three of the following:
Website: http://www.authorkarenrenee.com
Facebook: https://www.facebook.com/authorkarenrenee
BookBub: https://www.bookbub.com/authors/karen-renee
Newsletter Sign Up: http://eepurl.com/dsjfIH

THE LUCKIEST HAT

A Sweet Contemporary Thanksgiving Story

SARA WALKER

The Luckiest Hat

Could they find a second chance at love?

Happy with her modest circumstances and already having had her heart broken more than once, free spirited Hilde McQuire never planned to fall in love again.

When widower Dino Dudley planned his relaxing Thanksgiving vacation, he never imagined that an act of kindness would reward him with the second great love of his life.

Enjoy this heartwarming tale of two souls who meet in the most unlikely way on a windy beach in Georgia.

THE LUCKIEST HAT

"What's the matter with me? Who would wear such a hat on a windy, cold beach in November?" cried the woman as her hat flew away on an ascending gust toward the sloshing waves.

The sound of her voice carried across the empty beach and Dr. Dino Dudley couldn't help but smile at the picture the small woman made chasing her flyaway hat. The pair were moving fast in his direction and there was no chance she was going to catch up with her wide-brimmed possession before it landed in the water.

"No, no! Stupid hat! Don't do that! Not into the water!" She was jogging beneath it, pleading as the hat caught another updraft. The trailing ribbons tipped the front of the hat in a perfect imitation of a giant delta kite and gained more height.

"Tarnation!" The woman stopped to stomp a bare foot in frustration.

He squinted to see her better. She was slim and attractive, probably close to his own age of fifty-six with her long loose skirt now clutched in one fist as she jogged down the beach.

Glancing back at the sky, Dino realized the hat was on a trajectory that would bring it fairly close to his location.

"Tarnation is right." Dino scrubbed a hand over his short blonde hair, reluctant to get involved. People liked their privacy after all. But the infernal hat was heading his way, long colorful ribbons streaming close to the sand.

He really wasn't so young anymore and leaping would probably trigger his vertigo, but the pretty lady was in distress. And as a former Boy Scout, he'd always been taught to do the right thing.

Decision made, Dino set off at a fast jog toward the bright yellow hat, calling out. "I've got it!"

As soon as he was close enough, he leapt, barely managing to grasp the edge of the trailing ribbons. "What the...?"

Instead of just a fistful of soft cloth, he'd grabbed a cluster of paper flowers which were attached to the ribbons by shiny straight pins. One of which was now deeply imbedded in the pad of his thumb. The pain was so surprising that Dino missed his footing and fell face first into a tide pool of freezing water with his mouth wide open.

"Oh, oh! Are you all right?" The woman was there, hands mopping at the sand on his face.

Spitting and spurting like a big goof in his bright red shirt, long trousers and good walking shoes, Dino attempted to stand. Unfortunately, the leaping and subsequent fall had triggered his damnable vertigo and the horizon was bouncing in time with his struggling breaths.

"I just need a minute." Or an hour. Why was he even walking on the beach? Oh yes, this was entirely his son's fault. He'd called him a couch potato before pushing him out the door for a calm walk for his psyche. Well, his psyche was in trouble.

The woman pulled her yellow hat out from under his hand and crouched down in the water beside him. "Thank you for saving this. It's one I created myself and I didn't want to lose it."

"Glad I could help, but could you?" He opened his palm to show her the silver pin.

"Oh!" She leaned close, gently removing the pin before deftly sticking it in the side of the wet hat and using the bottom of her loose skirt to mop at the drops of blood on his palm.

"No worries. Believe me, it's fine." Dino wrapped one large hand around her wrist to still her movements, blinking to clear the sand from his eyes.

"What can I do?" She literally cooed that last word and something about that made him want to laugh, but instead he had to turn his head in order to spit out more sand.

"I'm okay." At least he would be when the horizon quit moving around and he could wash out his mouth.

He was sitting up now in the shallow tidepool with her crouched beside him, watching him with gorgeous sparkling green eyes. Most of her reddish blonde hair had escaped its clip and was spilling down around her pale face. She was a vision. The most beautiful woman he had ever seen.

That thought triggered a twinge of guilt. In thirty-four years of marriage he'd never glanced at any woman but his sweet Grace. Regardless that she had passed away more than three years hence, she deserved his loyalty; but, after all, he'd just noticed the woman was attractive, no harm done.

"We need to get you out of this cold water." The woman grabbed him under his arms and pulled while instructing him to move his feet under him.

Bossy little thing.

As soon as they were upright, she wrapped both her arms around his waist and leaned up on her tiptoes to brush soft lips over his cheek. "Just know that today you're my hero."

Instinctively he tightened the hold he had around her waist and raised his other hand to push back the soft tangles of her hair. "My pleasure to be of service to a lady in distress."

Thankfully, his infernal vertigo seemed to be settling but the late November wind was cutting right thru his wet clothing giving him a full body shiver.

Hilde looked up at the tall man with concern. He'd gotten a good dousing in the tidepool and seemed to be shaking pretty hard. They needed to get indoors and fast.

"Which way is your house?" Fully aware of the delicate nature of a male ego she added. "I'm really cold, do you mind if we get off the beach?"

When he didn't immediately respond, she simply wrapped her arm tighter and steered them both toward the sand dunes which stood between the houses and the ocean. She was grateful that he seemed steadier on his feet by the time they reached the wood boardwalk.

Dino pointed to the left. "Our condo is down there, on Waterfront Way, Number 134."

"I'll walk with you." Relieved he was talking again, Hilde guided them the short distance to the luxury condos. Her would-be hat rescuer had good tastes and a fat wallet if they were renting one of these units. Hilde's own small cottage was fine for her, but nothing like these.

She grinned, cutting a glance up at Mr. Good Deed. He definitely had money, and that was her main prerequisite for husband number four. Not that she wanted a number four. Besides, with her track record, this guy was probably a serial liar or worse.

Upon reaching the entrance to 134, the tall man was shaking so hard she thought she could hear his teeth rattling. Hilde was cold too, but she hadn't gotten as wet as him. Choosing not to dig in his pockets for the key, she rang the bell, assuming someone would be on the other side of the door. He had said 'our condo'.

Only a minute or two passed before the door swung open and a young child of probably four or five stared up at them.

"Hello. What's wrong with Papa?" Not waiting for a reply, she turned and bellowed back through the open door, "Daddy, something's wrong with Papa and there's a lady with him!"

Hilde could see over the child's shoulder as a man rushed from the recesses of the long hallway. Obviously related to her companion, with the same clear blue eyes and pale blonde hair.

"What happened? Dad, are you alright?"

Dino wanted to answer his son, but he was clenching his jaw to stop his teeth from chattering, and the interior of the warm dwelling beckoned. So instead, he pointed his free hand toward the big couch by the fireplace and still gripping the woman, shuffled in that direction.

His son leapt forward, positioning himself on the other side. "Dad, I think you need a hot shower first." He said as he began to tug all three toward the hallway.

"Papa, who is that?"

"Not now, muffin." Peter frowned over at the woman and turned back to his daughter. "Why don't you run ahead and turn on the shower for Papa? Then just go play in your room until I come get you."

Dino tried to slow the progress, but he was being tugged toward the hallway by his son and the woman was resisting being taken along with them all. He tightened his arm around the redhead when it seemed she was trying to shift away. He needed to know her name.

"Peter, wait."

"I should really go." Hilde looked up into two matching sets of crystal blue eyes.

"I understand. Thank you, ma'am and I appreciate you bringing Dad home."

"No. Please stay, at least sit with me." Dino implored.

"Shower first, Dad." Then Peter spoke to Hilde. "Would you mind waiting a sec while I get him situated?"

Dino's feet were planted, and he apparently wasn't going to cooperate until she agreed. In just a few seconds the pair had disappeared behind a closed door and Hilde was left alone in the foyer. She didn't want to track sand or sit on anything in her damp clothes, so she stood there, waiting, because she had said she would.

"Hello."

Surprise made her eyebrows go up. The little girl was back and peeking over the top of the couch.

"Well, hello to you."

"Papa's taking a shower."

"Yes, I heard them say that."

"This is our Thanksgiving vacation, but we have to go back home Sunday. When do you go home?"

Hilde smiled at the girl. "I actually live here, so I'm home already."

"Lucky!" Wide brown eyes watched her with the confidence of a well-loved child. "Do you build lots of sandcastles?"

"Well, sandcastles aren't easy, and I would need an expert like you. But I do love to fly kites."

Just then the girl's father returned with a harried look on his face. "Shawna, I told you to stay in your room and not bother the lady."

At the girl's crestfallen look, Hilde chimed in. "It's okay. We were just talking about kites and sandcastles."

Moving closer, he extended a hand in greeting. "I've no idea what happened, but I've never seen my father in such a state; he's adamant that you wait to speak to him," he said. "My name's Peter Dudley, and I see you've met my daughter, Shawna."

She took his proffered hand but stayed where she was. "I'm Hilde McQuire."

Peter gestured toward the couch and fireplace with its glowing gas logs. "Will you come and sit, so you can tell me what happened?"

Hilde shook her head and using both hands, she secured her long hair in a loose knot at her nape while she explained. "Long story short, I was walking on the beach and my hat decided to pretend it was a kite." She patted the soggy yellow bundle tucked in her belt before winking at a now giggling Shawna. "And your brave Papa leapt into the air to retrieve it, only he got soaked in the process. Really, I should be going, but would you please thank him again for me?"

Peter nodded as if he understood. "I wish you didn't have to hurry. Are you sure I can't at least offer you some coffee to warm up?"

"I'm good. My house is just a few blocks over, and I need to get ready for work anyway."

"You're a local then?" At her affirmative nod he continued. "Could I get your number or at least the name of your employer? Dad's the type of fellow who has to have closure on everything."

Admitting she was a food server might have bothered some women, but Hilde loved her job and her life on St. Simons Island, so she didn't hesitate to tell him where she worked.

"Anyone looking can find me every weeknight at the Seaside Bar and Grill. It's the new place over near the pier." She added with a conspiratorial wink, "And we have the best grouper sandwich on the island."

She turned toward the door before glancing back at Peter. "What's your father's name?"

THE RESTAURANT WAS THE NEWEST ONE ON THE beach, which of course translated to the most popular. The beach décor was typical dark shellacked wood with loopy fishnets hanging on the walls interspersed with pictures of old pirate ships.

"It's a little dark in here." Peter complained and checked his cell. "And it's only six o'clock."

"The music is nice." Dino glanced over at his stony-faced son. No doubt he was still annoyed that his elderly father wouldn't sit by the fire and rest a few more years before leaving the house again.

An antique jukebox was crooning an old Dean Martin tune and surprising for this hour, a few couples were slow dancing on the tiny dance floor in front of an elevated stage. The very old and the not-so-young smashed body to body, undulating in rhythm to the music. The scantily clad bodies of one couple displayed a veritable art show of tattoo swirls and figures across most of their visible skin.

Maybe he should get a tattoo. That would certainly irritate his family.

Dino turned to Peter. "Look, if you don't want to stay, I can meet you back home after dinner."

"I WANT TO STAY!" Shawna was swinging from his right hand, so he made a shushing gesture with his left. "Inside voices, my dear."

"But Papa, I see her." Shawna stage-whispered and extended a pink-tipped finger across the room.

Dino shook his head. "No sweetie, that isn't Ms. Hilde. Son, are you certain you got the right place?" He raised an eyebrow to indicate the rough-looking crowd near the long bar. "Perhaps this isn't the best environment for Shawna."

"I see her! Over there, with those men." Shawna tugged her hand free and took off across the room toward her new friend.

"Guess we're staying." Peter smirked at his father and followed his daughter.

Dino was gob smacked when he finally recognized his beautiful damsel from that morning. Hilde was no longer the demure vision from the beach. Her red hair was twisted up in a knot high on her head and she was wearing a tank top with tight pink jeans and thick wedged sandals.

A vision of female beauty holding a tray loose in her fingers with all the men lined up along the bar probably vying for her attention. He didn't know what to think other than his jealousy was completely illogical.

Hilde was looking their way when Shawna made a break for it, so she knelt to catch her up in a big hug. "Hello sweetie!"

"We came to see you!"

"Yes, and a wonderful surprise for me." She'd noticed Dino the minute his family had entered the restaurant. The trio were a little overdressed for a beach bar, but she really liked how Dino looked in his fancy suit and shiny shoes.

Glancing over the girl's head, her gaze immediately locked with Dino's and held as he crossed the room.

Perhaps number four might be a possibility after all?

Shrugging off that ridiculous thought, Hilde stood, still clasping Shawna's small fingers. "Hi Peter, Dino."

"Hello."

"Hilde." Dino stepped close, watching her in a way that made her heart beat a little faster.

Peter reached down to tickle his daughter and set her up on his shoulders before adding. "We came for the famous grouper sandwiches."

"Absolutely." She couldn't take her eyes off Dino. Sand free, he looked like a model from a TV commercial with his blue eyes and chiseled cheekbones and he seemed taller somehow. "I'm glad you're here."

Belated she glanced over at Peter and Shawna, "All of you. Come this way and I'll set you up at the best table in the house." Hilde tossed her tray on the bar and signaled the bartender. "I'll be back for the drinks."

When she moved to pass him, Dino stopped her with a warm hand on her arm.

"I came to see you."

This incredibly sweet man was so different from any she'd ever known, and she felt heat rise on her cheeks which was ridiculous because she was too old to blush.

"Thank you. That means the world to me." Simply wanting to touch him, she reached up and adjusted his collar and not knowing what else to say, she gestured for them to follow her.

She knew Dino would love the table she brought them to. It was located along the outside wall of the restaurant and had a clear view of the water through tall picture windows. Peter and Shawna slid onto the wide comfortable bench on one side and Dino took the other.

Instead of standing to write down their orders, Hilde perched companionably on the seat beside him, her pad and pen at the ready. "I'm glad y'all are here. So, grouper sandwiches for everyone? Or would Ms. Shawna prefer a grilled cheese?"

Dino grinned and stretched his arm along the back of the bench, not quite touching her. "Yes, and yes. Whatever you have on tap for us and a Sprite for Shawna."

"What about a Shirley Temple?" Hilde winked at the girl.

"Who's Shirley?" asked Shawna.

"A lady who made something delicious pretty famous. Want to try it?"

"Sure!" Shawna fairly bounced in anticipation.

"By the way gentlemen, dinner is on the house. She flicked her gaze back to Dino. "You rescued me today after all."

"On the contrary my dear, I think our rescue might have been a mutual event."

Hilde licked her lips and felt her heart beat a little faster.

"Well, tomorrow I'll be walking again, around nine if you care to stretch your legs." She grinned at him hoping he'd see the challenge in her eyes. "This time I promise to keep track of my accessories."

"I'm not sure." Dino felt a little panicked. Were they making a date? He didn't date. Grace was the only woman he'd ever dated in his entire life. What now?

"Why not Dad? Exercise is healthy, don't you tell your patients that?" Peter asked.

"Patients? Are you a doctor?" Hilde fixed her gaze back on him.

234

"Can I go too?" Shawna begged. "I'll be a help and we can look for things!"

"Hang on Shawna. Yes, I'm a chiropractor."

"Please, please can I go walking with you, Papa? I'll help if you fall in the water again."

Peter gave Shawna a quelling look. "Hush now."

Life was meant to be lived. Abandoning his internal debate, Dino reached a hand to cover Hilde's where it rested on the table. Her skin was incredibly soft and when she flipped her own hand over to thread their fingers together, he unconsciously moved a little closer.

He had eyes only for her when he spoke. "I'd be delighted to walk with you ladies in the morning."

Hilde grinned, delight clear on her face. "Fantastic. I'll meet you at nine sharp, on the beach side of the dunes. Now I'd better get your order in and back on the job or the folks around here will expire from thirst."

After watching Hilde walk all the way back to the bar and retrieve her tray, Dino turned to find his son considering him.

"What?"

"If I didn't know better, I might think you were interested in more than a grouper sandwich. What's going on, Dad?" Peter sounded concerned.

"I haven't had to say this in a long time, but son, you will just have to mind your own business on this one." Dino scanned the crowd again to get a glimpse of Hilde.

Maybe his son had a point. What would Grace think about him flirting with a virtual stranger? He and his beautiful wife had spent so many wonderful days on the beach, did he really want to replace those memories with new ones?

Dino found breakfast the next morning to be interminable with Peter being ultra-polite and accommodating, while Shawna was completely euphoric about the upcoming walk. He knew neither was aware of the guilt he was struggling with over the fact that he was even thinking about a woman other than his wife.

"Come on Papa, it's time to go meet our lady," squealed Shawna.

"Her name is Ms. Hilde. You go get your bucket and hat, and I'll see if I can locate my sunglasses."

"Hooray!"

Within a few minutes, the pair were headed out the door, Shawna skipping ahead with her bucket, Dino distracted by his guilt.

"Slow down, my princess. We're not going to a fire and I'm sure Ms. Hilde will wait for us." Watching Shawna's joyful antics lifted his spirits, though.

When they topped the last dune, Hilde was waiting in bright blue silk pants and a matching jacket with her red hair cascading over her shoulders.

"Look! She has a blue hat!" Leaving him staring, Shawna ran to hug Hilde like the best of friends. "I was afraid you wouldn't come. Papa was slow and I didn't want you to leave us. Your hat is so big!"

Dino caught up with the pair and smiled in apology. "Sorry, she's a little overexcited."

Hilde just laughed and reached for his hand.

The sun was shining and not a cloud in the sky, and her heart bubbled with joy. She'd woken extra early this morning, filled with anticipation of meeting this handsome and slightly awkward man. Something about him called to her.

Shawna grabbed her other hand. "Look! I have a bucket!"

"Smart thinking. But what will you put in it?"

"Seashells!"

"Good, and if we're really lucky, maybe we'll find some other treasures." She leaned down to whisper conspiratorially. "Like sea urchins and star fish."

"What's an urchin?" Shawna froze, eye's wide.

"You'll see. But anything alive we must put back in the water after we find it, okay?"

"Yes!"

The trio ambled down the beach, both laughing at Shawna's antics as she darted back and forth with the cold tide.

"Don't get wet! It's cold!" Hilde called and without considering, moved closer to wrap her arm around Dino's waist.

She was rewarded when he immediately wound his own arm around her. She didn't remember when she'd been this happy, even though she knew it would end soon. Dino and his family would leave after all, and she would stay. But for now, today, she would enjoy herself.

"Shawna, why don't you walk in the edge of the water to find better shells?" Dino suggested.

"Okay!" Shawna broke into a run and headed for the water, laughing and waving the bucket in delight.

Hilde tugged off her wide hat and tucked it in a pouch at her waist. "Do you mind if I ask how long you've been alone?"

"Of course not. My wife has been gone three years

now." He glanced down at her. "Three of the most miserable years of my life. I miss her, but I also miss having someone to talk to, you know?"

Hilde nodded thoughtfully. "Yes, I suppose I do. People look at you differently when you're single. Most of my friends are married and they don't know how to include me in their social activities without trying to find me a date or dinner partner."

"Exactly. With the friends Grace and I shared; it just isn't the same, either." Dino reached over to brush a strand of hair from her cheek.

"What happened to her?"

"Cancer. Took three years to take her from me." He brought her hand up to play with her fingers. "What about you? How long has your husband been gone?"

She grinned and flicked a finger. "Which one? Husband number one left me for his secretary." Another finger. "Number two was abusive." Another finger. "Number three loved alcohol too much and I left him."

Jerking to a stop he stared at her in consternation. "You've had three husbands?"

"Yes. Three husbands with no love, companionship, honesty, or loyalty. Guess I'm an idealistic woman with a remarkably poor judge of character. I don't want to just live with someone, I want to share a life." Hilde stood her ground, not sure how he would respond to her admission.

"Papa!" Shawna screeched as she hopped in their direction "I stepped on it! Ow, ow, ow!"

They both ran to meet the sobbing child.

Dino was attempting to inspect the bottom of her

wriggling foot when Hilde slapped a handful of sandy muck over it.

"This should help. The mud blocks the air from getting to it. She must have stepped on a jellyfish. They're out of season, but you never know when one will wash up around here."

"That is an interesting..." He paused. "Well look at that. It does seem to be helping." Shawna was calming down to hiccupping sobs, so he scooped her up to carry her back to the condo.

Without question, Hilde fell in step beside them, keeping her hand on Shawna's knee.

"Ms. Hilde?"

"Yes, sweetie?"

"Can we fly your kite next time?"

Dino and Hilde grinned at each other. The resilience of children was amazing.

"Of course, sweetie. Your Papa will get you fixed up in a jiffy and we can come back tomorrow, if you would like to do that." She directed her question to Dino.

"Absolutely I would." He nodded emphatically before turning his gaze back to his granddaughter. "And since you're such a brave girl, later today we'll go down to the pier and buy you one of those dragon kites. How does that sound?"

"With Ms. Hilde?"

Dino met Hilde's gaze. "I would like it very much if you would join our shopping trip. Can you make it?"

"Sounds like a plan to me." Hilde grinned, delighted to be included and excited at the opportunity to spend more time with this amazing man. Until she remembered what day it was.

She frowned. "Oh no, we can't go to the beach tomorrow."

"Why on earth not?" Dino asked.

"Tomorrow is Thanksgiving. We can't fly kites because I'm sure your family has plans." Hilde felt the joy puff away on the chill wind.

They walked in silence until Dino bumped his shoulder gently against Hilde. "Peter has plans. He and Shawna are going to drive back to the city and have dinner with his wife; she had to work this week. But I don't have to go, I mean, I could stay here with you. If you would like me to?"

"That's not fair. I want to stay with Ms. Hilde too," Shawna complained.

Their eyes met over the child's head and Hilde nodded, her eyes giving him his answer.

Shawna began to whine again, realizing she was being left out of the conversation and possibly the fun, so they were all relieved to reach the condo. As luck would have it, Peter was walking out the door just as they arrived, prompting Shawna to start bawling all over again as she reached dramatically for her father.

"Take her to the sink and I'll be right along, son," Dino directed.

Turning back to Hilde, something akin to loneliness in her expression made him reach out to wrap his arms around her in a tight embrace.

"Thank you for today." He buried his nose in her soft hair, inhaling a combination of sweet coconut and sun-warmed woman.

Pulling back far enough to press his forehead to hers, he spoke. "I hope you don't think I'm being too forward, I just wanted to feel you in my arms one time when I'm not staggering from vertigo and soaking wet."

"This is perfect." Hilde slid a gentle hand up to caress the hair at his nape of his neck. "This would be, too." She added before leaning up to fit her lips over his.

Dino took that as invitation to deepen his embrace, pulling her flush against his body to return her kiss with even more heat of his own. Their tongues tangled in a dance as old as time.

"PAPA!"

Hilde made no move to unwrap her finger when she spoke. "You'd better get going, the princess is calling you."

"Tomorrow then?" Dino stroked his hands over her arms, waiting for her response.

"Absolutely." She finally released him. Stepping back, she gave a jaunty wave before setting off down the walk.

Dino watched until she turned a corner, he really needed to find out where her house was located. Maybe he should be driving her home?

"PAPA!"

If the child could bellow that loudly, she was probably fine. So, with one last regretful look, he headed into the large kitchen. Shawna was perched on the side of the sink, her feet under the warm spray.

"How's my girl?" Dino leaned against the counter to inspect her foot.

"I think she's fine. See, just a little red. Can you stay with her and I'll run out to the car for the first aid kit? There's some ointment in there that should stop the stinging," Peter said.

Shawna was quiet until her father returned and that

should have been Dino's clue that the little tattletale was preparing her angle.

"Daddy, did you know that Papa is going to take me and Ms. Hilde to buy a kite today?"

"Is that so?" Peter arched an eyebrow in the way he did to show he was listening.

"Yes. And me and her are going to fly them. Only I have to go with you tomorrow and now they're going without me."

Shawna was working it. No tears, but she was squinching her eyes like she was trying to produce some. Dino stifled a chuckle; but kept a straight face when he plucked her out of the sink, in an attempt to head off any more revelations.

"Okay, princess. Let's get you dried off. I bet there is something good on Disney you would like to watch while you rest your foot, right?" Dino asked as he carried her toward the big couch.

Peter remained by the sink, his voice raised with concern. "Dad, I thought you were planning to go home with us tomorrow—for Thanksgiving with Kim."

"I've decided to stay here." Dino settled Shawna on the couch and flicked on the TV. Since she was the only one watching it, the channel was set to Disney and as luck would have it, her favorite princess movie was in progress.

The kid was good for at least an hour. His son, on the other hand, would need to be dealt with because he was waiting by the sink, expecting him to return to listen to all his rational arguments.

Resigned, Dino decided he could listen.

Peter snapped the lid shut on the first aid kit. "Stay

here because of Hilde? Are you serious, Dad?" He picked up a rag to wipe the sand out of the sink. "On Sunday we'll all be going back home, and you'll probably never see the woman again."

"The woman? Her name is Hilde, and it's my decision. Besides, it's only five hours to Atlanta." Dino crossed his arms and leaned a hip against the kitchen island.

"But what do you even know about her?" Peter snapped back, slinging the rag back in the basin.

Running a hand over his hair, Dino glared back at his only child. "I know quite a bit about her. She loves to fly kites and walk barefoot in the sand. She lives each day as if it's something to savor and for some reason she seems to really enjoy my company."

"Dad–"

Dino held up one hand in a dismissive gesture. "The three of you will be fine and I will see you all back here on Friday evening. End of discussion. I'm going to go take a shower."

BY THE TIME HE'D FINISHED SHOWERING, DINO realized he shouldn't be too upset with Peter. His behavior with Hilde wasn't exactly typical for him. He couldn't explain to himself just why she was so special, he just felt it.

Stretching out on his bed, he picked up his phone to call her.

She answered on the first ring. "Hey. I was just thinking about you. How is Shawna?"

Dino grinned at the sound of her voice. "She's fine—easy to distract with television."

Both were silent for a moment.

Hilde spoke first. "Are we still on for shopping this afternoon?"

"Definitely. Shawna and I are looking forward to it." He paused. "To seeing you."

Hilde didn't speak for long enough that he pulled the phone back to make sure they still had a connection and almost missed her next carefully measured words.

"I don't know what is happening here, but I'm really glad my hat flew away yesterday."

Dino felt his heart soar. "I'd say that it's a pretty lucky hat."

ABOUT THE AUTHOR

Sara Walker loves to read many types of books, but most of what she writes are sweet Christian romance stories. She is working on editing and formatting a three-book Christian Historical series and plans for all of them to be available on Amazon in 2021.

She loves to connect the stories in her novels with interesting and quirky characters who usually have to travel to find their happily ever after.

Sara enjoys small town living and still works fulltime in an office, when she isn't planting flowers or taking long walks with her husband. She also has two grown children and three grandchildren who don't visit as often as she would like.

Hearing from fans and fellow authors makes her day. Reach out anytime at sarajwalkerauthor@gmail.com.

Facebook: https://www.facebook.com/Sara-J-Walker-Author-117217430073094/

FAKING IT FOR THE HOLIDAYS

A Sweet Contemporary Christmas Short

LIA DAVIS

Faking It for the Holidays

Everyone knows Julius is in love with his best friend,
Tara.
Everyone except Tara, that is.
But when a miscommunication with his mother leaves
the wrong impression, Julius needs his best friend to
help him out of a jam. Will asking Tara to be his fake
fiancée for the holidays finally expose his true feelings
for her?

CHAPTER 1

Julius probably shouldn't be as happy as he was about his parents going on a cruise the week of Christmas. But he was. For the first time since he met his best friend and future wife—although she didn't know that yet—he would be able to spend a normal, quiet, holiday season with Tara.

Just the two of them.

Was it wrong that he wanted to spend Christmas with his best friend, alone?

They didn't have to listen to his parents, especially his mom, go on and on about how they should get married and give her beautiful grandbabies. It was embarrassing and made things awkward between them for the whole trip to Oregon to spend Christmas with his parents.

Tara had always been fantastic about his crazy family, which made her even more perfect for him. She never complained. She fit right in with them and humored his mom when she started in about the future of their lives and how they weren't getting any younger.

The whole thing made him hesitate to ask Tara to marry him. He didn't want her to think he was pressured into proposing, which he wasn't. He loved her from the moment they met as kids.

He wanted to show her how much he wanted to spend the rest of his life with her, without the pressure of his family lurking and watching them. Yessir, this year was going to be different.

He had Tara to himself.

His cell rang and he snatched it up from the kitchen counter where he was prepping movie-night snacks for him and Tara. It was their usual Saturday night "date" to make fun of bad movies. Not looking at the screen and thinking it was Tara, he said, "You better not be backing out on tonight."

There was a long few moments of silence. Jules' heart dropped to his feet. She wasn't coming over. He'd spent all week gathering the courage to finally tell her how he felt. That he wanted to spend the rest of his life with her and not as just her best friend. He wanted more. "Tara?"

"Oh, no silly. It's your mother. Don't you check the caller ID?"

Damn. "Mom. How are you? Are you on the ship?"

She let out a disappointing sigh. "Sadly, no. The cruise was canceled last minute. That means we're staying home for Christmas. You're coming, right?"

He ran a hand through his hair. No, he didn't want to go. He had plans, damn it. "I have plans with Tara."

"You know she is welcome. You always bring her

anyway." His mom lowered her voice and said something to his dad as she pulled away from the phone.

"I was hoping just to stay home this year and spend some time alone with Tara." Did that sound rude? He loved his parents, but he loved Tara too. And he hated doing anything last minute.

"Why is this year different? It's Christmas, we'll be home, so you and Tara can come to visit." Her voice cracked, and he felt like an ass. *And cue the mom guilt trip.*

"I love you, Mom. You know that. This year I had something special planned and now you're asking me to change my plans." He switched the phone to speaker and laid it on the tray of snacks before moving to the living room.

"What could you possibly be doing...Oh! You asked her to marry you. Or you're going to." His mom squealed a little and Julius started to panic.

"No. Mom, that's not what I meant."

"Don't try to backpeddle on me. I knew it would happen one day. You've been in love with that girl since you met. It's about time you asked her." She pulled the phone away and yelled, "Frank. Our baby boy is getting married."

"Mom, no. That's not—"

"Of course, it is. Now you and Tara *have* to come. I have to go call your sister. The whole family needs to celebrate together. Have you set a date? It might be too soon. We can talk more when you get here in a few days." Then she hung up.

Julius stared down at the phone as he put down the tray on the coffee table. What the hell just happened? How can he tell Tara that his mom just assumed he'd asked her to marry him? This wasn't happening.

His apartment door opened and clicked shut. Tara's soft voice drifted in from the foyer. "Honey, I'm home." When she reached the living room, she stood in front of him and froze. "What's wrong?"

He glanced up, drinking in the sight of her. Her dark blond hair was down with the ends curled. Her blue eyes held concern as she watched him. Shaking his head, he said, "Mom called. Their cruise was canceled."

"Oh, that's awful. She was looking forward to taking that trip for months." Tara sat beside him and nudged his arm. "Why does that bother you?"

"She wants us to go spend Christmas with her and Dad and the whole family."

Tara picked up a cracker and piece of cheese from the tray. "So we go. It's only a couple of hours drive."

He looked at her from the corner of his eye. When he just stared and didn't respond right away, she said, "Unless you don't want to."

Closing his eyes, he fell back against the sofa. He shook his head as he opened his eyes to stare at the ceiling. "We had plans to spend Christmas together, just me and you."

Tara removed her purse from her shoulder and sat it on the floor next to the coffee table. "Did you explain that to her? I'm sure with it being last minute and all, she'd understand."

He shook his head again. "I tried to tell her I wanted to spend Christmas at home with you and that we had plans. Then she assumed I asked you to marry me."

He said the last statement in a rush while watching for Tara's reaction. His besty looked him in the eye and burst out laughing. She fell back into the sofa as her laughter turned to giggles. "Where did she get *that* from?"

His heart sank. They'd never talked about their feelings for each other. As far as Julius knew, Tara didn't see him as more than a best friend. Frowning, he muttered, "Like I said, I was trying to come up with an excuse not to go, and she thought I was saying I proposed. She's calling the whole family right to 'spread the news.'"

His stomach soared, and he still didn't understand how the conversation with his mother went so wrong.

Sitting up, Tara kicked off her shoes and turned sideways on the sofa to face him. "Then, we pretend to be engaged."

"Seriously? You'd do that?" He searched her face for signs of pranking him. She wasn't. Her expression was serious, even though she still smiled as if the whole thing would be a game.

Hope bloomed in his chest. This was his chance to woo her. By pretending to be her fiancé, he was free to show her what it would be like to be his for real. Or the whole damn thing could backfire in his face.

"Of course. I bet she was excited about the news." Tara giggled again. "Who am I to break your mother's heart and ruin Christmas?"

Julius stared at her, drinking in the way her blue eyes twinkled as she smiled. Then he dropped his gaze to her mouth. He would claim those sensual lips soon. "You are amazing."

"I know," she said then pointed to the TV. "Which movie are we watching?"

"Something with action to make up for the sappy chic flic I suffered through last week." He picked up the remote and started the movie.

Tara poked him in the ribs. "You liked that sappy movie, even though it was cheesy. I caught you tearing up a few times."

"I told you there was something in my eyes."

Tara laughed. "Whatever. I know you better than anyone, Julius Clay."

Jules loved that laugh and had vowed to himself to make sure he heard it multiple times a day for the rest of his life. That was if she said yes when he proposed to her for real, that is.

⊱♥⊰

TARA HAD LOVED JULES FROM THE FIRST TIME THEY met in the first grade. They were closer than most couples, so it didn't surprise her that his mother jumped to the conclusion that he'd proposed.

What Tara found so funny was his expression when he told her that his mom thought they were engaged. Jules looked terrified. Tara wasn't sure if it was the idea of being committed to her, or he was afraid of her reaction to the news. Did he really think she wouldn't want to pretend to be marrying him?

Jules clearly didn't know her as well as he should. Then again, Tara had always kept her true feelings hidden. She'd rather just be his best friend than be rejected by him. However, the day would come when she had to realize that he may never ask her and didn't return her feelings. Her chest tightened at the thought.

But pretending to be his fiancée for the holidays was a perfect opportunity for her to show him just how much he meant to her. She had to know if he felt the same way. As much as losing him would hurt, she couldn't go on being just his friend. They were in their mid-twenties with their own careers, and soon one of them would find someone they wanted to get serious with.

She had to make a move soon or lose him to someone else.

"Other than being excited that we are getting married, how is your mom?" Tara pressed her lips together to keep from laughing. The situation thrilled her and made her giddy and nervous. She smiled and giggled when she was nervous. It was better than running in fear or crying.

"She's good. She sounded sad that the cruise was canceled, but that changed quickly." He rolled his eyes, making her laugh again.

Jules was looking forward to staying home this year but Tara never understood why he distanced himself from his family. She didn't have a family. Living in a foster home since she was a toddler made her see what others didn't realize they had—a loving family.

Sure, her foster parents were great and gave her everything she needed. But that stopped when she turned eighteen and was forced to get a job and "be an adult." Luckily, Tara had Jules's family for support.

"I could pretend to be sick, and you'd have to stay to

take care of me." Tara leaned her head on his shoulder and grinned at him.

He chuckled and wrapped an arm around her, holding her there. While they weren't shy about showing affection towards one another, something was different in the way he held her at that moment.

"Mom would move her holiday plans here and insist on taking care of you." He rolled his eyes. "We're trapped with those people."

"I'm more than okay with that." Tara settled against him, getting comfortable as the movie started.

With any luck, she would be engaged for real by New Years'. She just had to seduce Jules into seeing that they belonged together.

CHAPTER 2

Jules pulled into Tara's driveaway and parked his BMW next to her cherry red Jeep. His nerves hadn't settled down all week. It was hard to focus on work. Because he had such a great understanding boss, Jules was approved for the two-week vacation to spend with his family and new fiancée.

Todd was a close friend of his and Tara's and found it equally as amusing as Tara did that Jules' mom jumped to the conclusion that he and Tara were engaged.

Tara took a vacation during the last two weeks of the year every year, so she didn't have that to use as an excuse. Not that they had time to give his mom any more excuses.

When he reached the front door, Tara opened it and smiled. "Morning, future hubby."

He chuckled and moved past her to grab her suitcase. "You're having too much fun with this."

She shrugged and exited the townhouse. "It'll be fun."

After shutting and locking her door, he followed her to the car. "If you say so. Have you met my family?"

She laughed and got in the car, buckling her seat belt. When he got behind the wheel, he noticed she had a magazine. Upon close inspection, he saw it was a bridal magazine. "Where did you get that?"

"I pick up a few earlier in the week. I need to be prepared in case Mom and Susan start asking questions." Tara grinned, making her blue eyes sparkle like she had plans for the next two weeks.

Well, Jules had plans as well.

About an hour into the trip, Tara put the magazines away. "We need to get our story straight. So when did you propose? Was it super romantic? No, neither of us is very romantic. We're more spontaneous. You would just pop the question during a movie or something."

She knew him too well. That was why he came up with a plan to be romantic. A plan that was now in the crapper. "How about I surprised you with a romantic walk on the beach at sunset and dropped down on one knee?"

Tara's eyes widened. "That would be so you to do something completely out of the norm. And I would have cried happy tears for days."

He knew she would. That was why he'd planned to do just that. He wasn't so sure he could still do it when he proposed for real.

"What about the ring?"

His heart stopped for a beat, and he almost patted

his jeans pocket to check to see if it was there. "We'll tell them it's being sized. It was too big."

"Right, but don't you know my ring size?"

He glanced at her, and panic stirred within. He knew her ring size because he snooped through her jewelry box and sized one of those she wore on her ring finger. But he didn't think she knew that. "I don't. I've never bought you jewelry. Plus, I'm a man."

"That's so true." She giggled and changed the station on the radio. "Are we waiting to set a date?"

"Maybe?" He glanced at her again, wondering if she'd thought about all this before.

"Let's go with yes. It would make sense that we wait to set a date until we spoke to your family. Plus, we'd have to save up money because I...don't have parents that would pay for the wedding." She turned to look out the window.

On instinct, he covered her hand with his. "Knowing Mom, once you say that to her, she will offer to pay for the whole thing."

"But that's not right. We should pay for a part of it."

He chuckled. "You can argue that point with Mom and see how far it gets you."

Tara scrunched up her nose. "We'll just plan to pay for things before she does."

Jules smiled to hide the churning in his gut. While his mom would happily pretend things go her way, his sister needed more convincing. Susan was too intuitive for her own good. And, he hated lying to his family.

Tara woke as soon as the car engine turned off. Blinking away the sleep, she looked out the windshield at the two-story home. It hadn't changed much since they were kids. It had the same soft beige painted exterior and navy-blue shutters and trim.

When she reached for the door, Jules gripped her forearm, drawing her attention to him. "What is it?"

He stared into her eyes, watching her. "I...There's something I need to tell you."

Pounding on Tara's window made her jump out of her skin. Turning, she spotted Susan motioning to the door lock. Her muffled voice came through the window. "Let me see it."

Laughing, Tara took off her seatbelt as Jules unlocked the doors. All the while, Tara was silently cursing Susan for interrupting them. Whatever Jules wanted to say made him look far too serious. When she stepped out of the car and sent him a curious look, he shook his head as if to say not now.

Pushing away her worry and curiosity, for the time being, Tara faced Susan. "See what?"

Susan took her right hand and frowned. "The ring. Where is it? And don't tell me my cheap-ass brother didn't buy one."

"I bought one." Jules moved to the trunk and pulled out their bags.

Tara looped her arm with Susan and walked with her into the house. "It's gorgeous and too big, so it's at the jewelers being sized. I was afraid I'd lose it."

Susan looked disappointed, but she nodded. "I'll let him slide this time."

"Tara!" Jules' mom rushed down the stairs. Once she

was on the ground floor, she pulled Tara into a hug. "Welcome to the family. Then again, you've always been family."

"Hi, Mom." Tara had always called Mrs. Clay, Mom.

"How was your drive?" She released Tara to give her son a tight hug.

Jules kissed his mom on the cheek. "It was good. Tara snored the whole way."

Rolling her eyes, she playfully punched him in the arm. "I don't snore."

He leaned in until their lips were inches apart. Tara's heart pounded, and she held her breath for a brief moment. Desire flooded her body and pooled in her core. Just the idea that he might kiss her in front of his family made her all hot and bothered.

"You do too." He flashed a brilliant smile at her, then kissed her forehead before backing up. "I'm going to take our things to *our* room."

Oh shit. The reality that she and Jules would be sleeping in the same room and the same bed hit her. A giggle bubbled from her as her nerves made her insides shake. "You do that."

"You two are too cute!" Susan motioned for them to the living room. "You both look so much in love. Of course, we all knew you loved each other since you were kids."

Tara jerked her gaze to Jules as he jogged up the stairs. Had he loved her as long as she had him? His family seemed to think so.

She was going to find out right after dinner. After all, if he really wanted to marry her, why the hell were they pretending to be engaged?

CHAPTER 3

They'd been there for two days, and Jules hadn't had five minutes alone with Tara. His mom and sister took her shopping or were talking to her about wedding plans. As he told Tara, once his mom found out about her idea that they'd pay for the wedding themselves, Mom said, "Hell no."

Jules was sitting beside his dad across from the women and snickered, causing Tara to stick out her tongue.

It seemed like every time he tried to get her alone, either his mom or sister needed her for a minute. Finally, Jules got tired of it. He stood up and walked over to Tara and took her hand. "We have plenty of time to talk about wedding plans. We are here to celebrate the holidays."

He pulled Tara to her feet and out of the room. As he grabbed their jackets, he heard his sister protesting. "Where are you going?"

"For a walk." He handed Tara her hat, then ushered her out the door.

Tara watched him for a little while then asked, "What was that about?"

He let out a breath. "They were monopolizing your time."

"They usually do." She paused, then added, "But they do seem worse this time. Not that I'm complaining. I love your family."

"I know." He stuck his hands in his pockets. The right one had the small box with the ring he'd picked out months ago and had been too chicken to ask her. He decided that he was going to stop torturing himself and ask her.

What's the worst that could happen? She could rip out his heart and stomp on it.

When they reached his dad's workshop, Jules opened the door, motioned her through. Closing them inside, Jules stared at her. There was a knowing in her eyes like she knew exactly why he stole her away from his family.

Before he spoke, she moved forward and placed her hands on his chest, then slid them up to wrap her arms around his neck. "Susan said they've known that we loved each other since we were kids."

His breath hitched, and he watched desire fill her blue eyes. "Yeah."

She threaded her fingers in his hair, and he fought off a groan. "Does that mean you are in love with me?" she whispered.

All the tension rushed out of him and he gripped

her hips, pulling her closer to him. "I've been in love with you since we met."

He crushed his mouth to hers, drawing a moan from her as she tightened her hold on him. He swept his tongue inside her mouth as the taste of her rocked through him. A groan echoed through the room, and he could'nt tell if it came from him or Tara.

For too long, he'd fantasized about kissing her, touching her, and making love to her. She tasted as sweet as he imagined.

Lowering his hands, he gripped her ass and lifted her off the ground. Instantly she wrapped her legs around his waist.

Breaking the kiss, he locked gazes with her. "I've never wanted anyone but you."

"Why did it take you so long to realize that?" She gave him a crooked grin.

"I was afraid you'd think I told you how I felt because of how Mom goes on about how perfect we are." He frowned. Now that he said it out loud, it sounded like a lame excuse.

Tara brushed the hair from his forehead. Her legs were still wrapped around him, so he walked to the old worn chair. Tara stood and curled up in his lap once he settled there. "One thing about you is you are as stubborn as your mom. No one could influence your decisions. So your fear doesn't make sense."

He snuggled into her. "I was also afraid you didn't feel the same way, and I'd lose you forever."

"I'm pretty sure you are stuck with me. Mom and Susan are determined to make it so." Tara framed his face and kissed him. "I've loved you from the moment we met, too. So it's safe to say it was love at first sight even though we weren't old enough to know what it was that drew us together."

He nudged her to stand. When she did, he scooted out of the chair onto his knees, then pulled out the box from his pocket. Tara gasped and put her hand over her mouth.

Opening the box, he met her stare. "I know this isn't the most romantic spot, but will you marry me?"

Tears streamed down her face, and she bobbed her head up and down. "Yes! And this is a perfect place."

Taking the ring out of the box, he slid it onto her finger. She laughed and said, "It fits perfectly."

"Of course it does. I snooped through your things and sized your finger while you fell asleep once." He picked her up and pressed his lips to hers.

"Of course you did." She held out her hand to admire the one caret teardrop diamond ring. "How long have you had this?"

"About a month."

She laughed and kissed him again. Just then, the door to the workshop opened, interrupting their kiss.

Susan stood in the door with a wide smile. "Thank God, I thought you two were faking it."

Tara wiggled out of his embrace. She walked to Susan and held out her hand. "We were, but he just proposed for real!"

"Congrats for real then," Susan said and glanced at Jules. "Mom and Dad want to know if we're opening gifts tonight or in the morning."

Jules shrugged. "We always open them on Christmas Eve. Why change now?"

Susan stepped outside. "We weren't sure if you two would be taking off to have alone time or not."

Jules winked at his sister and hooked an arm around Tara's waist. "We could always sneak off after we open gifts."

Tara laughed nervously. "I like that plan."

Susan rolled her eyes and went into the house, leaving them alone on the porch. Jules cupped Tara's cheek. "I'm looking forward to spending the rest of my life with you."

"Me too." She kissed him quickly. "I love you."

"I love you, too." He pressed his lips to hers again, deepened the kiss.

Tara broke the kiss and looked out into the yard. "Look, it's snowing."

Fat snowflakes fell as they held each other on the porch. "Merry Christmas."

ALSO BY LIA DAVIS

Paranormal Series

Shifters of Ashwood Falls

Bears of Blackrock

Dragons of Ares

Gods and Dragons

Dark Scales Division (Co-written with Kerry Adrienne)

Shifting Magick Trilogy

The Divinities

Witches of Rose Lake

Coven's End (Co-written with L.A. Boruff)

Academy's Rise (Co-written with L.A. Boruff)

Lucifer's War (Co-written with L.A. Boruff)

Singles Titles

First Contact (MM co-written with Kerry Adrienne)

Ghost in the Bottle (co-written with Kerry Adrienne)

Dragon's Web

Royal Enchantment

Marked by Darkness

His Big Bad Wolf (MM)

Their Royal Ash

Tempting the Wolf

Hexed with Sass (part of the Milly Taiden Sassy Ever After World)

Claiming Her Dragons (Part of the Milly Taiden Paranormal Dating Agency)

Contemporaries

Pleasures of the Heart Series

Single Titles

His Guarded Heart (MM)

ABOUT LIA DAVIS

Lia Davis is the USA Today bestselling author of more than sixty books, including her fan favorite Ashwood Falls Series.

A lifelong fan of magic, mystery, romance and adventure, Lia's novels feature compassionate alpha heroes and strong leading ladies, plenty of heat, and happily-ever-afters.

Lia makes her home in Northeast Florida where she battles hurricanes and humidity like one of her heroines.

When she's not writing, she loves to spend time with her family, travel, read, enjoy nature, and spoil her kitties.

She also loves to hear from her readers. Send her a note at lia@authorliadavis.com!

Follow Lia on Social Media

Website: http://www.authorliadavis.com/
Newsletter: http://www.
subscribepage.com/authorliadavis.newsletter
Facebook author fan page: https://www.
facebook.com/novelsbylia/

Facebook Fan Club: https://www.facebook.com/
groups/LiaDavisFanClub/
Twitter: https://twitter.com/novelsbylia
Instagram: https://www.instagram.com/authorliadavis/
BookBub: https://www.bookbub.com/authors/lia-davis
Pinterest: http://www.pinterest.com/liadavis35/
Goodreads: http://www.goodreads.com/author/show/
5829989.Lia_Davis

A GHOST OF A CHANCE ON LOVE

ON LOVE

A Sweet Contemporary Christmas Story

GLORIA FERGUSON

A Ghost of a Chance on Love

When Kate Peterson needs someone to portray Santa for the grand reopening of her family's business, she doesn't have to look far. Her employee, waiter Rico Santos, fits the bill, but will he accept the job? And, can the matchmaking antics of Kate's ghostly mom bring the unlikely couple together in the nick of time for a Christmas Eve romance? Find out in this feel-good romp about taking a chance on love under the mistletoe.

CHAPTER 1

"That's when the Christmas Magician will perform for our guests." Mixologist, Kate Peterson, set her glass of iced tea on the zinc bar top in the nearly deserted pub.

"Please don't ruin our Christmas Eve reopening next week with a silly magic show," waitress Tracy Jones, replied.

Kate fingered a coaster bearing the Peterson Distillery and Pub's logo. "We've all had a rough year and the fire two months ago only made things worse. Everyone in Rendezvous Beach deserves some joy and a little hope for a magical Christmas."

Tracy's eyes, as green as a glass of Crème de Menthe, grew big. "You think that magician could find me a boyfriend?"

"Perhaps. Oh, and someone has to dress up as Santa and distribute presents to the employees."

"I know just the guy to play Santa."

"I hope you're not going to suggest Rico."

"You must've read my mind."

Kate shook her head. "After he failed to show for the evening shift last week, I don't think we can count on him."

"His car battery died. And his *abuela* got sick. And he lost his cell phone. Give the guy a break. He'd make a perfect Santa. He's kind, generous, and, has that amazing six-pack. Though on second thought, it'd be a shame to disguise it with a king-sized pillow and red and white suit."

Kate draped a gold garland around the old-fashioned lantern at the end of the bar. "It's kind of late to hire someone else for the job. Do you really think he'd be interested?"

"You're his boss. He'll do whatever you tell him. He's *loco* for you."

"Crazy? Maybe. But not over me."

For the past month, Rico, the pub's finest part-time waiter, begged her for a second date. The first was a terrible mistake, the result of losing a bet with Tracy. Relaunching Kate's family's business demanded lots of energy and time. Dating an employee four years her junior was no longer an option.

"If you don't ask Rico to be Santa, I will." Tracy wiped the bar and rearranged a stack of cocktail napkins, that was leaning like the Tower of Pisa.

"Okay. You win. He's downstairs trimming the tree. After we set up the furniture, I'll talk with him."

"Take along some mistletoe, just in case."

"In case of what?"

"You need to bribe him with a kiss."

"Sounds like trickery to me."

Kate wouldn't coax Rico into the Santa gig with a smooch. If he were the type of stand-up-guy she believed him to be, he would offer his assistance. No kisses needed. And no strings attached.

The women arranged the pub's furniture, keeping tables, chairs, and stools far enough apart to comply with Florida's lingering recommendations on social distancing. Kate longed to hear laughter ricochet and glasses clink again through the halls of the century-old ice plant, turned distillery. She'd operated the place for the past five years with her brother, Bill, and all she wanted for Christmas was their clientele to return.

In droves.

❧

KATE ADMIRED THE FRESHLY CUT EVERGREEN TREE Rico Santos had set up in the recessed alcove of the distillery's lobby. "You chose a nice one."

Twinkling dark eyes met hers. He wore tight jeans and a snug white T-shirt, which outlined his famous abs. Below rolled-up sleeves, muscles bulged. Hot didn't do justice to the apparition before her.

"I'm glad you like the tree, but I'm not finished decorating it." He gestured toward the stack of boxes, marked Xmas.

She fanned herself with her hand as heat rose along the back of her neck. Luckily, she left the mistletoe behind. No need to tempt Fate with her heart pumping double-time.

"*Qué pasa?* You're not still mad at me for letting you

down last week when I didn't show for work, are you? Tell me you're not going to fire me."

She slid her hand into her jeans pocket and fidgeted with her key ring. "Uh, no. You're not fired. Stuff happens. I'm only glad you weren't lying dead on a back road, somewhere. Instead, I want to hire you for a special assignment. It requires you wear a uniform."

His fingers smoothed his short ebony hair. "Security, huh? Well, I can't wear my uniform on official business until I graduate from the Police Academy."

She laughed. "That's not what I had in mind. I'd like you to play Santa Claus."

His chocolate eyes teased, and she considered risking a second date with him, until she recalled their first had been a total disaster.

"Santa Claus? For real?"

"Yes. I'd like you to hand out presents to all our employees at the grand reopening."

"Do you get a present?"

She shook her head. "No, of course not."

"Too bad. Say, does this Santa job come with bonus pay? You know, like a supplement for hazardous duty?"

Kate shrugged. "I . . . I guess Bill and I could arrange that."

He reached his hand toward her to shake, and then pulled it back. "Oh, we're not handshaking anymore. I nearly forgot. Well, if it makes you happy, you've got yourself a Santa. *Feliz Navidad!*"

"Wonderful. I'll find you a nice red suit."

His brow arched in a suggestive sort of way. "When I wear it, are you going to sit on my lap and tell me what you want for Christmas?"

She wriggled her nose, hoping to make his proposal disappear. "Not everyone believes Santa makes wishes come true."

He winked. "I bet *you* believe he does."

A shiver of delight traveled up her spine. She felt as giddy as a lovesick teen.

He reached for a box on the floor and unpacked an angel wearing a gold and white dress. "She's a blue-eyed blonde, like you. But you're *mas linda*."

She cleared her throat; she knew just enough Spanish to realize he was still hitting on her. She couldn't let her self-control reach a point of no return. "Work calls. I'd better get back upstairs."

She turned and walked toward the wrought iron staircase leading upward to the pub, relieved she'd found her Santa. Her employees would get the gifts they deserved, and a little happiness. Mission accomplished. Well, almost.

She crossed her fingers.

Santa Santos still had to show up.

❦

AFTER RICO LEFT FOR HOME, KATE SWEPT THE FLOOR in the lobby near the Christmas tree, and tidied things for the night. Suddenly, the atmosphere grew as cold as a frozen daiquiri. A hazy mist encircled her with the presence of a ghostly spirit long gone. "Mom? Is that you?"

"Were you expecting someone else? Aunt Helen, maybe?" an eerie voice asked.

"Don't sneak up on me like that. You scared me half

to death!"

"You shouldn't raise your voice to your mother. Your boyfriend is nice, but what you really need is a husband."

"Can you please mind your own business?"

Her mother flipped a gauzy silver shawl over her ethereal shoulder. A burgundy flapper dress peeked from beneath it, accented by a long strand of pearls. Her gloved hand grasped an ebony cigarette holder. She inhaled and then blew out a puff into Kate's face, making her cough.

"Matchmaking *is* my business, dear," her throaty voice announced.

"He's going to be my Santa," Kate said.

"So, I heard. You'll make the perfect couple with you as Mrs. Claus."

"No! No Mr. and Mrs. Anything! You haven't been hitting that spiked eggnog again, I hope."

"Now, whatever gave you that idea?"

She heard a loud hiccup just as the chill dissipated and the mist vanished from the room.

Leave it to her mom to try to find her eldest daughter an earthly soulmate from beyond the grave. Kate would find her own Romeo.

On her own terms. And in her own time.

And it would *not* be Rico.

CHAPTER 2

What did he agree to do? Playing the part of Santa on the night before Christmas would be Rico's worst nightmare. Crowds made him nervous. Besides, the guys at the Academy would laugh their behinds off when they found out about his upcoming role.

But he couldn't resist Kate's request. Whenever she asked him for a favor, he always folded. Maybe it was that hushed tone in her voice. Or her big blue eyes. Or--

-

Trouble was it didn't matter. She refused to go out with him a second time, because he was her employee, and, she was busy. He was running out of ideas to woo her. She tossed the dozen red roses he sent her last week into the wastebasket without a second thought. He doubted his agreeing to play Saint Nick would garner a second chance at love with her either.

But, heck. He was Santa. And he still had a trick or two up his sleeve and a heart full of hope. And a secret. Since he was close to graduating from the Academy, he planned to give Kate his two-weeks notice soon. His days of waiting tables and working shifts at the distillery were just about over. She wouldn't have an excuse to turn him down any longer, because she wouldn't be his busy boss. The police chief would be. And instead of lugging a menu, he'd be toting a gun.

As soon as he finished work, he was headed home to celebrate his good fortune with some sugar cookies and milk.

⚜

BACK UPSTAIRS AFTER SPEAKING WITH RICO, KATE polished the shot glasses and stemware and stacked them on a counter behind the bar to prepare for the reopening. Try as she may, she couldn't get Rico off her mind. They had chemistry. She couldn't deny that. She needed to act like his boss, not some star-struck schoolgirl.

Tracy emerged from the kitchen off the bar with another tray of clean glasses to stack. "How'd it go with Rico tonight?"

"Great. He agreed to be Santa."

"So, the mistletoe worked?"

"I didn't need it."

"Oh, really? Handsome guys like him don't agree to prance around as Santa for the heck of it. He has a serious crush on you."

"Nah, I don't think so."

"I *know* so." She flipped a lock of chestnut hair behind her ear.

"What should I do?"

Tracy slung a towel over her shoulder and shot her a smile. "If it were me, I'd follow my heart. If you like him, go for it. And if you don't, tell him, so he can move on."

"That's just it. I do like him. But, being his boss makes me want to stay away. And he's a lot younger than me. Honestly, what would we have in common?"

Tracy's brow furrowed. "I'll pretend you didn't ask me that question."

"I'm afraid to give him another chance."

"I wouldn't let fear stop me. Go for it. Who knows? You just may fall in love with the guy."

Yeah. Go for it. Easy for Tracy to say. She lived her life on a high wire. For her, taking risks was second nature. Kate yearned for that spunky sense of adventure. "Maybe I will. Go for it, that is."

Tracy beamed. "Good. Besides, it's almost Christmas. You deserve a little joy. And, maybe even a kiss under that mistletoe."

⚜

THE NEXT DAY AFTER EATING LUNCH IN THE distillery's kitchen, Kate caught up with Rico. "Hey, I've been looking all over for you. Can you help me make a couple of batches of gin in the lab? We're short two dozen bottles to put on the gift shop shelves for the reopening."

"What about Doug? Has he been drinking up all the missing alcohol?"

"I doubt it. He doesn't like the taste of the stuff. Anyway, he had to go home. The baby's coming early.

With your help I can get the extra batches made in half the time, just like we did in February when he got sick. Remember?"

"February seems like an eternity ago."

Her lips crept upward. That was so like something her mom would say. "I have all the formulas written on note cards, so we can't make a mistake."

"Good, because if we mix ingredients in the wrong proportion, we could give someone a very bad hangover."

She bit her bottom lip. "Or worse. Things could turn deadly."

"Now you're scaring me."

"Just trust your gut and follow me to the lab. We got this."

Actually, she was the one who was scared. This wasn't Rico's area of expertise. What if he did make a mistake? It was a good thing Bill had insisted on buying that expensive liability insurance policy last year, just in case. She hoped they wouldn't need it.

Hours later, inside the windowed lab in the center of the distillery, Kate set the six bottles of gin she and Rico had finished mixing and processing into a wooden crate on a nearby shelf.

"That first batch wasn't so hard to make, was it?" she asked.

He looked odd wearing a white lab coat, latex gloves, booties, goggles, and a hair net. She didn't mind wearing a matching outfit. They almost looked like twins. Except, he stood about five inches taller than she did.

He grinned. "If I'd known mixing these concoctions

was this easy, I would've asked you for a promotion to this department months ago."

"I hired you last Christmas. No one gets promoted until they work here a year. We're all incredibly lucky to just be hanging on to our jobs."

He stared at her and then nodded. "Right."

She laid out the ingredients to prepare the next batch of distilled spirits: juniper berries, coriander, anise, and such. "The key to this process is being precise. You measure each ingredient exactly and mix it all for a specific amount of time. No more. No less. Later, process and savor the creation. Any oversight can ruin it."

"Kind of like love."

She jerked backward. "Love?"

He flashed her a huge smile. "Yeah. You bring a couple together, add a secret ingredient, and create a special feeling. One you can't find with anyone else. It's magic."

She stared at him. The fumes from that first batch must have affected his brain. But in a way, love and alcohol did go together. It was too bad, that try as Rico may, love between them wasn't practical.

The pair continued working, measuring, and mixing until the final batch of gin was finished.

He heaved a sigh. "Do we get to taste the fruits of our labor?"

"Not until the party tomorrow night when you strut around as Santa."

He frowned.

"You're not going to change your mind, I hope. I'm depending on you. Everyone is."

"I'll be there. You can count on me."

As they exited the mixing laboratory and placed their lab coats and outer gear into a laundry bin, a niggling feeling came over Kate. This would be their shining moment. They were relaunching their business toward its destiny.

Rico better not let her down.

After walking a few steps beside him through the shadowed, narrow hallway that led past company offices to the gift shop, he turned toward her. "What's next, boss?"

"Setting up tables for the buffet. Can you help with that?"

"I can help you do a lot of things." He slid in close beside her and she backed up to the wall in the tight passageway.

"But only if you want me to," he added.

Uh-oh. She was in trouble. He leaned in so close she could smell his musky cologne. Her head felt woozy, like she would faint. Those alcohol fumes had no doubt adhered to the clothes she wore under the lab coat, because she was getting dizzy. At least she wasn't seeing double. Yet.

"How about a little kiss for Santa?" he asked, caressing a strand of her hair.

She recalled the goodnight kiss they shared at her front door after their first date. Her body tingled for hours afterward until she finally drifted off to sleep, solo in her bed that night with visions of sexy Rico swirling in her head. She missed that feeling. She longed for another kiss.

In a moment of weakness, she recalled Tracy's advice

about taking a chance and going for it and shrugged. "Why not?"

Big mistake.

That's when he came in for the kill and pressed his lips against hers. She savored the sensation of his mouth upon hers. Moist. Tender. Teasing. With a hint of steamy desire brewing just below the surface, just like she remembered. She was in heaven. And on the fast track to hell.

"Hey Sis, you got a minute?" Bill said, as he swung open the closed door leading from his office into the hallway where the couple stood.

She pulled away from Rico and fixed her mussed hair. "Oh! Gosh! Sure. I was just telling Santa, I mean Rico, thanks for his help today."

"That's a strange way to say thank you. Rico, please excuse us. I need to talk to my sister in private. In my office."

That didn't sound good. She hoped Bill wouldn't give her another one of those big-brother lectures. She had enough of him looking over her shoulder, watching her every move for years. Trying to protect her. She was a big girl. He had to butt out of her personal life.

Inside Bill's office, she slid into a chair across from him.

"What're you doing, Sis?"

She shrugged. She had no defense. She longed for another kiss from Rico.

"Listen, I know you like the guy. But, like I tell our staff, no public displays of affection at work. And you, young lady, are no exception to the rule."

Did he just call her young? She was thirty. She co-owned the business. She didn't feel young. Except, when she was with Rico. "We were practicing."

"Practicing what?"

"I wanted to make sure if any old ladies try to sneak a smooch with Santa at the party, he could deliver the goods."

"Rico looks like he can deliver the goods, all right. But you can't be kissing your boyfriend on company time."

"He's not my boyfriend."

"It doesn't matter. Just don't make out with our employees here at work. Better yet, I'd recommend you end the relationship ASAP. We can't take a chance on getting sued to Timbuktu and back. Not during our recovery phase."

"You want me to make signs to remind everyone no PDA?"

"No. We have enough signs instructing people how far back to stand and where to wait in line. No more signs. Please."

"Then, we're done?"

"We're done."

She stood and turned to exit.

"You know, I really like the guy", Bill said. "He's hard-working, congenial, and as honest as the day is long. Rico definitely has potential to go up the ladder with this company. Don't mess that up for us, okay?"

Mess it up? What Rico had was the ability to make her forget all about her brother, her business and showing up for work. She sighed. "Well, let's just keep that between us."

Bill winked. "Deal."

Kate shut the office door after stepping into the narrow hallway, and then looked both ways. Thankfully, Rico wasn't anywhere in sight. Yet the presence of another spirit hovered nearby.

A white feathered headdress sat slightly askew atop her mom's ghostlike head. "You have a problem with the condenser. It's not working."

"What're you talking about?"

"The condenser had a meltdown."

"I just saw Bill. He didn't tell me that."

"He doesn't want you to know. He's called the mechanic."

Kate bit her fingernail. "What if he doesn't get it fixed in time?"

She pointed to the dial on her glow-in-the-dark watch. "That's just it. You two don't have much time. The reopening is tomorrow night."

"How about some supernatural intervention to get the condenser up and running soon?"

Her mom flicked a piece of lint from her shawl and tapped her cigarette holder, causing ashes to drift to the ground. "What's in it for me?"

Kate swallowed hard. Sometimes her mother's requests could be unreasonable. "What do you want?"

"You already know what I want. I'd like to see you and Rico together. In the meantime, I'll settle for you adding my brother, Al, to the party's guest list."

"Uncle Al? Oh, I don't know. He's such an . . . exhibitionist."

"Look, sweetie-pie. Do you want that condenser fixed or not? Just tell me."

Did Kate have a choice? It was crunch time. Their

success tomorrow depended on selling as much liquor as possible at the pub and in the gift shop. Getting the condenser fixed would enable them to meet their quota and possibly exceed their goals. It was a no-brainer.

"Okay, Mom. You do whatever you have to do to get things working again, and I'll pencil Al in on the guest list."

"Call him. Right away."

"Consider it done."

"I knew you'd come to your senses sooner or later. Now, I'm hoping you'll see that Rico is the right man for you, too. Start working on that relationship and give him a little TLC."

"You're giving me a headache. My brain hurts."

"It's not your brain I'm concerned about. You need to open your heart to love. In the end, you'll thank me for bringing you two together. Mothers always know best. You'll see."

A wispy kiss brushed against Kate's cheek.

"Bye, Mom. I gotta' go."

She couldn't share her mom's vision. She had a distillery on life support to bring back from the brink.

As the image floated away, she wondered if her mother had been behind the equipment malfunction. She certainly seemed to have the power to do so. Well, if she *had* been the culprit, she would have the power to fix it. Maybe things weren't so bad after all.

Kate dialed Uncle Al's number on her cell, crossing her fingers and hoping he wouldn't answer.

CHAPTER 3

Finally, the lights dimmed and then grew brighter in the Diamond Pub after the Christmas Magician completed his act at the reopening. Granted, it was a bit amateurish, but the guests took it all in stride and applauded the card tricks and his making a rabbit disappear from a hat and reappear again. This was the night they'd all waited for. The good news was that Mom had come through and got the condenser operating in time to complete the quota of distilled spirits they'd put up for sale.

Kate reached for the microphone again and greeted the gathering of about a hundred customers and staff. They were the most heroic people she knew. After all they'd gone through this past year, all she could say was thank you. It wasn't enough. That's why she purchased the gifts for them, out of her own pocket.

Kate cleared her throat. "Well, we all know why we're here tonight. To honor our accomplishments and officially reopen this place that we all love so much. It's been a hard year, but we worked together and helped each other every step of the way. We're family now. And I'm proud of every one of you."

Nods and shouts of approval emerged from the crowd. Tears welled in the corners of Kate's eyes. On the far side of the room sat Santa's empty throne, beside the baby grand piano bench, bearing the traditional cookies and milk. A white sled awaited, containing brightly wrapped packages with familiar names written on gift tags.

But where was Rico? Kate scanned the staircase yet again, searching to see if he had finally made an appearance. Thus far, no Santa. She couldn't stall much longer. Would she have to pass out the gifts herself?

Suddenly, Uncle Al lifted a brown cloth shade from a lamp on a table nearby, occupied by a pair of mannequins dressed as Mr. and Mrs. Claus. He grasped Mrs. Claus and danced around with her, swinging her out and back in jitterbug fashion, while the music from the speaker blasted *Rockin' Around the Christmas Tree*.

This is exactly why she hadn't wanted to invite him. After too much hooch, he went off the rails, and she always had to bring him back on the track. She maneuvered over to Al and Mrs. Claus and pulled the mannequin from his firm grasp. "Uncle Al, may I have this dance?"

His gray eyebrows shot upward. "You betcha', honey."

She returned the mannequin to its chair across from Mr. Claus and then latched onto Al's hand. He swung her around like a sack of Indian River grapefruit. In truth, he was a good dancer, just like her mom.

"Ho, ho, ho!" a cheery, deep voice cried from behind the bar. "Merry Christmas, everyone! Merry Christmas!"

Kate knew that voice. It belonged to Rico. He slid out into the room and waved to the crowd. *"Feliz Navidad!"*

She hadn't asked him to speak Spanish and give away his identity but then again, she hadn't asked him not to. She was just grateful he showed up.

"Oh, Santa. Over this way please." Kate gestured toward the throne and sled overflowing with gifts.

Where did that mistletoe dangling from the ceiling above Santa's throne come from? She hadn't noticed it hanging there before. Maybe Tracy did a little last minute decorating? Well, she shouldn't have bothered. Kate would not sit on Santa's lap and tell him what she wanted for Christmas. And he wasn't getting another kiss tonight. Bill's words about no PDA on company property still reverberated loud and clear in her ears.

Rico nodded and followed her to the throne. She guided him to sit down.

"Oh, thank you, Miss. What a nice surprise."

"No, you're the surprise. I didn't know if you were really going to make it, Santa, coming all the way from the North Pole."

He stroked his long white beard. "Yes. I had a little trouble getting my car, er, I mean sleigh, to go. But Rudolph came to my rescue and led me and the other reindeer here tonight."

He must be referring to his best friend, Rodolpho. She'd met him one night at the pub when he came to pick Rico up for a ride home. As Santa called out the names on each gift, the recipient came forward and embraced the present with open arms. And Tracy had reported earlier that the gift shop had nearly sold out of their vodka, whiskey, gin, and rum. Their business was starting to come back, and she owed it all to her family, patrons, and employees.

After Rico had passed out the gifts, the group clapped their hands in rhythm, shouting "Kate, Kate, Kate."

Rico motioned for her to come forward, and she walked toward him. A big smile graced his face. He'd retrieved another gift, wrapped in red foil, from inside the piano bench after setting aside the milk and cookies. The gift was tucked under his arm.

"What's that?" she asked, as she scooted in beside him.

"It's your Christmas present. All the staff chipped in."

Her face warmed. "Oh, gosh. You want me to open it now?"

"Open it. Open it," the guests chanted.

She tore away the foil and slipped the lid from the box. Inside, it was stuffed with cold, hard cash. Fifties, twenties and ten-dollar bills were folded into the shape of a liquor bottle with the Peterson Distillery label on it. "There must be at least five hundred dollars inside. Wow. I hardly know what to say."

"Just say thank you," Rico said.

"Thank you, everyone." Humongous tears of joy rolled down her face and onto the collar of her lipstick red sweater, which matched her skirt. Rico slipped her a handkerchief, monogrammed with an *S*, fished from his red jacket pocket. She mopped at her tears and waved toward the people gathered around her. What she cared about most was the overwhelming love and support that emanated toward her from the crowd. She locked arms with Bill. "You're the best staff, friends, and family I could ever ask for."

Rico whispered in her ear. "Make a Christmas wish."

She closed her eyes and wished that her business would completely recover and that her family and staff would receive the happiness they all deserved. And, that she would find love after all. Just like her mom wanted.

Rico put his arm around her and pulled her close and then pecked her on the cheek. "I hope you don't mind Santa stealing a little kiss. After all, we're standing under the mistletoe. And, it's almost Christmas."

To her surprise, it felt good to have Rico standing at her side, his broad arm cradled around her back, supporting her. She wondered again who put the mistletoe above them, but when the room suddenly grew cool and a mist formed over Santa's head, she figured her hunch was right. Her mother had been behind it all along.

"Merry Christmas," she half-whispered to her mom.

"Same to you, honey. And don't forget to keep me posted on how you two are doing. I don't want to miss a thing."

Rico leaned toward Kate's ear. "How about that second date?"

She paused.

Kate knew Rico wouldn't be an employee much longer. He'd turned in his two-weeks notice late this afternoon. When he graduated from the Police Academy, she planned to be there.

She nodded. "Why not take a chance?"

Kate couldn't see into the future, but if she could, she'd trust that everything would be okay, and that she'd be happy with a man she loved. Maybe, it would be Rico.

After all, mothers really did know best.

ABOUT GLORIA FERGUSON

Gloria Ferguson, aka Glo, is a Romance Writers of America Pro and author of sweet romance and romantic mystery. She is a former finalist in RWA chapter contests, in particular: Pages from the Heart and Romancing the Tome. She loves writing stories with a humorous tone that always end with a happily-ever-after.

She lives in Northeast Florida where she enjoys playing piano, eating dark chocolate, and walking on neighborhood trails, accompanied by voices of her characters swirling in her head. She likes kicking around with writer pals and former teaching colleagues from her years as a school music teacher in Aruba and central Florida.

She values having received the Carol Quinto Service Award twice for her work with the Volusia County

Romance Writers chapter. She is grateful for the friendship and support of fellow FCRW members.

You can contact her at the following:

Website: http://gloferguson.com/
Newsletter: http://gloferguson.com/newsletter/
Blog: http://gloferguson.com/scrapbook/

HIS CHRISTMAS ROSE

A Sweet Historical Christmas Story

MAGGIE FITZROY

His Christmas Rose

Penniless and alone, young Rose Robinson accepts a position as caretaker to the matriarch of a wealthy Vermont family just before Christmas in December 1899. Grateful to have a place to live, she is also relieved that she will not be spending the holiday alone and braces herself to be content. Until she realizes she is falling for the handsome heir to the estate. A man that she, a servant, has no right to love.

HIS CHRISTMAS ROSE

VERMONT, DECEMBER 1899

A t least she wouldn't be alone at Christmas.

Leaning her head back against her seat, Rose Robinson took comfort in that truth, at least. The position of caregiver to the frail and elderly Eleanor Cardelle had come along just in time, and for that she was grateful.

Not to mention that she would also have a roof over her head and food to eat. Her room at Cardelle Manor wouldn't be much of course, but it would be far better than having no place to live at all. Or maybe worse, becoming a charity case. Rose shuddered at that thought as she turned to stare out the train window at the wintery Vermont countryside streaming past.

Dazzling white hills roll toward the sky, where light lavender clouds float high. Rose smiled. A might trite, but not a bad first line for a little ditty about her journey from Boston to Woodbridge, Vermont, and her new home. Hopefully, the matriarch of the Cardelle family wouldn't be so demanding of her time that she had none left for composing her beloved poetry.

"What is your destination, dear?"

Startled, Rose turned and looked at her seat mate, a middle-aged woman with a mop of silver-brown curls, who had been so quiet that Rose had assumed she was asleep. "Ma'am?" Rose said.

"Forgive me for being nosey, but I was just wondering where you are going."

Rose smiled. "Oh, I get off at the next stop, Woodbridge."

"Wonderful. Me, too. You'll love our small, charming town."

"I'll be working at Cardelle Manor, which I believe is on the outskirts," Rose said. "As caregiver and companion to—"

"Old lady Cardelle, of course."

Rose widened her eyes. "You know her?" It would help to learn something of her employer before they met. Other than that, she was vastly wealthy, one of the few facts the employment agency had conveyed before hastily signing Rose on.

The woman laughed. "Not personally, she's not exactly in my social circle. But I've heard plenty about the Cardelles. Miss Eleanor's a widow. Lives with her son and daughter-in-law and granddaughter, Lucy. But I understand her handsome grandson, Jack, has also returned for the holidays. *That* has set many a young maiden's heart a-pounding. Every eligible young lady in town wants to marry him, now that he's available again."

Rose wondered, but didn't ask, why Jack Cardelle was available again. What could it matter? She would likely soon find out, and anyway, she was not an eligible young lady, the daughter of a respectable family. She was the daughter of a man who'd died drunk and penniless. She was hired help.

"Don't worry dear," Rose's seat mate said, her eyes twinkling. "You look frightened, but no need. The Cardelles are quite nice. And Woodbridge is sure to embrace you."

"You think so?"

She gave a nod. "After all, small towns can be stifling places, where everybody knows everybody else. So, a pretty young thing like you? You're sure to set hearts a flutter."

ROSE HAD EXPECTED A SERVANT TO MEET HER AT THE station, so she was surprised that Jack and Lucy Cardelle came instead.

Lugging her wicker valise down the train platform, she spotted them immediately. Seated side-by-side atop a two-horse, four-seat carriage, they were watching passengers disembark and—based on her seat mate's descriptions—Rose knew them immediately.

"Lucy's about eighteen," the chatty woman had shared. "Cute lass, with blonde ringlets. Her brother's hair is darker, light brown, you might say, and wavy."

Brother and sister were both strikingly good looking, and fashionably well-dressed. Lucy wore a pale-pink velvet cape, with a white-fleece-lined hood, from which some pretty blonde ringlets peaked. Her brother was gripping the horse's reins in gloved hands, garbed in a fitted, tan wool coat that flattered his trim physique.

Rose heaved a sigh as she glanced down at her ill-fitting gray coat, patched in places along the hem, repairs she hoped weren't too obvious. She set her suitcase down to tie her bonnet ribbons tighter in a futile attempt to warm herself against gusts of frigid wind.

But her gloves were too large for her fingers. Fumbling awkwardly, the ribbons became more tangled and her bonnet fell forward. Frustrated and embarrassed, she yanked it off to fix the ties, and pieces of her dark-brown hair came unmoored from their pins and whipped her cheeks.

Rose watched the train pull away in a bellow of smoke, leaving her standing alone.

Jack Cardelle hopped down from his perch and holding his top-hat down with one hand, sprinted toward her. "Miss Rose Robinson?"

She nodded, then he formally introduced himself. "My sister and I were sent to get you, as our stableman has the afternoon off."

His eyes were an arresting slate-gray, and he wore his hair longer than fashionable. Clean-shaven, he had angular cheekbones and a strong, square chin. He looked to be in his late twenties, and Rose didn't doubt for a moment that every eligible young lady in town would love to capture his fancy.

She offered a shy smile. "Thank you for meeting me."

"We were expecting someone much older," he said

with a puzzled frown, as if trying to decide if she was who she claimed to be.

"I'm twenty-one," Rose said, lifting her chin to convey confidence she suddenly no longer felt. "Young, yes, but I assure you I'm an experienced caregiver. I nursed my father for many years until he died...." She swallowed hard. "Just last month."

"I see," he said, lifting her valise. A deep line appeared between his brows. "Is this all you have?"

In the world, she thought. "Yes," she said. "It's not much, but all I need."

The young woman in the carriage was shouting her name. "Miss Robinson, is that you?" Beaming, she waved. "Come over here, I'm excited to meet you."

Rose raised a hand and waved back. She turned and met Jack Cardelle's bemused gaze.

"My sister, Lucy...she wants everyone to be her friend, so she really is excited to meet you." He shrugged. "But she was also afraid we wouldn't be able to find a caregiver for Grandmother two weeks before Christmas. Since your predecessor quit with no notice."

❧

"WELCOME, DEAR," ELEANOR CARDELLE SAID WITH A smile as she leaned forward in her wheelchair to squeeze Rose's hand.

Rose beamed at the warm welcome she'd not expected. Given that the prior caregiver had left abruptly, she'd worried the matriarch might prove cranky and difficult. Instead, the regal, silver-haired woman seemed nice. As did her son, Charles, and daughter-in-law, Julianna—Jack and Lucy's parents.

Lucy had insisted when they left the train station that Rose take the seat beside her brother in the carriage. A polite offer, but Rose would have preferred sitting in back.

She'd found Jack intimidating, with no idea what to say to him as he sat upright and tense, focused on the horses, occasionally glancing her way as they moved through town.

Fortunately, his sister had made up for the awkward silence between them, chatting away about her friends and their plans for the holidays. Ice skating. Sledding. Parties. Dancing. Rose envied her.

Then Rose's heart leapt when they turned into the Cardelle estate. It was beautiful. Acres of snowy woodlands, and at the end of a long drive, the family's grand, gabled, three-story mansion.

After meeting Eleanor Cardelle, who asked Rose to call her Lady Eleanor, a housemaid led Rose to her room on the third floor. It was modest, with a small window overlooking a winter-white forest. It also had a maple armoire and a bed with a plump mattress.

Rose grinned as she opened her valise and unpacked her few things. She'd never had a room of her own.

LADY ELEANOR HAD A WING ON THE FIRST FLOOR AND Rose met her there the next morning to help her dress and settle into her wheelchair. Then she pushed her to the dining room for breakfast, where Rose saw they'd be eating alone.

"I'm in the habit of rising earlier than everyone else," Lady Eleanor explained between bites of poached egg. "I live a rather routine and boring existence, as you will see, but I have a feeling you'll fit in just fine. After this, we'll go to the library, beside the sunroom, where you can read to me, and then it will be time for lunch, and then my nap, and then a stroll around the estate, and then dinner."

"Goodness," Rose said. "And what shall I do while you are resting?"

"Whatever you like, my dear."

Rose beamed. She'd have time for her poetry after all.

"Perhaps Lucy will invite you to join her on some of her excursions," Lady Eleanor said. "But don't expect to see much of my grandson, Jack. He's been horribly moody, claiming he dislikes Christmas now, after all that nonsense that happened last year." She sighed. "Such a pity."

Rose opened her mouth to ask what had been a pity, then hesitated, wondering if it was her place, when Lucy burst into the room.

"Grandmother! I've a most marvelous idea," she cried. "I know Rose is *your* companion, but I would like her to go ice-skating with *me* this afternoon."

Lady Eleanor smiled. "Wonderful idea."

"And Jack must come, too. It will be good for him."

Lady Eleanor clapped her hands. "I agree."

Rose felt her cheeks redden. "But I have never been ice-skating–"

"But you must go," Lucy said with a grin. "I insist."

❧

W~HY~ IN THE WORLD HAD HE LET L~UCY~ TALK HIM into this?

Jack Cardelle glided across Woodbridge Pond, passing hordes of skaters, including quite a few young ladies trying to catch his eye.

He hadn't been there in a year, not since breaking it off with Franny, and it seemed the whole town was there now. He was in no mood to pretend to be having fun.

He skated in a large circle, pleased that at least he still knew how. Then his gaze landed on Rose Robinson, who clearly had no idea what she was doing. Why in the world had Lucy invited her? She didn't fit in with the well-dressed crowd his sister went with and was a pitiful sight as she tried to put one foot in front of the other without falling.

Jack watched her wobble, move a few inches, then wobble some more. She was brave, he gave her that. Even dressed in that sad coat of hers, struggling to remain upright in Lucy's old skates, she was still the prettiest woman on the ice. Who, he realized, could use a few tips on skating.

"Miss Robinson," he called, gliding toward her, "you look like you could use some help."

She looked over, startled. "Mr. Cardelle," she said, giving him an embarrassed smile. "I suppose I could. I've never done this before."

"I can tell."

He winced, realizing how condescending that must

have sounded, but she didn't seem to mind. They locked gazes. She was stunning. Large, powder-blue eyes ringed with dark lashes. Shiny, wavy chestnut-brown hair. Cheeks, rosy-pink from the cold. Her smile widened and his heart did a flip.

There was something about her, he'd noticed that the moment they met. Beyond her beauty. Why was she working as a paid companion?

"Hold onto me," he said, offering his arm. "It will be easier for you to practice that way." He grinned, "While remaining upright."

She took it, tentatively laying a gloved hand on his wrist as she lifted her chin and looked out at the groups of skaters. "I haven't fallen yet," she said.

"No," he said, "and I'll try not to let you."

She was a quick learner, or maybe it just seemed that way, because time evaporated as together, they moved farther and then faster across the pond.

They passed other couples, many flashing polite but puzzled smiles, obviously wondering who the new woman was on his arm. Lucy, skating with a young man Jack didn't recognize, flew by and waved.

Franny, skating alone, glided past and glowered.

"I want to try on my own," Rose declared with a gleam in her eye as she let go of his arm. "I think I can."

Jack gave a nod and let her go ahead of him, admiring her courage. "You're doing great," he shouted, then wondered how long her newfound confidence would keep her from falling. Better follow, just in case.

It was a good thing he did. She hadn't gone far when one of her ankles slipped out from under her, and she went flying. Flailing her arms to try to regain her balance, she landed in a heap.

Alarmed, Jack skated over and helped her stand. "Are you alright?"

"I don't think so." She grimaced.

He was gripping her arm and felt her start to fall again.

"I think I twisted my ankle."

Jack slowly lowered her back down onto the ice. "I can carry you," he said, hitching his chin toward a bench at the pond's edge. "Over there. Okay?"

"Okay."

She didn't weigh much, which was fortunate, because it allowed him to maintain his balance.

She was in pain, though, her eyes welling with tears.

He lowered her onto the bench, and she looked up at him, her lower lip trembling. "I think it's just twisted. But I'll be okay. I have to be."

"We'll call for a doctor," Jack said. "Don't worry, you'll be fine."

"But don't you see?" Her voice was breaking. "I will have to be fine. For the sake of my job."

❧

How could she have been so foolish? Believing she could fit into the glamorous lifestyle of the Cardelles?

But Lucy had invited her to go skating. And Jack had kindly given her lessons. And for a brief few hours, on an afternoon that had seemed a wonderful dream, Rose had allowed herself to believe it was real.

She sighed. Now, here she was, lying in bed with her ankle wrapped and propped up, unable to help Lady Eleanor, let alone herself.

"I don't know why my predecessor left, but now you'll need to replace me, too," Rose sadly told Lucy, who was hovering over her, holding the crutches the doctor had left.

"Don't be silly. You heard what the doctor said, your ankle is only twisted. In a few days, you'll be fine."

Rose let out a deeper sigh.

"And anyway, she left of her own accord," Lucy said as she went over and leaned the crutches next to Rose's window.

"What?"

"The caregiver before you. She ran off with a carpenter from town, who'd come to the mansion to do repair work. They eloped, claiming they were in love, just up and left for parts unknown. Which is why Jack asked the employment agency for someone middle aged or older. Which is why he was disappointed, at first, to see you were not."

"At first?"

"I think he's warming up to you," Lucy said as she held Rose's gaze and smiled. "I think you're good for him."

Rose felt her cheeks grow hot and looked away.

"It's difficult to find good help this time of year," Lucy said. "Will you miss your family?"

"I don't have one. It was only me and my father and he died the day after Thanksgiving." Rose pressed her lips together. "This job was a Godsend."

"Oh. I'm sorry."

"Don't be. He'd been sick for a long time. My mother passed away shortly after I was born and then my father became melancholy and started drinking and lost his business—a quarry that had been in our family for generations."

"Oh, you poor thing."

"Please don't feel sorry." Sympathy was the last thing Rose wanted. "I'm just very glad to be here," she said, "and regret being a burden."

Lucy waved a hand. "You're not. And we're glad you're here, too. As I said, you're doing Jack some good."

It was Rose's chance to ask. She took it. "Your grandmother mentioned that Jack has been moody lately, dreading Christmas because of something that happened last year. Is that what...?"

"Yes..." Lucy's smile faded into a frown. "Our family had a big party planned for Christmas Eve, where everyone expected Jack to propose to Franny Witherspoon, his sweetheart. She's the daughter of a Woodbridge banker, and they'd known each other since childhood. Jack's an attorney over in Burlington, where he owns a townhouse near his office, and everyone expected that he and Franny would marry.

"Oh." Rose widened her eyes. "What happened?"

"At the very last minute, Jack told us to cancel the party, to which much of the town had been invited. He couldn't go through with it, he said. Wasn't sure he loved her. Franny was mortified. As was her family, and ours. It was scandalous, the way he went about it, everyone said." Lucy pursed her lips. "Now you know."

"Oh..." Rose said. "I'm sorry."

"Don't be." Lucy gave a wry grin. "I never liked her anyway."

❦

THE DOCTOR WAS RIGHT.

After two days in bed, mostly spent composing poetry, Rose was able to stand again, and walk with only a slight limp.

Lucy, bless her heart, had assumed her duties with Lady Eleanor during that time, and cheerfully brought Rose her meals. She also brought exciting news about Jack, that he was eagerly going out again with friends, and had even gone sledding.

"He's smiling once more and it's wonderful to see him back to his old self," Lucy said. "I told you that you were good for him."

Lucy's wonderful news about Jack didn't exactly gladden Rose's heart, although she knew it should. To her secret shame, when she hadn't been writing odes to nature and friendship and grief and love, she'd been thinking about him. The way he'd looked at her, with a sparkle in his eye, as they glided together amidst the other skaters. The concerned warmth he'd conveyed when he lifted her up and carried her across the frozen pond. How wonderful it had felt to be in his arms.

It was magical. But how could she think it had meant anything to him? To think so was ridiculous. He was a wealthy professional, heir to a vast estate. His father was a lumber baron, and he and his sister would someday inherit it all.

How could a man like Jack Cardelle ever care for a

woman who had nothing and was a nobody? He had shown kindness to her, and that was all. It was clearly his nature to be nice, and that was all.

Lady Eleanor smiled broadly when Rose limped into her room and announced she was back to work, ready to help her dress. "I'm so glad, dear," she said. "I've missed you. But I'm so glad to see you're better. Looking even lovelier than before."

She was being polite. Rose wore the same pale-blue gown she'd had on under her dowdy coat when she'd arrived. While she owned a few undergarments, she had only two dresses to her name, the other a slightly less-worn olive-green frock, which she was saving for Christmas.

Rose's eyes lit up as she pushed Lady Eleanor into the dining room. In her absence, it had been decorated for the holiday, with streams of holly around the windows and doorways, and poinsettia bouquets on the table.

Then her gaze slid to the man sitting at the end of the table. Jack.

"Good morning," he said. "I thought I would join you for breakfast today." He stood and took the handle-bars of his grandmother's wheelchair from Rose, and as he did, their fingers lightly brushed together. A delicious shiver raced through Rose's body.

Lady Eleanor beamed. "Goodness, Jack, I don't think I've seen you at breakfast since you were a boy. We're honored."

"I agree," Rose said as she took her seat. She could think of nothing else to say and wondered how she would be able to eat. Would they notice if she didn't?

They would surely notice if she started choking on her food, because she suddenly found it hard to swallow and her heart was racing.

Jack seemed not to notice. Or maybe he was just being polite to his grandmother. Because as the cook served breakfast, he directed the conversation to the elderly woman, giving Rose a chance to compose herself.

When they finished, as the cook whisked their plates away, he turned back to her. Although, he, too, seemed oddly ill at ease. "How did you find your past two days, Miss Robinson?" He cleared his throat. "Uhm, I mean, I hope you found something to amuse yourself...I mean, I hope you weren't too bored."

Rose flushed. It was kind of him to ask. "Thank you, but no...I used my time to write poetry."

He lifted an eyebrow. "Oh, so you're a poet?"

She nodded, embarrassed. "I like to think so. Literature was my favorite subject in school—and poetry gives me great pleasure."

"I'd love to see some of what you wrote, wouldn't you, Grandmother?"

"Indeed," Lady Eleanor said. "Perhaps you can read some of your poems to us in the library."

The library? Rose hadn't expected Jack to accompany them there. But whether or not that had been his plan, he insisted she go up to her room to fetch some of her work.

He and Lady Eleanor proved polite listeners. After she read three of what she considered her best poems, they applauded, and Rose nodded her appreciation as her cheeks burned hot.

"You're quite talented," Jack said, lifting a corner of his lips in a smile that made Rose blush even more. "If you don't mind, I would like to join you again for breakfast tomorrow, and then Grandmother and I can listen to more of your works."

Really? Rose couldn't believe her ears.

"Marvelous," Lady Eleanor said. "I should love that."

<hr/>

PLEASE, PLEASE DON'T LET ME BE HUMILIATED ON Christmas, Rose thought as she and Lucy made their way through crowds of shoppers in downtown Woodbridge.

Lucy had insisted Rose join her, to help pick out gifts for family and friends. But her selections were so extravagant that Rose was ashamed to realize she couldn't afford anything for anyone in the Cardelle family, when they had all shown her such kindness.

For the past three days, Jack had joined her and Lady Eleanor for breakfast and library-time, and also for lunch, before going off to spend his afternoons and evenings with friends. It had been heavenly. And nerve-wracking.

Rose found herself flattered when he praised her writing, curious as to why he even cared, and then bereft when he left to go off to parties and dances with his social set. Which included, she assumed, many of the eligible females in town vying for his attention. She tried, and failed, to stop her envious imagination from running wild.

"There's Jack now. Oooh, I wonder what he got

me?" Lucy cried as her brother came out of a hat store, carrying a package.

He bowed as shoppers streamed past. "Lucy, Miss Robinson. Are you enjoying yourselves?"

"Immensely," Lucy said, holding up packages in both hands, then nodding her head at others Rose was carrying for her.

"I'm glad," Jack said, then hesitated, as if not sure what to do or say next.

"Care to join us?" Lucy giggled. "Unless you have plans to meet someone else."

He grinned. "I don't, actually. And yes, I'd love to tag—"

A young woman in a lavender coat and matching feather hat ran up to him. His smile froze. "Franny..." he said in a strained voice, "hello."

"Jack, Lucy," she said, not even looking at Rose. "Merry Christmas to you both."

Franny. Rose stared at her. She was pretty, in a pinched, high-strung sort of way. Or maybe she just looked pinched because she was still furious at Jack. *If that's the case*, Rose thought, she could have just avoided greeting him by crossing to the other side of the street or turning around and going the other way.

Instead, she held out a brown-paper package and ripped some of the wrapping off. "See what I got your grandmother," she said, looking at Lucy and then Jack as she held it out. She gave a strained smile. "Won't she love it?"

It was a vase. A very expensive-looking one.

Jack looked shocked, and not pleased. "You

shouldn't have, Franny. You needn't have gotten her anything. She's—"

"Oh, but Jack, dear, I wanted to." She sniffed. "I love her still, even if..." Her eyes darted to Rose, then quickly away. "I shall deliver it to her on Christmas Eve." She gave a stiff smile and darted around them. "See you then."

"I hope not," Lucy whispered.

Rose frowned. She had nothing to give Lady Eleanor. Or Lucy or Jack or their parents.

Then it came to her—she would write each of them a poem.

❧

JACK WANDERED INTO THE FAMILY GREAT ROOM AND stopped to contemplate the empty space next to the fireplace.

He felt a pang of guilt. According to family tradition, the Christmas tree should be there by now. For the past twelve years, ever since he was fifteen, it had been his job to go into the woods behind the mansion and chop one down.

Someone—likely his father—had moved a large chair to make room for this year's tree. And now, here it was Christmas Eve, and they didn't have one yet.

Memories of how the room had looked a year ago entered Jack's mind. Sparkling. Festive. Garlands of holly. Candles. Mistletoe. Red and white flowers. With a giant spruce, grandly decorated, its top star touching the ceiling. Ready for a party that never happened.

And now...

He frowned. He'd been ignoring gentle hints that it was time for him to go fell a tree. Clearly, no one had wanted to press it until he was ready.

Jack snapped his fingers. Well, now he was ready. And this year, he wouldn't go alone. He'd ask Rose to go with him.

Lucy had told him about Rose's impoverished childhood. She'd probably never enjoyed a truly happy Christmas. Not the kind he had been fortunate to know, anyway.

She'd been enthusiastically embracing so many of the activities he'd always taken for granted. Skating, despite falling. Going shopping, despite clearly having no money.

In the past few days, she'd also cheerfully joined the family in other activities: baking cookies, going sledding, singing carols—always with a sparkle in her eye.

It did his heart good.

Lunch had just ended, and Rose had gone to help Grandmother get ready for her nap.

Turning toward his grandmother's wing, Jack hurried to catch Rose, and did just as she was leaving the bedroom.

Rose put a finger to her lips as she closed the door.

Jack grinned. "Go get your coat."

She widened her eyes. "Why?"

"Because," he said, "you need to help me find the perfect Christmas tree."

"OH, THIS ONE'S PRETTY," ROSE EXCLAIMED AS SHE dashed over to a tall pine. "What about this one?"

Jack grinned. "Nah, too scrawny."

She twirled around and pointed to a squat fir. "This?"

He laughed. "Nope. Too short."

"How about this one?" Rose dashed over to a towering spruce with full, majestic branches. Her smile did something to his heart that no woman's smile had ever done before. "This one's perfect."

Jack gave a quick nod and hurried through deep snow toward her, brandishing his axe and flashing a wide grin. "I agree heartily. You have good taste in trees, Miss Robinson."

She beamed, her eyes dancing, as snowflakes drifting from the sky landed on her hair. In her rush to join him on his quest, she'd forgotten her hat, and locks of her shiny-brown curls had come un-pinned.

They locked gazes.

"Please call me Rose," she whispered, stepping toward him.

He grinned. How long had he been wanting to do that? He moved closer. "Rose. And Rosy...I might even call you Rosy..." his grin widened. "Because your cheeks have a tendency to turn rosy-pink when the slightest chill kisses them. Did you know that?"

He wanted to kiss her.

"It's not the cold...Mr. Cardelle. It's me blushing, whenever I'm near you."

"Jack."

"Jack."

And then he did kiss her. Reaching for her hands, he

took her into his arms and put his lips to hers as feelings of love and passion flooded through him such as he'd never felt before.

This was love. True love. He was ready, and he sure hoped she'd say "yes."

He pulled back and looked into Rose's amazing face. "We better start lugging that tree to the house," he said, his voice husky, "or they'll come looking for us."

HE'D KISSED HER. ROSE HAD NEVER KNOWN SUCH happiness. Her entire body was aflame. But what had the kiss meant to him?"

As they dragged the tree they'd chosen together through the snow, she had to ask.

"Jack," she called. "Don't you care...you must know... that I'm penniless. Don't you care...that I'm one of your family's servants? A nobody..."

He dropped his end of the tree.

She dropped hers.

He rushed over to her.

She melted into his arms again, and then he kissed her forehead, her cheeks, her lips.

"I don't care about any of that," he whispered in her ear, "and I never have. You're unlike anyone I've ever met, and I'll embarrass myself now by saying I've loved you since I set my eyes on you at the train."

She shook her head, hardly able to believe her ears. "How could you? I'll not fit in—"

He kissed her gently and silenced her arguments.

"I'm not looking for a dalliance. Would you consider me suitable for marriage, Rose?"

She gasped, then beamed. "Me, marry you? Are you sure? But, of course! You, sir, are *all* of my dreams come true."

He laughed, then kissed her again. "And you've just given me my best Christmas ever," he said. "My Christmas Rose."

ABOUT THE AUTHOR

Maggie FitzRoy is a former journalist and magazine and newspaper editor with a bachelor's degree in history from Ursinus College and a master's degree in education from the University of Virginia.

A lifelong, avid reader of fiction and nonfiction, she loves creating historical romances that sweep the reader into the past—where love is an adventure.

Her debut novel, Mercy's Way, takes place in 1845 on the Oregon Trail. Her second, Beacon Beach, brings the seaside resort town of Cape May, New Jersey alive in Gilded Age 1886.

Maggie is currently working on her third novel, a romantic suspense set in exciting, jazzy 1923 Miami Beach.

She has also written two nonfiction books featuring Northeast Florida history.

Maggie lives in Ponte Vedra Beach, Florida. When she's not writing, she enjoys travel, swimming, choral singing and reading a variety of fiction and nonfiction genres.

For more information, and links to her on Facebook, Instagram and Twitter, visit her website: maggiefitzroy.com or email her at maggiefitzroyauthor@gmail.com

AN ELF'S CHALLENGE

A Sweet Contemporary Christmas Story

VICKEY WOLLAN

An Elf's Challenge

Angelina Tinsel, Toy Painter, doesn't know her father forbid Zack Holly, Woodworker, from speaking to her. A generations-old feud between the two departments causes ongoing elfin-relations issues. An all-seeing Santa knows about the elves' attraction and decides encouraging it might help end the fighting. When Santa's Claus High assignment lands Angelina in the woodshop, how will she work past family loyalties and stereotypes to find love?

CHAPTER 1

"I think you're lost, miss. This is the woodworking shop. Aren't you a painter?"

Angelina rounded on her heels when she heard the male voice crack as he ground out the word "painter." *Why do woodworkers dislike painters so much? Oh yeah, the feud between the departments.* But it was the woodworkers who had repeatedly marred the pristine efforts of Santa's artists by dragging unwanted sawdust into the Paint Drying Zone.

"Hi. Right. Took a wrong turn—on purpose. Doing a research paper on operational efficiency for school." Angelina dared to peek in the direction of the voice then stared at the floor. *Double darn, drat and why me?*

Figures her mystery host would be Zack, the hottest woodworker—no, hottest elf—at the North Pole. "I'm Angelina, a senior at Claus High. You don't know me."

He wrinkled his nose and raised an eyebrow. "Aren't you the paint foreman's kid?"

Ugh, he knows my dad. That can't be good. "True enough, but that's not important."

She riffled through her backpack to find the letter with the official Claus seal while she took in the view of his uniform. His beige all-in-one was a bit tight across his chest and the dark-tan leather apron did little to hide the V shape from the width of his shoulders to his waist. Her hand shook a bit as she thrust the paper up at him. *He's tall for an elf.*

"I have permission to look around." She couldn't help but smile once she stepped closer to him. Of course, he smelled of wood, oak to be exact, but there was a hint of musk that clouded her ability to think straight.

"I'm due for a break. I'll give you the five-cent tour." With a nonchalant wave of his arm, he strolled toward a flight of stairs to a balcony that circled the room.

Angelina struggled to re-zip her pocket and gather her wits but managed to climb ten steps without tripping. On auto-pilot, she grabbed her phone and started a video with sound. She turned the camera where Zack pointed and did her absolute best to pay attention. The shop was much cleaner than she expected. If she were to believe the gossip, there should be piles of dreaded sawdust at every machine and in every corner.

"Want a soda?" Zack opened the glass door to a mini-fridge sitting on a counter.

"Diet, please. Nice of you to offer." Her hand brushed his when she accepted the can. As the heat of a blush rose in her cheeks, Angelina realized he hadn't noticed the contact. Her whole body went as cold as the metal in her hand.

Zack chuckled, leaned against the railing, and took a long, slow sip. "Relax, kid. I'm a woodworker, not a whack-job. You don't get out much. Do you?"

The "kid" comment was getting on her nerves, but he had a point, she was acting a bit weird. "Why are you being so nice to me?" She stared straight at him and lifted her chin. Angelina was determined not to be the first one to blink. Then, she noticed *he* hadn't blinked either.

"I can do this all day. Remember, sawdust in my eyes regularly – no biggie." Zack raised his lids and brought his nose inches from hers. "You had me at operational efficiency. I'm hoping you'll return the favor, let me into the Paint Drying Zone." He winked.

Angelina's mouth went dry. No amount of soda could fix it. "Of course!" *Oh, dear. What did I just do? What will my father think of me bringing a dust-covered woodworker into the paint shop?*

❦

ZACK WAITED AT THE BACK DOOR OF THE PAINT SHOP as Angelina had asked. He brushed the natural-wood rose he had carved as a thank you gift for the hundredth time to ensure he would not carry one-molecule of dust with him. *Santa has your back. Names can never hurt you. Stay calm.* Zack spritzed his mouth with peppermint Binaca and tugged on the cowlick in his hairline.

When the door opened, Zack jumped with such force he nearly dropped the rose, and then almost broke the stem trying to catch it. "Your promptness is an appreciated courtesy," she said.

Zack relaxed once the sparkle from her red hair came into view. Elves that were gingers were a rare thing indeed. He missed viewing that glorious radiance *and* her inner beauty ever since he graduated from Claus High last year. His nerves caused him to call her "kid" when he'd wanted to call her "girlfriend" for years.

"Street clothes instead of your uniform, good call." Angelina's head swiveled left and right before she grabbed his sleeve and hauled him into the paint workshop. "My father's not due back for another hour. What would you like to know?"

She began to stride away, but Zack stopped her by shoving the flower under her nose. "A gift of thanks. No sawdust! I promise."

Angelina gasped, and then studied the details of the carved grooves. As she clutched it to her chest and swayed embracing it, moisture gathered in her eyes. "What a thoughtful present! Is it made of oak wood? It's beautiful." She turned her gaze on him. "Thank you. I'll treasure it always."

Zack grinned, but then unleashed a mammoth smile. "Yeah, it's oak. You're welcome. Got any wet paint I should be aware of?"

"The Paint Drying Area is through that door, so we're good in this room."

Zack took the liberty of inspecting the airbrush guns and assembly-line conveyor-belts. "Can you please show me your newest and oldest pieces of equipment?"

Angelina pointed to a workbench with rows of rainbow-colored paint jars and brushes in every width appropriate for toy making. "That has been in this room for hundreds of years." She giggled. "It's wood with about a thousand coats of clear varnish. No splinters and it's washable."

"I gotta check the maker's mark." Zack dove under the bench and looked at the backside of the support beam.

"What are you doing? There's nothing to see there!" Angelina yanked on his pant leg.

Instead of trying to escape, Zack took her by the hand and encouraged her to duck down for a better view. "My great, great grandfather made this work-bench. See the H.H. branded into the wood? Henry Holly was his name. Painters and woodworkers used to get along, you know."

"What's the meaning of this?" shouted the paint foreman. Zack peeked out to see the old man's wrinkled face get redder with each word.

Zack saw the old-fashioned curled-up toes on the elf shoes and rolled his eyes. *Ugh, the foreman, her father. The man that forbade me to speak to her after school.* He sighed. *You're a man now. Be the bigger man.* He scrambled to his feet and tried to shake the foreman's hand. "Mr. Tinsel. Great shop you have here. Very impressive."

After Mr. Tinsel stepped back and shoved his hands in his pockets, Zack's wrist went limp, but he stood tall. "Santa asked me to tour your fine shop. I've created a negative air-flow contaminant-removing entranceway. It debuts at the elf appreciation dinner this weekend."

"Hogwash! It'll never work." Mr. Tinsel gave Zack his back and rounded on Angelina. "How dare you pull this stunt while I was in a meeting? I vary my schedule to expose slackers. I never expected you would be one of them."

Zack's chest tightened as he watched the beautiful, smart young-woman grow pale and tongue-tied. He opened his mouth to defend her, but she gave him a look that begged him to stand down.

"As I said, Santa approved this visit. I look forward to seeing you both at the celebration." Zack bowed at the waist and backed his way to the exit.

Angelina took such care to hide the rose in the side pouch of her white painter's pants while he was talking, it gave him pause. *How could trying to fix things make such a mess? How would her father punish her for breaking his long-standing anti-woodworker rule?*

❧

LATER THAT NIGHT, ANGELINA DIDN'T DARE SAY A word during dinner. Her father glared at her, and her mother kept looking away and swiping at the tears that rolled down her cheeks.

After completing her evening chores, she was alone in her room. Angelina retrieved the rose she had stowed away under her pillow. She kissed it and pretended she was kissing Zack.

He didn't have to make this gift for her. She thought back over their few conversations. He had always been kind to her, but she caught him starring at her often. She figured it was because he hated painters or was drawn to her hair. Not in a good way, but in a freakish-fascination-for-the-outcast kind of way. Angelina was so caught up in her thoughts she didn't hear the soft knock on the door.

Her father seized the rose from her before she saw

him. "Did he make this? Give this to you? He's only trying to get on Santa's good side. Can't you see he's using you?" With a ballistic throw, Mr. Tinsel pitched the flower into her roaring fireplace before he marched out and slammed the door.

Angelina sat in her bed unable to sleep. Who should she believe? Santa spoke highly of all the elves that worked for him. Other departments didn't treat the woodworkers with such disdain, but her father had told her so many awful stories. Why would he lie?

CHAPTER 2

The only thing that could make Angelina smile was seeing herself in the mirror wearing her new dress for the annual dance. The uniforms were color-coded so everyone would know who was on duty and where they worked. Street clothes were always red and green, but for special occasions, the elves added silver and gold. This year's dress design was her best. The all-red gown was just the right hue that wouldn't clash with her hair and had a dusting of silver around the neckline to help make her blue eyes sparkle.

Who was she kidding? Her shoulders drooped as she dragged herself into the living room to wait for her parents. They would force her to stay with her kind–the painters. Very few friend-elves would realize her dress was the newest design. Dancing would be out of the question, especially if Zack was anywhere near her.

She bit her lip and squeezed her eyes shut. The rose had burned into ash, Zack would never talk to her again, and her life was laid out in front of her based on her parent's wishes. She had no say, no offering of her opinion. The only way she knew how to make her life bearable was to be quiet, smile and nod. *How can I be true to myself and make my father happy? Hopeless.*

After Christmas, the three-story barn where the sleigh was usually stored was converted into a ballroom. The balconies used to load toys had tables and chairs close to the rail so the elves could see Santa as he and Mrs. Claus gave the state of the North Pole speeches. Disco balls and linen tablecloths transformed the unadorned space into an ornate party hall. Angelina sat up straight and feigned attention to every inventory-related word uttered by Santa, but her gaze searched for Zack.

Maybe he had a work deadline or was ill or just maybe her father had his invitation revoked! She became more afraid each time she allowed her mind to conjure possible reasons why she couldn't find him. Angelina hugged herself and looked through the moon roof. The sleigh garage was built to take advantage of as much natural light as a northern latitude could offer. The aurora borealis' glistening ribbons of color might be the only thing she enjoyed tonight.

❦

ZACK TAPPED HIS TOE AND TUGGED ON THE CUFF OF his tuxedo shirt behind the stage's curtain, while listening to Santa sing his praises. *This demo had better go off without a hitch.* A trickle of sweat rolled down his back when a spotlight blinded him as the heavy red velvet parted to reveal him and his invention. *Good thing*

Santa can explain how it works as well as I can. All I have to do is be the test subject.

Walking with purpose, Zack picked up a bucket of sawdust and dumped it over his head, then stepped through the entrance of the sawdust remover. With the flip of a switch, the air vortex began and then sucked everything not attached to him into the side vents. He exited and started shaking his head and brushing his forest-green satin coat. No debris was left on him to fall away. There were gasps from the elfin community followed by a standing ovation.

Zack exhaled, not realizing he'd been holding his breath. Santa, then Mrs. Claus gave him a big hug. He practically floated to the dance floor level where he was mobbed by shop foremen wanting their department to be next recipient of the magical-door installation.

The recognition of his invention was nice, but he couldn't enjoy it. His mind wandered to Angelina. Zack had watched her dutifully climb the stairs behind her father. Her dress was stunning. Without her there as a part of his life, his recent success felt empty.

❦

THE FOLLOWING MORNING, ANGELINA AND HER parents were called to Santa's office. Angelina jumped out of her skin when the door opened. Both he and Mrs. Claus had solemn faces as they entered. *Oh, no. This can't be good.* Her lower lip began to quiver. Pulling words from thin air, her father launched into idle chit chat that seemed to put himself at ease. But everyone else remained as stiff as the wooden walls.

"I've made a point of having Mrs. Claus and your family serve as witnesses to this conversation for a reason." Santa took a seat and combed his mustache with his fingers. "You know I can see elves just like I see children, right? See them sleeping, being bad or good." The big man paused until he received a head-bob from each elf on Angelina's side of his desk. Mrs. Claus stepped closer to her husband and took his hand.

"I don't enjoy doing this, but for the sake of the children all around the world, I must. Mr. Tinsel I'm putting your shop on a Work Improvement Plan." He cleared his throat and opened a file on his laptop. "The work is fine, but your attitude is dividing the elfin community. I won't tolerate it anymore."

"Whatever do you mean?" Angelina's father shouted and threw his hands in the air.

Santa closed his eyes and pinched the bridge of his always-rosy nose. "I know your parents brainwashed you to despise woodworkers, but if Angelina can see past the old feud then you need to break this cycle of hate."

Her father stood up, but both she and her mother grabbed his arms and pulled him back into his chair. "We will make a change right away, sir." Mrs. Tinsel spoke before Angelina had a chance to form words.

"I mean it. The manager of plastic dyes can absorb all things needing color tomorrow." Santa harrumphed. "Your shop gets Zack's negative airflow door, first. Don't blow it." With a yawn and a stutter step, the usually jovial man made a hasty exit with his loving wife in tow.

Angelina found her voice. "I had no idea this was going to happen and before you say a word Dad, remember he sees you. Got it? He always sees you!" *I need a miracle. How can I get my father to change?*

❦

ANGELINA BARGED INTO HER FATHER'S OFFICE unannounced clutching a stack of papers to her chest. "Dad, did you review last year's annual toy production report?"

"Leave me alone. Can't you see I'm trying to think?" Mr. Tinsel grumbled and shooed her toward the exit.

She took one step back and her stomach roiled. After she solidified her footing, Angelina took her deepest breath ever. "You need to think differently."

"How dare you! I put a roof over your head and fed you all these years just to have you take Santa's side when things get tough? I taught you better than that." Mr. Tinsel got up and tried to leave his office with a huff, but Angelina stepped in his path.

"I love you Daddy, but the numbers don't lie. The children are no longer asking for the toys we make."

"It's a phase. They'll come back to the classics if they have any sense. Now step aside."

Dropping typed pages all over the floor, Angelina grabbed the lapels of her father's coat. "Santa will do what he must to keep giving the children the toys they want. Even if that means closing your shop and forcing you into retirement." She gasped for air as tears rolled down her face. "Please, take off your blinders. You need to see what is going on, not what you wish was true."

"You've always been a head-strong girl. Figures only a girl would throw such fantasy in my face. My decades of work speak for themselves. Santa will see the error of his ways." Mr. Tinsel picked up Angelina by the shoulders and moved her just enough to bolt past her, out of the workshop with the door slamming behind him.

꧁꧂

ANGELINA COULDN'T SLEEP. HER FATHER HAD NOT come home for dinner. Her mother sat in her rocking chair and wrung her hands, staring at the fire as it danced its usual dance.

She sat in her bed and did her best to find a solution. As she flipped and flopped around, she heard a rustling sound but assumed it was her sheets and comforter.

Someone cleared their throat. "Maybe I can be of assistance?"

Angelina had never heard that woman's voice before, so she sprang into a seated position like a jack-in-the-box.

"Who are you?" Angelina rubbed her eyes.

She could see the lady but also see *through* her. The intruder was a mature elf with bright white hair and a veil of sparkling gold dust all around her. But she was dressed in a traditional elfin celebration dress. Her gown had many layers of ruffles in red, green, silver and gold. Her smile was brilliant and enchanting. Angelina's jaw dropped.

"I'm a spirit of elves past. I'm your great, great grandmother – on your father's side." She paused while she pondered her next words. "Think of me as a defender of history. You can call me Lizzy."

348

Angelina tapped herself on her cheek to make certain she was awake. "How is history going to help me?" She yawned and snuggled back under her covers.

Lizzy hovered closer to her bed. Angelina could see the family resemblance. The vision looked like her dad. *Maybe Lizzy can haunt my father into thinking straight!*

"I'm all ears. Literally." Angelina pointed at her over-sized ears and chuckled. "Is elfin humor still funny to ghosts?"

Angelina felt something stroking her head and shuddered. "Did you just do that?" She raked her fingers through her red locks. "Wow, I guess I'm not dreaming."

Her guest smiled a bit and then it widened. "Sorry. I used to have ruby hair too. It's a blessing and don't let anyone tell you otherwise." Lizzy patted Angelina's coiffeur one more time, and then straightened a few flouncing bunches of material. "You can only save yourself. Your father will hold fast to his beliefs even if it destroys everything around him."

Angelina's eyebrows vaulted toward the ceiling. "That's not what I wanted to hear. I was hoping you had some extraordinary magical powers."

"Zack was right. Painters and woodworkers used to work so well together. But you need to think about your future. If the Paint Shop closes what job will you get when you graduate from Claus High?"

The question stumped Angelina. She would work with her family. Everyone did. Choose another line of work? How would she begin to do that? Now her brows pinched together, and her mouth went dry. "Can you tell me what I should do?"

"Oh no, deary. Only you know that answer. I'm just

here to tell you it's okay to have those thoughts. You have many talents."

Angelina was enveloped in a warm hug. She felt the love and support even though she could barely see Lizzy. "Everything will be just fine if you put the needs of the children around the world before your own."

The apparition began to float away. Angelina reached out to her, then lunged for Lizzy, but she was gone. "Wait come back!" Moisture gathered in her eyes and threatened to spill onto her cheeks.

The voice of the spirit returned but not the translucent being. "No tears, darling. In your mind just list all your strengths and talents. The answer you seek will present itself."

Oh, joy! I've never been very good at the self-love thing. Angelina tossed the covers over her head and curled into a ball.

"I can paint within the lines, I'm creative, organized, follow instructions, and can coordinate color combinations..."

When her wake-up chimes sounded, Angelina knew what she needed to do.

CHAPTER 3

W hile continuing to go to school, Angelina secretly arranged for a temporary housing swap. It would be like studying abroad for a semester.

She started working part-time at the North Pole commissary and lived with the manager of the bakery. *Santa and the elves will always need to eat. I can decorate cakes and all sorts of confections as good as any elf born into the job.* With this new direction for her future, Angelina found an inner peace she didn't know she had lost.

"I'd like to put in an order for a birthday cake for my mom, please."

Angelina finished a pink flower made of icing and looked up. She sucked in air and dropped both her arms. Her icing bag hit the counter with a splat. The other arm hit a spatula, sending vanilla cake batter flying, much of which landed all over her apron, but a bit of it landed on Zack's chin. He scooped it up with his finger and tasted it.

"I kept sneaking by the Paint Shop hoping to run

into you. Santa sees everything, right? He called me to his office, thought I was gonna get fired. Instead, he told me where I could find you. But I do need to order a birthday cake. I'm rambling, so I'll shut up now." Zack licked his lips and gazed at his new sneaker-style elfin-shoes.

"It's so nice to see you. I mean, talk to you without, you know. Anyway, I wanted to tell you the demo was amazing. You must be flooded with requests. It's so incredible that you got to do what you wanted with your career and help so many elves in the process." Angelina picked up the order pad and began to fill in his name. She flipped to a page in a book of pictures. "I think your mom would love this design."

Zack looked at the cake, then at Angelina, back at the cake, and then he found his shoes interesting again. "That's perfect. You're good at your new job. It suits you."

Angelina sighed. "I'm still learning, but I'm getting the hang of it." She tried not to giggle as she watched Zack fidget while she completed the order form. When she forwarded his copy, he took her hand instead of the paper.

"Ya know, bakers date woodcutters." He bit his lip, but then broke into a broad smile.

Angelina put on her best poker-face. "I heard that." With a nonchalant shrug, she added, "Everybody dates everybody except painters and woodworkers."

"Yeah, but that's not what I meant." He pulled her to the end of the counter between them and stepped closer. He bent down to put his mouth to her ear and in a whisper asked, "Would the newest baker like to go on a date with this woodcutter?" With the hand not still clutching hers, he pointed at his broad chest.

"Oh, you mean me? I am a baker now, aren't I?" Angelina began to twirl her hair but found a few curls still covered with batter. "Um, sure. I'd like that. You can pick me up here or the baker's house." Before the joy she felt was able to sink in, she saw her new boss heading her way. She pulled her hand out of Zack's and ran back to her post in record time.

She looked back to see Zack standing with the yellow copy of the order in his hand and a confused look on his face.

"Ms. Tinsel, your father is out in the cafeteria and says he would like to speak to you." The head baker patted her on her shoulder and pointed toward a door. "I'll be right here if you need me."

Angelina stumbled in place. Her knees went slack, and she steadied herself by leaning on the display case. "Is it okay if I take my break now?"

"Of course. You're doing a great job and can keep this position as long as you want." Her boss smiled and left without another word.

Angelina took off her apron and cleaned herself up as best as she could using the glass case as a mirror. She passed Zack and said nothing. *He may not want to date me if my father is going to continue to be a problem.* She heard him shuffling behind her and stopped. He plowed into her back and had to hug her from behind to keep them both from toppling to the ground.

"Sorry. I'm going with you." He turned her in his arms. "I'll give you privacy, but I'm not going to let you out of my sight. I want to be close by for moral support." Before letting her loose, he hugged her tight.

Angelina let her head slump to his chest. She found strength being close to him. Having him as her protector made her feel a sense of calm. "I got this. Thanks for hanging around." She saw her father and walked with purpose until she was at his side. She glared at him but remained silent.

Mr. Tinsel looked pale and had dark circles under his eyes. "Thanks for seeing me."

"Of course. You'll always be my dad." Angelina stood up straighter and thought of her visit from Lizzy. The list of her strengths and talents was longer than she could have imagined, but until she was asked to list them, she hadn't recognized how much she had to offer the elfin community.

"Your mom tells me the two of you have chatted often. That's good. She needs you. She's been helping me see the error of my ways as well." He lifted the corner of one side of his mouth, but it didn't look entirely like a smile. "I wanted to let you know that whatever happens with The Paint Shop, your room will always be open to you. Be a baker, date whomever you want, but please still be my little girl." He swallowed hard before speaking again. "I think I've convinced Santa for a second chance."

He stepped forward with such speed; it surprised her when he took her into his arms for a warm, affectionate bear-hug. "I'm okay with losing my job, but not my daughter. Please tell me you and I are still good...."

The lump in her throat made it difficult, but she finally replied. "We're good." Tears streamed down her face and she felt moisture on his face when he pulled her even tighter.

Then as quickly as he had reached for her, he pushed her away from him and cleared his throat. "You've got work to do. Do your new shop proud. You're a Tinsel after all." He gave her a faux punch in the arm. "Mom will set up a family dinner real soon."

Angelina swallowed hard, couldn't catch her breath. Her mouth moved to make the words, "I love you," but no sound escaped. She stood there for a moment replaying the scene. She would have a job she could enjoy and not lose her place on the Tinsel family tree. She could live with that. Then she remembered Zack had to be standing nearby, watching alone.

"Everything will be okay." Lizzy's words rolled around in her mind and Angelina tucked them away for safekeeping.

She swiped away the tears and smiled the most honest smile she had worn in years. When she started back to the elf she would soon date, he motioned her to join him in a secluded alcove of the cafeteria. When she reached him, the look of true caring on his face nearly had her burst into tears again.

"That seemed like it went better than I expected it might." Zack leaned against the wall.

"It did. I think this is the best thing for us all, including the elfin community." With those words, her frayed nerves stopped throbbing. She relaxed and exhaled. "Thank you so much for being here, though."

Zack nodded, then reached into his pocket. "Oh, Santa also told me you might want a replacement one of these?" With a steady grace, he presented her a hand-carved rose made of natural-oak with as much attention to detail as the flower that had gotten throw into the fireplace.

Angelina accepted the gift and held it to her nose as if it were real. "Thank you. The first one was beautiful, but this one means so much more to me because when that rose burned, my dreams of us being accepted went up in smoke. Now I have a new life, a new start and a new rose. Having you in my life is an even bigger gift!"

A bold idea popped into her head, so she went with it. Going up on her tippy toes, she kissed him. His lips parted to greet hers and the feeling it gave her was magical. The happiest elf ever.

THE END

A Snowflake Christmas - Can a blooming love that becomes forbidden survive fears and rumors?

ABOUT VICKEY WOLLAN

Vickey Wollan caught the writing bug in elementary school, and her thirst for reading novels started in junior high. Although her career included journalistic and public relations writing, she recently jumped with both feet into writing romance stories.

She writes heartwarming, sweet, contemporary romances that tickle the funny-bone and wrap up with an always satisfying happily ever after.

Vickey lives in Central Florida, but her travels inspire her stories. She likes the outdoors and sports, so she creates heroines who are strong and multi-talented, but are still attracted to sexy modern men who appreciate the love of a capable woman.

With a background in wellness, she allows her creativity to emerge during a good workout. When not writing, she enjoys reading, hiking through the beauty of nature, or chilling-out with her husband.

She appreciates hearing from readers. Reach out to her at vickeywollanauthor@yahoo.com

Social media links:
Website: https://vickeywollan.wordpress.com
Newsletter: https://mailchi.mp/dd2e4421315a/vickey-wollan-newsletter
Facebook author page: https://facebook.com/vickeywollanauthor
LinkedIn: https://linkedin.com/in/vickeywollan

Made in the USA
Coppell, TX
18 March 2021

51914760R00203